Praise for Angela Jackson

WINNER OF EDINBURG
FESTIVAL FIRS

WATERSTONES SCOTT

AMAZON RISING STAR FINALIST

A wonderful, home-grown success
**Nick Barley, Director of Edinburgh International
Book Festival**

Reviews of *The Emergence of Judy Taylor*

The Emergence of Judy Taylor is a heart-wrenching yet dryly funny tale of relationships and second chances
Grazia

I couldn't put this book down. It was funny, witty, heartbreaking and wise, and never once cloying or sentimental. It is steely-eyed and sympathetic at the same time. Angela Jackson is a generous writer, and her warm and captivating prose engages and enfolds the reader
Angela Newton

An enriching read. A brilliantly observed, original take on universal themes of love, life and relationships.
Matt Cain, author of *The Madonna of Bolton*

Think a northern Nora Ephron with a smattering of Edinburgh magic
Kristin Pedroja

This book is beautifully written and paced, alive with rhythmic and true dialogue; like Anne Tyler to a Miles Davis soundtrack. Does what all good fiction should do, forces you to stop and think and to question the choices you make as you sleepwalk through life
Tim Court

Reviews of *The Darling Monologues*

With all of these women's stories, there's a humour, hope and big hearts at the core of even the darkest aspects of their tales. This is where Jackson's genius for revealing character through apparently simple stories shines. She is a brilliant storyteller, and has a natural, human warmth which shines through in all of her characters
edinburghfestival.org

Meet Lily, Sadie and Ruby, acutely observed characters brought to life by their creator, award-winning writer Angela Jackson. Fresh from the pages of her novels, these women and their relationships are fully revealed in three frank and darkly funny monologues. Sex, secrets, birth, death, infidelity and Russian Red lipstick – no subject is out of bounds. Compelling, with a northern nod to unsentimental compassion and wry wit
The List

The Darlings

ANGELA JACKSON

Lightning Books

Published in 2021
by Lightning Books Ltd
Imprint of Eye Books Ltd
29A Barrow Street
Much Wenlock
Shropshire
TF13 6EN

www.lightning-books.com

ISBN: 9781785631337
Copyright © Angela Jackson 2021

Cover by Nell Wood
Typeset in Book Antiqua and Bauer Bodoni Std

British Library Cataloguing in Publication Data
A catalogue record for this book is available from the British Library.

Printed by CPI Group (UK) Ltd, Croydon CR0 4YY

For David and Tom
And for Scott, as it turns out

The curious paradox is that when I accept myself
just as I am, then I can change
Carl R. Rogers

It's about acceptance, isn't it?
Jeremy Hardy

Chapter 1

WHEN MARK DARLING was fifteen years old, he killed his best friend.

In an attempt to score a perfect six, he swung a cricket bat with such force that his young hands lost their grip on it. He laughed as the bat zoomed through the air, until it hit Fergus Banks on the head with a firm thwack.

Mark's body clock shifted. He shut out the daylight, slept sun up to sun down. At night, fuelled almost solely by junk food, he lurked online, clicking and scrolling his way around, while documentaries buzzed at low volume from the television. His parents tried to help, via a conveyor belt of therapists, but each time he described the accident, it served only to burn the sounds and images more deeply into his brain.

One icy winter's night, his parents took a bend too fast, and two police officers delivered the news that he was now truly alone in the world. So, from that point, he learned how to toke and drink himself to oblivion. It was easy to pass a decade or so that way.

Then came Sadie. Slowly, carefully, mercifully, she rescued him, patched up the parts she could mend, and lived with the rest.

Mark is a comedian.

chapter 2

'I WAS PERFECT. We all were, once.'

Mark looked out into the darkness. Someone sneezed.

'My parents never missed an opportunity to tell me how wonderful I was. And now, the world never misses an opportunity to put me straight.'

A mild ripple of laughter.

'That's the way it is. If only my parents had said: *Look Mark — we're gonna be honest with you, and it's for your own good. Your drawing of the house and our family? It's shit. You've drawn our arms coming out of our heads. It's anatomically unfeasible. Your little story about the fluffy kitten who got lost? It's mawkish. It's woefully punctuated. Some of your letters are the wrong way round!'*

Laughter.

'Sports Day? Son, we were mortified.'

More laughter.

'Nativity play? We think you dropped baby Jesus on purpose. Attention seeking.'

He was on a roll. He paced the stage.

'Truth! You know? I just needed them to be honest. But parents are liars! They put the terrible drawings on the fridge, or — worse — they frame them! They actually hang them on the same walls as real art. They even get them made into little drinks coasters now. Who wants to see that kind of crap every time you pick up your coffee?'

He shielded his eyes from the glare of the spotlight, and spotted a friendly face.

'This woman here is looking very guilty.'

He haunched down, despite his knees. 'You have kids?'

The woman shouted something. He didn't quite catch it. He cupped his hand to his ear. He could feel the momentum slip. She held up four fingers.

'Four? Jesus, what, you have no telly?'

A laugh. A potential seam. As the laughter died down, before he had the chance to riff on it, she shouted her response.

'Quads.'

Quads. He didn't know what to do with it. Nothing would come. He felt beads of sweat on his upper lip. He could hear chattering.

'And is your fridge covered in crap drawings?'

Her response was lengthy and inaudible. The sound of breaking glass from behind the bar distracted him;

he looked across, ran his fingers through his hair and attempted to hold onto his thread.

'Course it is. That's the law. They draw a picture, you crack out the Blu-tack.'

Laughter. Low level but sustained.

'You're ruining their lives, you know that, right? They'll get into the real world and their teachers, the other kids, Twitter — everybody will make it their business to put them straight on the many ways in which they're not perfect. And it's all. Your. Fault.'

He picked up his beer and just before he took a swig, he muttered close into the microphone:

'Mummy.'

Big laugh.

He splashed his face with cold water then ran a green paper towel across it. He was covered in sweat; his shirt clung to him. Someone banged on the door. He opened it. A man in a wheelchair tried to get past him.

'Oi!' said Mark, rubbing his shin.

'This is the disabled toilet, you prick.'

'I know what it is,' said Mark.

'Well, get out!'

Mark started to gather up his stuff.

'I don't know if you know, but this is the only place we comedians can–'

'You're not disabled. And you're not a comedian. Fuck off.'

Mark strode through to the bar. Another comic was on stage now, getting bigger laughs. She was doing a bit about trying to send a parcel and being sold a mortgage at the post office. The warm laughter of recognition filled the room. She laughed along, shaking her head. She picked up a ukulele and started to sing about the decline of the high street. The audience joined in on the second chorus. Mark ordered a beer and leaned back against the bar. As she strummed the final note and shouted her thanks, the club manager, Eddie, appeared from the shadows, handed him a couple of folded twenties, and patted him on the shoulder.

'Better.'

'Cheers. I've been working on it.'

'You should've done something with the quads.'

Mark winced and took a swig of his beer.

'Don't bring 'em in if you're not ready.'

'How will I know when I'm ready if I don't have a go?'

'You're a late starter. Some of the best were on stage at eighteen. What are you, thirty-five?'

'Thirty-eight.'

'Exactly. You need to cram to catch up. Go to gigs, watch YouTube, Instagram, make notes. If you want to make this your life, you have to throw your life into it.'

'He said if I want to make it, I need to shift up a gear.' Mark was sitting on the arm of the sofa, gently rubbing Sadie's feet.

'What, like, be funnier?'

He stopped rubbing. 'No. I'm already funny.'

She started laughing. 'You are. Go on.' She put her hand on his to encourage him to keep rubbing.

'Shift a gear, as in, maybe look at it as more of a full-time job.'

'A full-time job?'

'I got a lot of laughs.'

'You have a full-time job.'

'I was absolutely storming at one point.'

'You can't have two full-time jobs.'

'I have the chops, Sade. You know? People don't laugh if you're not funny. I'm funny.'

'There's only one of you, though.'

'Exactly. I was like: *Mate, that's mad. I've got responsibilities. An IVF loan, a baby on the way —* '

'The kitchen ceiling's falling in.'

'Yeah. That's what I said. *We live in a money pit,* I said. *I'm just gonna keep it part-time for now, until it's more profitable than the day job.*'

Sadie's chest started to rise and fall again. 'No rush.'

'No rush.'

A clunk followed by a series of clicks signalled the ancient central heating turning off for the night. It would be too cold for them to stay unblanketed for much longer. She changed position, kissed him. 'Once the baby's here, I'll come along again, see how the act's developing.'

'Yeah.'

'You could do a bit now. Some of the new stuff.'

He scratched his head, sent his hair skew-whiff. 'I think it only works on stage. It's like a magical thing that happens up there, you know? I can't just switch it on.'

She made space for him on the sofa. 'Hey, some

good news. Dad knows someone who can look at the kitchen ceiling. Art.'

'Art?'

'That's his name. Art. He says it might be nothing, but it might be dry rot. You need to catch it early because it can spread. And then things start crumbling. Literally, the house could fall down.'

"Why does none of that sound like good news?'

'Apparently, Art knows his stuff and might catch it early. And it might not even be dry rot.'

Mark let out a long sigh. He switched on the television, and they eased themselves into mutually comfortable positions, loosely intertwined under a chenille throw. A documentary was on, and they let it play, watching a man carefully repair a broken vase. The narrator had a soporific tone.

Rather than discard it, there is an opportunity for the fault to make the original stronger. Done well, using gold foil and resin, the final vase will be more valuable.

'How can a broken vase be worth more than the original?' said Mark.

Sadie shifted slightly, folded closer into him.

The television mumbled on. *Kitsugi is the art of precious scars. The gold renders the fault lines stronger than before.*

'Until you drop it again,' said Mark. He stroked Sadie's head and she made a soft, grunting sound.

He looked up at the ceiling, and willed it to stay right where it was.

chapter 3

IT WAS THE MILDEST and brightest of Saturday afternoons. Cloudless. Convertible car hoods were still fastened tight shut — it was March in Edinburgh, after all — but windows were cracked open, jackets unbuttoned.

Mark was inching along in city-centre traffic, looking forward to relaxing with an afternoon bill of Sky Sports. In the car boot, there was a paper bag containing seventy-two twenty milligram Citalopram tablets, and three bulging supermarket bags: two that Sadie would approve of, and one she would not. He would stash the contents of the latter — M&Ms, liquorice wheels, jelly beans and the like — in the hold-all at the back of his wardrobe as soon as he arrived home, and would consume the supply incrementally, secretly, over the course of the week. It gave him a kick to buck the nutritional system, to have a secret source of comfort.

He stopped at a red light, and undid the top button of his jeans, allowing his soft belly to spill out more freely. He ran his hand over weekend stubble, and wondered if that faint pinprick on his earlobe might still be receptive to an earring. Sadie had not been a fan, so it had gone the way of his days-of-the-week socks and novelty t-shirts. He massaged the lobe between his finger and thumb, and angled it towards the mirror to check for a hole. It was then he caught sight of a grey hair, blatantly sprouting from his temple. He tilted his head and the hair stayed grey. Not blond, not bleached, not sunkissed. Grey.

Once indoors, he located Sadie's tweezers, and started to pluck at what turned out to be a small crop, only stopping once he heard her arrive home. She always managed to close the front door with a solid thunk and click, whereas he could only get it to shut with a slam or, at best, a struggle. He ditched the tweezers and emerged into the living room as she breezed in, post-massage. She hugged and kissed him. She tasted of spring, of loose limbs and ungreyed hair.

'I'm just going to take a quick shower.' She started to raise her voice as she walked away. 'My orange dress needs a quick iron before Mum's party. Can you just…'

Shit. The party.

Mark followed her. She was holding her hand under the heavy spray, waiting for the perfect temperature. She playfully flicked a splash of water at him. Her bump was distinct now, and he noticed little red veins across her chest.

'I found a grey hair. Well, a few, really – all scattered.'

She stepped under the shower. 'Yeah, I've seen them. They're sweet.' She arched back slightly and turned her face upwards so the stream hit her neck and breasts.

'You've seen them? The greys? Why didn't you say?'

'Could you just pass me that shower gel please…' She stretched out her hand.

'How long have I had them?'

She squirted a generous blob of gel into her hand. 'If you're not ironing my dress, do you want to come in?'

'I'm too young for grey hairs, and now you're telling me they've been there for a while!'

'You're not too young! It'll be ear hair next!'

He joined her because he'd never, ever refused before, because saying no might mean the start of something else, and because, at some point, there would be ear hair, which he couldn't face thinking about.

Later, after ironing the dress, he dug out a pair of linen trousers he'd bought on holiday in Italy a couple of years ago. As he fastened them, he noticed they'd shrunk slightly. He pulled at the fabric, wondering if it might give a little. He decided to wear them with his edgiest t-shirt — he'd bought it at Stockbridge Market a couple of years ago, from a designer who sourced the best biodynamically-grown cotton, and used organic fabric paints to apply her artwork onto each t-shirt in a darkroom while listening to music. Each garment was a unique work of art. This particular design had been painted to a traditional Chinese folk tune, using chopsticks instead of a paintbrush. That's what she'd told him, anyway, and he'd been more than happy to hand over seventy quid for the t-shirt and the story.

•••

Sadie jostled the large gift bag she was carrying.

'Can you ring the doorbell? I'm a bit constrained here.'

Mark had offered to carry it — he'd offered to carry it twice, in fact — but he knew Sadie had wanted the drama of handing it over.

The approaching figure of Sadie's brother, Nick, appeared through the stained glass. Anyone could see he was no stranger to the gym, the climbing wall, the marathon route, the fast lane at the pool, the army assault course and kickboxing classes, even through heavily pitted opaque glass and molten leading.

'Welcome to what I'm calling the pre-party drinks reception,' said Nick, waving a glass of champagne. 'An opportunity for the non-pregnant to pre-load before the hoi polloi arrives. You look gorgeous, Sade.' Kiss, hug. 'Shall I take that?' Sadie frowned and held tightly onto the bag. 'OK. Come on in, and Mark can tell us all about his bold choice of outfit.'

Mark flipped his middle finger. Nick grabbed him in a bear hug and rubbed his head with his knuckles, causing Mark to grunt and struggle.

Sadie edged past them along the hall, and deposited the bag onto the kitchen table, where her sister, Ava, the baby of the family at fifteen, was scrolling through her phone and nursing a smoothie. She kissed Ava's head.

'Your hair smells weird.'

'I've stopped using shampoo. I've cut out all parabens. You should do the same. What's in the bag?' said Ava.

'Mum's birthday present. Where is she?'

'Upstairs with Dad, getting ready. I got her a smoothie maker. What did you get her?'

'It's a surprise. What are parabens?'

'Endocrine-disrupting preservatives.'

Ava slurped the green concoction and returned to consulting her phone. Mark walked in and winced.

'Jesus, Ava, what are you drinking?' he asked.

'Smoothie. What d'you get Mum?'

'Oh, Sadie made her a dressing gown–'

'It's not a dressing gown! And it's a surprise, so wait and see.'

Ava took another sip of her smoothie. 'Nick's winning so far. Platinum bracelet. She said it was too much, but then she put it on, and kept holding it up to the light.'

Sadie cleared industrial quantities of apple cores and fruit peel from the work surface. 'There is no *winning*, Ava. It's Mum's birthday, not Wimbledon.'

Ava rolled her eyes. Mark sat down next to her.

'We've not seen you for a while. How's school?' he asked.

'You saw me five days ago.' She spoke without looking up from her phone.

'Did you finish the art project?'

She looked up, surveyed him. 'What's that t-shirt all about? It looks weird on you.'

'Says the girl drinking swamp water.'

Ava stirred the smoothie slowly. She drew the teaspoon out and examined it.

'Bryony Jones has been hassling me. Don't you play football with her dad?'

Mark made a terrified face.

'Exactly,' said Ava.

'So what have you done to upset her?'

'Wasn't me. Mum put something bad on her term report.' She turned her attention back to the swamp juice.

'If you ignore her, she'll probably stop. Or you could report her.'

Ava wiped her forearm across her mouth. 'She's not stupid. There's nothing I can report.'

'Right,' said Mark. 'What does your mum say?'

Ava gave him a withering look. Mark picked up her smoothie and downed it in one before plonking the glass on the table, wiping his mouth and making a baulking face.

'I was drinking that!'

'Well, I've saved you the bother.'

He took the glass to the sink and squirted plenty of washing up liquid into it before filling it to the brim with hot water. He tried to pick up the conversation with his back to her; she always seemed more comfortable talking without having the added pressure of eye contact.

'So. Boyfriend.'

Silence.

'Michael, is it?'

'You're talking about Michael Deluna. He's not my boyfriend.'

'Crush. He's your crush.'

'Shut up.'

'Deluna. Deeeluuuuna. Hmm. What's he like?'

Sadie wiped down the cupboards, so Mark returned to the table and started to flick through a magazine, as though he was only vaguely interested in her response.

'He's clever. He's going to study astronomy at university.' A beat. 'That's your cue to make a lame joke about star signs.'

He looked up from the magazine: 'Are you still a Virgo?'

'Lame.'

Violet appeared at the kitchen door. She was birthdayed up — indigo dress and heels — and her make-up was slightly smudged. Sadie waylaid her with hugs and kisses.

'Happy birthday, Violet,' said Mark, pointing to the gift.

She opened it gently, and pulled out a floor-length midnight-blue kimono, hand-embroidered with sixty white gardenias.

'One for each year,' said Sadie.

'It must have taken you…'

'It took her a year,' said Mark, fully aware that Sadie would very much want her mother to know how much time and effort she'd put into it, without having to tell her herself.

Violet wrapped herself in the robe, twirled around.

'It's not silk is it?' said Ava, squinting at it suspiciously.

Violet stroked the fabric.

'Because you know how silk is made, right?' said Ava.

'It's lotus silk,' said Sadie.

'No carbon footprint,' said Mark, giving a thumbs-up to Ava.

'Where's Dad?' said Sadie.

Tony walked in, on cue. 'Nice dressing gown.' Violet unfastened it, and he stepped forward to help her out of it.

'Sadie embroidered an average of one-point-two gardenias on it every week for a year,' said Ava, without looking up.

They all looked at her. The doorbell rang, and she pushed her earbuds in.

Over the next hour, almost everyone from the length of the street arrived, and a few from further afield. The house babbled with catch-up and gossip, punctuated by loud exclamations and bursts of laughter. As the evening wore on, every time a group of people left, more turned up. There were enthusiastic attempts at dancing, but the majority of those who felt sufficiently moved by the music displayed all the allure and rhythm of eggs on a rolling boil. Mark circulated, keen to allow everyone the opportunity to hear his best material.

Tony tapped him on the shoulder just as he was in the throes of trying out a new bit on a squiffy group of teachers. The intrinsic authority of the tap caused him to stumble slightly.

'Can you help me bring in more wine from the garage?' It sounded like a question, but it was really an instruction.

He followed Tony through the door under the stairs along to another door that led into the garage, and made an involuntary sound as a sticky spider cobweb attached itself to his face. Tony turned back to give him a withering look.

Mark wiped the dust off a wine bottle.

'Don't touch anything,' said Tony.

He wiped his hand on his trousers, then stood still, waiting for instructions.

'Sadie's looking tired,' said Tony.

It felt like an accusation. He stayed silent.

'She needs her rest now. Enough sleep.' He picked up two cases of wine and tilted his head for Mark to do the same.

'You get the red.'

Mark scanned the boxes for clues.

'Right. Erm, now, what's this, Chenin…'

'That's white,' said Tony, before kicking two cases. 'Those. Take those.'

Laden to capacity, Mark followed his father-in-law through the garage side-door back into the house. Tony put down his cases to wedge the kitchen door open for Mark, and held his arms out to take a case from him. Unable to see this, Mark tripped over the cases on the floor, and lurched forwards. Tony put his body up against the cases, stopping Mark and the wine from falling to the ground.

'Get the first half breathing,' said Tony.

Mark looked at him, nonplussed.

'Open one of the boxes. Uncork all of the wines in that box.'

'Right. And what shall I do with the corks?' asked Mark, rubbing his hair, trying to remove all traces of cobweb.

Tony sighed in response. Mark had never understood why he had always elicited such irritation from Sadie's dad. There was something about not being good enough, of course, but it ran deeper than that.

'Put the white wine in the fridge,' said Tony.

'The whole lot?'

'As many as will fit.'

Tony effortlessly uncorked two bottles of red wine, looking at Mark's t-shirt as he did so.

'Oh, there's a story to this.' He stretched his arms out to give Tony a better view. 'I got it done by an artist at Stockbri–'

'And fill up the bowls when you've finished.'

'Bowls?' Mark looked around the room.

'Crisps, nuts, olives – that kind of thing. They're all over the house.' He strode out of the room, holding two bottles of red between the meaty fingers of one hand, and several wine glasses in the other.

Once Mark had carried out the instructions, before rejoining the party, he treated himself to a very large glass of dark ruby Grand Cru Bordeaux.

chapter 4

MARK ROLLED TOWARDS Sadie and placed his hand gently on her belly. She pressed his fingers more firmly over her womb.

'I read an article online that said it's like water ballet in there now. It'll be throwing all kinds of shapes. A bit like you last night,' she said.

He turned over onto his back and laughed.

'The attempt at Northern Soul was impressive. All that kicking. A shame about your trousers.'

'They'd shrunk.'

She laughed and pulled his hand back onto her belly, placing her own over it.

'It's the size of an avocado now.' Her voice was bed-whispery.

'Wow,' said Mark. 'An avocado.'

They lay in silence for a few moments. Mark's hand slowly made its way up to Sadie's swollen breasts.

'I keep thinking about what it'll be like, you know, after the baby's born,' said Sadie. 'Can you imagine?'

Mark let out a little exhalation, not quite a laugh, and repositioned his hand back down to her belly.

'What if I turn out to be a rubbish dad?'

She nuzzled into him.

'Not gonna happen.'

'You say that now, but...'

She kissed his good heart. 'Not. Gonna. Happen.' She wouldn't let it happen. Not after all they'd gone through to get here. Years of gut-wrenching anguish, as period after period arrived dead on time, or, crueller, a day or so late. Walking on eggshells through forty grand's worth of IVF, cycle after cycle. Fixing a baby monitor to the wall of a carefully decorated nursery, in the hope that it would, one day, be switched on. The maybe-gravity-will-do-the-trick headstands after sex. The maybe-a-change-of-diet-will-do-the-trick glut of chicken, lentils, liver and caviar. The endless temperature checks. The boxer shorts. The silent prayers and bouts of retching tears.

'You're a natural. You're brilliant with Ava; she loves you. Everyone's kids love you.'

'That's different from being a dad, though.'

'I know that,' she kissed him. 'Come on,' she said, patting him out of bed.

They did the breakfast dance. He put bread in the toaster and set to making the coffee, she semi-circled past him to the fridge for butter, marmalade and milk.

He reached over her head for two cups. She picked out two knives, two teaspoons, and passed them to him. He placed them on the table, moved the fruit bowl to one side. They took their seats simultaneously. Mark troughed straight into breakfast, as Sadie surveyed the bundle of wires hanging from the kitchen ceiling.

'Did you chase up Vince?'

Mouth full: 'Vince?'

That was a no. She knew that was a no. 'The electrician. His number's on the list.'

Mouth half full: 'The list?'

Every week, she'd draw up a weekend list, adding to it most days: 1. Meter reading; 2. New shower head (square?); 3. Present — Sarah; 4. Tiles — take discount code; 5. Low-odour washable paint. And so on. And every Saturday morning, Mark seemed surprised at its existence.

Mouth empty: 'You know when I fell over the dog last night?'

'You didn't chase him?'

'The dog?'

'Vince.'

'I'll do it later. So, last night. I go flying over your dad's stupid dog, and everyone — everyone — rushes to make sure the dog's OK. What's that about?'

Sadie was already dialling Vince's number.

'Nobody — *nobody* — asks me if I'm OK. And then I hear you laughing in the kitchen.'

'Hello Vince. This is Sadie Darling. Just wanted to know if you'd managed to get the fitting for the kitchen light. The painter's saying it's dangerous with the wires just hanging out, so I hope we'll see you this weekend. Bye.'

'What painter?'

'We need to look at cot bumpers this weekend. We can swing by that new baby place after we've picked up the missing bracket fitting from Ikea. Then you have a haircut at two.'

He ran his fingers through his hair. 'I've been thinking of a change. I've become that "same again" guy. I was thinking of–'

'Then we need to pop in to see Mum and Dad. Make sure the dog's OK.'

Chapter 5

As THE DAYS LENGTHENED, new ranges of soft furnishings started to roll off factory production lines fast. It was Mark's job to tempt young professionals and other credit-worthy individuals into Re:Klein to feel the comfort of the Hamptons, Provence and Tuscany ranges, to consider the inadequacies of their own cat-plucked, weirdly stained five-year-old sofas compared to the bouncy new specimens on offer. Once he'd lured them in, it was the salesforce's job to flatter and do whatever else it took to close the deal. An afternoon of copywriting stretched ahead.

'Is sumptuousness a word?' asked Mark, addressing the office at large.

'It means squashy, doesn't it?' said the intern, Nisha, who had eschewed her undemanding general role and now worked mainly as Mark's assistant.

'So, which is the squashiest of this new lot, does anybody know?'

There was some shrugging and shaking of heads. The sales director, Don West, crawled from under his stone, and scowled in Mark's direction.

'Why don't you bloody well go and find out, Lardarse? And get yourself a dictionary while you're at it. If I've added this line up once I've done it half a dozen times.'

'Yeah, Don. I'll leave you to your big sums. And, by the way, nobody buys dictionaries any more. That's what the internet's for,' said Mark, pushing his tongue under his bottom lip.

'That's not what I use the internet for,' said Don, a lecherous grin cracking open his pockmarked face. He guffawed, stood up, adjusted his stirring tackle, and headed for the toilet as Nisha summarised the lot on Twitter.

The Tuscany range was the most sumptuous, Mark could see that at a glance, even though it was covered in plastic and tucked away in a dark corner of the stockroom. Overstuffed and overdesigned, it came in two fabrics and ten colourways, and included a double reclining option for an extra couple of hundred pounds. It would fly out in droves as long as he could get people to come in and sit on it. The Hamptons was this season's safe bet; unassuming design in three tasteful shades, none darker than a buff envelope, perfect for any child-free couples who happened to be wandering around the retail park looking to be tempted. The Provence was the season's wildcard. Retina-blasting colours on a chrome frame, this was a range for the heavily medicated or the visually impaired.

Mark weaved through the sofas, and eventually found a dark nook. He curled onto a Tuscany and closed his eyes. Inevitably, the dry sound of the thwack of a cricket bat came. He silently chanted: *I'm OK, I'm OK, I'm OK.*

When he got back to the office, a lively discussion was mid-flow, bouncing across cubicles. Those with headsets had them half-off or around their necks, some were standing and almost everyone was grinning.

'Can someone google it?' asked Don.

'Don has blood in his piss,' said Nisha, excitedly, as Mark passed her desk.

'You've got haematuria, Don!' shouted someone.

'What's that, then?'

'It's blood in the urine.'

'I know that, you stupid arse! I've just sodding well told you that! I want to know what it is. Why have I got blood?'

'It might be your prostate!' shouted someone else, rather too gleefully.

'Bladder stones!'

'Infection!'

'Renal disease!'

'Urinary tract disorder!'

'Have you been eating beetroot?'

The Finance Director sidled in and signalled to Don

that she wanted a word. *Now.* Don gave her a thumbs-up and waved for everyone to shut up.

'All right, all right!' he said, gathering up a sheaf of papers. 'I bet there was beetroot in that sodding kebab last night,' he added, as he trailed out.

A few took the opportunity to pause for speculation and to make up jokes. Others quickly returned to what they'd been doing before the blood.

'Nish, can you find out how much a door drop for an A4 flyer would be for EH3, 4 and 5, please?' said Mark.

Nisha nodded.

'Get a couple of quotes, if you can.'

'Shall I draw up some comparisons on prices and reach – that kind of thing?'

'Yeah, great. Can you look at some tightly targeted online stuff, too?'

'I've got an idea for an Insta campaign.'

'Go for it,' he said.

His phone vibrated in his pocket. It was a photo of a yoga class on a beach, sent from his old friend, Dean, who was now living the dream in California.

Finally been persuaded to start my day with these guys. #hardlife

He shoved the phone back into his pocket.

'Fancy having a crack at some copy writing later?' asked Mark.

'Sure. What is it?' said Nisha.

Mark lowered his voice. 'I need a few paragraphs that'll tempt all those bored couples to come in and buy two sofas, one of which they'll eventually shove on Gumtree because it gets in the way of the telly. Are you with me, Nish?'

'You know consumerism is wrecking the planet?'

'It's also paying my mortgage and your equally hefty student loan.'

'Don't you ever feel guilty?'

'It's my default state,' he said.

chapter 6

MARK AND SADIE'S WEDDING anniversary fell on a Tuesday, and they had tickets for that evening's preview of an exhibition of silica-preserved body parts. It wasn't a traditional way to spend an anniversary, but it was also the final day of a Scottish fashion retrospective that Sadie hadn't yet seen.

'We can zip in, then go on somewhere nice for something to eat,' she said.

She had developed a habit of speaking with her right hand splayed across her bump. Sometimes, usually when contemplating, she would rhythmically rub the bump in such a way that made him think she might, at any moment, start patting her head with her other hand. It wouldn't have surprised Mark in the least to discover that Sadie was, in addition to everything else, effortlessly ambidextrous.

They arrived early enough to avoid the preview throng. 'OK, you can go and look around the body parts while I check out the Jean Muirs,' she said, hand on bump. 'Meet you back here at quarter past?' Mark kissed her cheek before walking towards the signs that warned visitors they may experience distress at the contents of the next room.

It was silent in there. He crouched in the half-light, drawn to the tiny fingernails of a sixteen-week-old miscarried foetus. He read the blurb but it offered no clue as to why this particular exhibit came to be here, and he suddenly felt sorry for the poor sod who would have been charged with the task of asking the grieving mother if she would give permission for her child to be drained of blood and injected with silica gel before being sealed in a tube and put on display. A flat, uniform nap of down covered its almost transparent skin. He peered at the perfect pink fingernails again. Smaller than shirt buttons, thin as rose petals.

It was then he caught sight of someone familiar. He stared at her: Ruby Suddula. He skidded back two decades. *Thwack.* She adjusted her skirt, and his mouth remembered a snog at the end-of-term school disco, when she had twirled his hair and his heart around her forefinger. He could almost feel acne re-pustulating his chin and brace wires threading around his teeth.

Ruby murmured to a couple standing next to one of the large exhibits. She moved around, pointing out various bones, joints and muscles of interest. Eventually, the couple moved on, and Mark walked towards her. She smiled at him, ready to answer his questions.

'Ruby.'

She looked intently at the face of the man who knew her name.

'Mark,' he said.

'Darling,' she said. She stifled a wow and half-hugged him. As they separated from the awkward tangle, Ruby held onto his arms and leaned back, as if to take in the full Mark Darlingness of him.

'I didn't recognise you without your rugby kit.'

'Football,' he corrected her. 'Captain.'

'Oh, yeah, football.' A smile.

No mention of cricket. But he heard it. The thwack, the scream, the sirens.

'You still play?'

'Sometimes.'

She arched a brow.

'Are you still doing the art?' *Doing the art.* Jesus.

'I am still *doing the art.* Yes. Third floor. All me,' she said, pointing upstairs.

'Really?'

'There is no third floor.'

She was always sharper than him. At school, she had run quiet rings around most people.

'So what are you doing?'

'I'm a stand-up.'

'A comedian?'

'On a good night, yeah.'

'Impressive. Brave.'

'Only if you're not funny.'

A cagoule approached her, checked her name badge through his unfeasibly smeared glasses, and launched into a question that was more of a comment. Ruby handled it expertly, answered politely, and turned her beam back to Mark.

'Someone said you were a writer.'

He let out a loud nervous laugh. A woman nearby shot him a filthy look.

'Well, not really *writing* writing,' he said, using air quotes for the first time in his life. 'No great novel yet.' He checked to make sure she wasn't smirking. She wasn't. 'I do a bit of daytime work for an interior design company. Promotional stuff about reclining sofas and chairs, mainly.'

'I have one of those reclining chairs.'

He would, one day, come to realise that he should have walked away then, that he should have said: 'Look, it's been lovely seeing you again, and I am impressed and delighted to discover that you have clearly maintained your level of superiority over me in every way, but I am going to say goodbye and scoot back into the other room to my pregnant wife. I'll doubtless take a moment later this evening to think of you in that reclining chair of yours, but I really do have to go.'

But he did not say any of those things.

c**hapter 7**

SADIE WAS A MENDER, a fixer, a hell of a stitcher. She spent most of her daylight hours from Monday to Friday, and sometimes Saturdays, next to a large curtainless window in a tiny studio, repairing the rips and frays of everyday life. As each winter approached, squally showers and gusts would rattle at the old casements, and she would haul an oil-filled radiator from the storage cupboard, and wheel it past the two mannequins to take up a minimum four-month stay next to her chair. The smell of murderously hot dust for the first couple of days was always a reminder that hail, snow and ice were on their way. Some mornings, if she'd cycled in or had spent ages at the bus stop, she would place a thick blanket on the radiator and warm it to toasty hot before draping it over her knees and starting work. Once summer finally arrived, she would squeak the sash window as high as it would open and let the sound of traffic and pedestrians drift in. Often, on such days, a fragment of a conversation would ooze into the room, and she would allow her mind to wander, conjuring up context and characters and happy-ever-afters.

All the studios in this former textile mill were occupied by furniture upcyclers, card-makers, lino-printers and other artists. Between them, they shared the services of Woody, a retired civil servant and now photographer, who made coffee, ran errands and cleaned in return for minimum wage and varying degrees of use of the space. They also shared petting duties of Woody's black, retired greyhound, Dandelion (Dandy by those who knew her best) who loped from studio to studio for strokes, naps and the odd nibble on something tasty.

The only time Sadie closed her door firmly shut was when she had a customer with her. People would bring in their favourite dress or jacket and wonder if there was any way she could, please, make it like new again, bating their breath as they handed it over. And she would squint at it, hold it away from her then peer at it close-up, test the strength of the fabric, turn it inside-out, and grate her teeth over her bottom lip. Then, slowly, gradually, the corners of her mouth would turn up, her eyes would crinkle and she would say yes, promising to make everything OK. And they would breathe again, thanks to this woman who could turn back time, who could restore what had been damaged. She would see them out, knowing full well that their earnest resolution to be more careful in future would vanish as soon as they became reabsorbed into the real world.

It was no longer a novelty to have people strip down to their stretch marks and crinkles soon after hellos were exchanged, but she never took for granted the secrets she was privy to, people's dramatic and careless moments. She discreetly nipped in and let out the clothes of yo-yo dieters, often rethreading her needle through neat lines of tiny holes she'd made just months before. She never asked and tried not to judge as she meticulously mended what people had undone. She re-attached post-break-up torn suit sleeves and furiously ripped pockets, she smelled and touched where even lovers' noses and hands never had cause or inclination to venture. She learned not to ask how or why, and to turn a blind eye to what fell out of pockets. Occasionally, she would stitch over a stain that would cause her such consternation she felt justified in applying a surcharge. 'Right, you dirty bastard, it's the filth tax for you!' she would say, and her voice would cause Dandelion to wander in.

Private customers, particularly those who paid the filth tax, were few and far between; most of her business was impersonally couriered to her in boxes from local theatre companies – royal robes, dwarf costumes, burlesque outfits, the occasional pantomime horse's arse. But, as summer drew to a close, as the days shortened, she would stock up on the palest silk thread to prepare for the annual influx of still pristine summer wedding dresses, which she would cut and refashion into elegant cocktail gowns, flippy party dresses and christening robes. November was her busiest month. She would arrive early and leave late, often taking stitching home: panto costumes, school Nativity garb, Christmas party outfits. Those short, poorly lit days, occasionally fuelled by a glass or two of communal mulled wine, were when she received most sharp pinpricks – tiny reminders to be careful, always be careful.

This morning, with spring in the air, she opened the windows. The breeze quelled her nausea but was not strong enough to keep her awake. Surrounded by soft fabrics, bobbins and quilted linings, she closed her eyes for a moment and leaned back. Three hours later, she was still asleep.

'So this is how you spend your days, is it?'

Mark nuzzled into her hair, kissed her.

'Oh, my God! What time is it? What are you doing here?'

'It's lunchtime. I had a meeting around the corner, so I thought we could go to Urban Angel.'

She blinked slowly, still half-asleep. 'We haven't been there for ages.'

'I know. Get your coat, sleeping beauty.'

The place was busy, but the table they used to sit at when they'd first got together was empty.

'Our old table,' said Mark.

Sadie wasn't able to pull her chair in as tightly to the table as she once could, and apologised to the woman sitting behind her.

'It'll soon be a table for three,' said Sadie, hand on bump.

She said it with a laugh, but a mild panic hit Mark. Of course it would soon be a table for three, he knew that. It just hit him sideways, the mention of the baby in the context of sitting at the table where they'd once dated. He looked down at the menu, reading nothing.

'Asparagus risotto,' said Sadie.

Mark looked up. Sadie pointed to the blackboard.

'On the specials. Your favourite.'

A waiter appeared.

'Can I get you something to drink?'

'Whisky,' said Mark.

Sadie laughed.

The waiter stood poised with his pencil.

'Whisky?' said Sadie. 'Have you taken the afternoon off?'

Mark tried to compose himself. He smiled and pretended it had been a joke.

'I'll have a sparkling water, please.'

Sadie held up two fingers – a request for the same.

The waiter retreated.

'You OK?' Sadie reached over to hold his hand across the table.

He nodded and tried to smile, overwhelmed at the realisation that he would almost certainly be a terrible father.

A moment. They looked out of the basement window at the feet of people with somewhere to go.

'Do you remember the time you made me laugh so hard, right here at this table, that we had to leave?

Didn't even finish our desserts.'

He exhaled a small, quiet laugh. He was a psychological wreck. What could he offer a child?

'You sure you're all right, hon?' She said it quietly, leaning towards him.

He opened his mouth; his nostrils didn't seem capable of taking in enough air now.

Sadie held his gaze, stroked his forearm and repeated a phrase that she'd said to him so many hundreds of times over the years. 'It's OK. Everything's going to be OK.'

He sat up straight. The voices in his head quietened as he surfaced. Sadie quickly changed the subject. This was their pattern. He would buckle, she would reassure him, he would surface, she would distract, and everything would be smoothed over until the next time.

'There was something on *Woman's Hour* about subliminal bonding today.'

Distraction. He made a *go on* face.

'I only caught the end of it. A woman came up with a set of questions to make people bond with you.'

'That sounds very dodgy.'

'It's for people who don't know how to date face-to-face. They hook up online, then meet in real life and they've no idea what to say to each other, or how to behave.'

'Vomiting within the first ten minutes worked for us.'

'Not ideal first-date material, apparently. Anyway, the questions are along the lines of: Would you like to be famous? What's the one thing you'd ask a fortune-teller? If you could change anything about the way you were brought up, what would it be? That kind of thing.'

The waiter returned with the drinks. They ordered food and he went away again.

Sadie held her hands out, palms up, inviting him to speak.

'Are you trying to bond with me?' he said.

'Well, the famous one's a no-brainer. I'd hate it. Imagine sitting here and everyone gawking at you, taking photos of you eating. Ugh! Who'd want that?'

'I would.'

'Really? Famous for what?'

'Comedy,' he said. 'I'd like to be famous enough that the audience cheers before I've even walked onto the stage. Famous and rich.'

'You know you've actually *spent* more than you've earned on comedy so far? That website designer's invoice was one of the funniest things I've seen.'

The ribbing was good-natured, but it stung a little.

'So what would you ask the fortune-teller?'

Mark took a sip of water, and considered his list of questions.

'Nothing.'

'Not even the lottery numbers?'

He shook his head.

'You might as well ask this table.' He knocked on the wood. 'Nobody — nobody — can predict the future.'

chapter 8

'YOU'VE NEVER MENTIONED her before.'

'I've not seen her since we were kids.'

Mark and Jonny were resting at the base of a huge climbing wall, having scrambled up, across and down it a few minutes earlier.

'So Sadie's never met her?' said Jonny, lunging deep to stretch out his hamstrings.

'Nope.'

'How's she doing?' Jonny arced his hands over his belly to make a pregnant shape.

'She's great. She's great.' Big grin.

'And what does she make of Ruby?'

The grin disappeared. 'I've not mentioned her.'

Jonny shook his head, gave him a knowing look. 'Secret.'

Mark shrugged, and hoped Jonny might have a magic wand in his kit bag.

Jonny Salter had never been married. He felt unable to offer any useful relationship advice. His only serious girlfriend had left him a couple of years ago. As she packed her belongings, she relayed in a resigned, monotone voice how she loved him but she hardly saw him, and when she did, he was spent, exhausted from teaching all day.

It transpired that there had been a significant level of dissatisfaction on her part for some time and, as she folded her skirts and rolled up her sweaters, she took the opportunity to get a few things off her chest. She hated the way he hung up his suit within moments of arriving home, then slobbed around in boxers and a t-shirt for the rest of the evening — it showed a lack of respect for her. She didn't think he ate nearly enough vegetables, she thought his taste in humour was too slapstick, she was sick of listening to his nineties music, she had no interest in rugby, and, by the way, why was it always her who had to write and post the Christmas cards? She complained about how their sex life had dwindled to a Saturday-night fumble, followed by him lifting her on top as he lay there 'making those weird encouraging noises'. Did he realise, she asked — and did he even care — that she often lay beside him sleepless and despondent? He was a nightmare to live with during the academic term and too unadventurous for her liking in the summer break. She suspected all the itching he did was due to athlete's foot, and seriously recommended he should have that odd toenail seen to, and, by the way, it wasn't against the law for a man to use moisturiser. Was he aware of how annoying it was, the way he breathed through his mouth when he was reading the Sunday papers? Also, in the interest of full disclosure, it turned out she wasn't overly keen on his mother.

It was a fair list. He didn't dispute any items on it, and he could see her point about his mother.

During the intervening years, he had met women at parties and had been set up on a few dates but nothing had really taken. He was never short of someone to snog, and had rolled around on a few beds, but had quickly lost heart. He still took his suit off as soon as he got in from work but no longer 'slobbed around' in his boxers — instead, he wore soft sleeping shorts and paraded around bare-chested. His vegetable intake had increased; he had discovered pak choi, Chinese artichoke and yard-long beans. Bottles and tubes of high-end products lined his bathroom shelves these days. Last summer, he spent three glorious weeks in Sri Lanka, where he'd tracked leopards, witnessed migrating elephants and had allowed himself to be thoroughly seduced by the tour guide. And nobody, these days, except his mother, complained at not receiving a Christmas card from him.

'Do you moisturise?' said Jonny.

'What?'

'Your skin. On your face. Do you use moisturising cream, that kind of thing?'

'Er, sometimes.'

'There you go. Buy yourself some proper products. Those assistants on the counters make you feel great. And then you walk away, no complications. You go back when the bottle's empty.'

'What does this have to do with anything?'

'If you want someone to stroke your face, laugh at your jokes...'

'Hang on–'

'You should start with a scrub, then a serum. The moisturiser goes on top. Get to Harvey Nics. Or Space NK on George Street.'

Mark laughed. 'Right. Noted.'

Jonny stretched, as Mark sat in a small heap.

'Do you think I should say something to Sadie? About Ruby?'

'Depends.'

Mark wiped his face with his towel before taking a long drink of water.

'She was there — Ruby — when the accident...'

Jonny nodded.

'Did she mention it?'

Mark shook his head.

'Maybe she's forgotten. What was it, twenty-odd years ago?'

Twenty-three years of guilt. Twenty-three years of trying to make up for killing his best friend.

'She was a few feet away from where Fergus was standing. As the bat left my hand, I laughed. I saw her laughing, too. Until Fergus went down. I haven't seen her since.'

Chapter 9

ONE, TWO, THREE, FOUR, five, six, seven, eight, nine.
One, two, three, four, five, six, seven, eight, nine.
One, two, three, four, five, six, seven, eight, nine.

Ava liked to count out her run in nines. Three was her magic number, and what could be better than three threes. If she didn't end her number of steps on a nine, she'd do a little jog at the doorstep, just to be safe.

One, two, three, four, five, six, seven, eight, nine.
One, two, three, four, five, six, seven, eight, nine.
One, two, three, four, five, six, seven, eight, nine.

She broke into a sprint. She had designed herself for this, keeping her hair short, her nails trimmed, her kit not too loose, not too tight. No piercings, no jewellery, no make-up. Sweatbands, Skinful gloves, skort.

Onetwothree, onetwothree, onetwothree.
Onetwothree, onetwothree, onetwothree.
Onetwothree, onetwothree, onetwothree.
Onetwothree, onetwothree, onetwothree.
Onetwothree, onetwothree, onetwothree.
Onetwothree, onetwothree, onetwothree.
Onetwothree, onetwothree, onetwothree.
Onetwothree, onetwothree, onetwothree.
Onetwothree, onetwothree, onetwothree.

Eighty-one. Tap on thigh, knee, heel. Start again.

On her coach Emma's advice, she was including short, explosive elements to her cardiovascular training. Emma was also trying to make their one-to-one sessions more fun, which Ava ended up liking, despite her initial reservations. Earlier that week, she'd had Ava running around the court keeping three balloons simultaneously afloat. She couldn't think about that right now, or she'd lose count.

One, two, three, four, five, six, seven, eight, nine.
One, two, three, four, five, six, seven, eight, nine.
One, two, three, four, five, six, seven, eight, nine.

On difficult days — and there were many — she would find a quiet spot where she could hold her breath as she counted to a high square number. The more difficult the day, the higher the number. The release, the outbreath, made her feel alive, powerful.

Just as she arrived home, Mark emerged from the house carrying a bag stuffed with home-grown vegetables.

'Sadie asked me to pick these up from your dad. Hope I've not left you short of ingredients for one of your concoctions.'

Ava bent almost double, hands on her waist.

'Good run?'

She straightened up, surveyed him.

'You should run.'

'I *do* run. I play football. We run all over the pitch. That's the game.'

'So why are you still a bit fat?'

Mark looked down at his stomach. 'You want me to come running with you?'

'No way! I'm just saying, if you're fat, you'll probably die young. Not that you're young.'

'How's the tennis?'

'Dad said you would've killed the dog the other night if you'd have landed a couple of inches to the left. And Mum said you fell because your trousers were inappropriately tight.'

'Well, thanks for the rays of sunshine. I'd better be getting this veg home, so I can let it rot in the fridge while I gorge on pies and chocolate.' He rubbed the top of her head. 'Stay honest.'

He walked away, feeling every gram of the extra few kilos he was carrying.

'Can you set up the Wii for me for next week?' she

shouted. 'Inter-school finals.'

Without turning round or slowing down, Mark held a thumb aloft. He'd spend an hour later that evening, setting up the spare room for Ava to stop in on the way home from school to play tennis against fierce virtual opponents. He'd put his own games away, ensure the floor was clear so she could leap and bound about, he'd place the tennis games in front of the console, and leave a small pack of hand wipes next to the controls because he knew she wouldn't trust they were sufficiently germ-free.

'And no bottled water! I've stopped drinking it.'

He turned back.

'Water?'

'*Bottled* water.'

He raised his palms, puzzled.

'The planet,' she shouted, by way of explanation.

He'd look online for the best water filters, and would pick one up at the weekend. He wouldn't win many prizes for being the best husband but he felt sure he'd storm the brother-in-law category.

chapter 10

HE WAS BACKSTAGE. Backstage, where there was never a mirror, let alone one lit by strips of bright bulbs. Where the air smelled of stale sweat, terror, and cheap disinfectant if you were lucky. The holding area for the desperately insecure, the unloved, and those with something to prove. The place that could give New Year's Eve a run for its money when it came to making people feel horribly alone, despite the noise. This one had a notice on the wall:

PLEASE PUT YOUR RUBBISH IN THE BAG PROVIDED
NO DOGS

The bag provided contained a large empty cider bottle and a Co-op sandwich wrapper. There were several Haribo sweets scattered around the room, as though someone had ripped into the bag teeth first and hurriedly tipped most of the contents right into their mouth. It wasn't impossible that the remaining gummy bears, hearts and strawberry jellies might still be eaten tonight, particularly those that had only fallen as far as the table, even though there was no telling how long they'd been there; sugar was sugar.

Mark sat on the only chair and focused on a poster of Las Vegas. He'd been square-breathing since the early days. Top left corner, breathe in; top right corner, hold; bottom right, breathe out; bottom left, hold. Repeat until sane. His backstage playlist emanated from his phone, tinny and slightly distorted over the muffled sound of the act currently on stage. Now and then, a swell of laughter would blast under the gap at the bottom of the door, reminding him of what he was going out there for.

A young man walked in — no knock — and held up five fingers. Mark nodded.

'Milk's milk, right?'

The warm wave of laughter lapped over him, bathed him.

'So, yeah, we're gonna be green parents. Absolutely. We're all about preserving the environment, looking after the planet for the next generation. Oh yeah, we've bought loads of books and magazines on it. A few trees' worth. That we carried home in plastic bags.'

Another wave, smaller this time.

'You do what you can. Oh, and we've stocked up on

gender-neutral toys. We're on track to be the parents everybody hates. You know, avocado smash and hummus at the birthday parties. Piano lessons. Solvent godparents who own allotments and have learned Polish so they can patronise the cleaner properly.'

A swell.

'But I've had to stand my ground on the light sabre. I'll be honest with you — and I think I'm not alone on this — part of the reason I want a kid is for the light-sabre duels. I mean, that's the dream, right: two light sabres in the same house?'

A ripple.

'Maybe I'm missing the point. I dunno. I've opened a lot of the stuff already — just checking the quality — also, those Lego kits are not going to build themselves. And, you know, even Lego is environmentally sound these days. Oh yeah. The latest bricks are made with ethanol. Ethanol. You know what that is? It's a chemical extracted from sugar cane. *Sugar cane Lego.* Incredible.' A beat. 'I mean, I think it tasted OK as it was.'

A sip of water. A moment to take in the love. The warmth. The wave.

'But my wife says, 'Mark! Mark, you need to focus less on the toys, and familiarise yourself with those instruction videos on the parenting app.' And she's right. So, this app has short films where very thin, immaculately dressed men show you things like how to change a nappy in a place where facilities are limited. So you might be in the park, which is where they do their demonstration, or, I dunno, in the off-licence, comedy club…wherever. These guys can get a baby from shitball to peachy in a flash. They're geniuses.'

Pause.

'And they also have tips on how to stop your child choking on that delicious piece of Lego.'

He held his arms out, let the warm waves of laughter wash over him.

Chapter 11

SADIE HAD NEVER FELT SO RIGHT. So at one with everything. Not in a hippy-karmic-lotus-position way. Shit, no. But there were fleeting moments when she definitely felt connected to the roots of the trees in the Botanic Gardens and the nesting birds in the branches. Her blood ran hotter. She felt passionate about everything, from litter to #positiveparenting, and had the Twitter scars to prove it. And, just lately, she would take every opportunity to drop chocolate biscuits and toothbrushes into the supermarket food bank, picturing underprivileged kids enjoying the comfort of sweet, branded goods while also having the means to look after their teeth.

She'd long discarded her headphones, in favour of judgementally eavesdropping. She would surreptitiously tilt her head to listen to parents chatting to their toddlers or making unfathomable baby talk with rubber-limbed infants. She baulked as performance parents took to the stage in the fruit and veg aisles: 'How many bananas are in the bunch, Freddie?' 'What colour is the broccoli, Sophia?' *God save me from that.* And she'd wince at those who treated cafes as crèches, oblivious to their kids' antics as they smeared butter everywhere and ran around the legs of harassed staff. She calibrated her own parental instincts against the behaviour of these unwitting models. Often, she was only a short step away from holding up gymnastic-style score cards.

'Everyone thinks their way is the right way,' said Grace, shifting slightly onto her left bum cheek to take pressure off her ruined perineum. The Wonder Spot was buzzing with families. Sadie devoured a slab of coconut and lime loaf, while Grace made her way more moderately through a wedge of carrot cake. 'But it's hard, you know. Especially when you've had no sleep, and you've spent half an hour bundling the baby up to go out for bread and milk, then have to unbundle her because she's taken the opportunity to fill her nice clean nappy with what can only be described as the devil's own shite.'

'I just think there's no excuse for being on your phone when you could be bonding with the baby, that's all,' said Sadie.

'Come back to me on that in a few months' time,' said Grace. 'I've definitely looked at my screen while one of the kids has been up to mischief.'

'You were probably online shopping for nappies,' said Sadie.

'Nah. I was probably getting myself on a waiting list for some magic serum to stop me looking so bloody knackered all the time.'

It was easier to let Grace off the hook for the lapses because she was, in the main, a great mum, if you didn't count the time one of her kids managed to shut the other in the fridge, or the time she didn't fully screw the top back onto the wine and Katie had to take two days off nursery with a hangover.

•••

'I heard something on *The Food Programme* today, all about organic greens and superfoods,' said Sadie, enthusiastically cutting huge leaves of the stuff into ribbons. 'Apparently, one portion of kale contains all the amino acids you need for a day.'

'Really?' Mark had only a vague idea of what an amino acid was.

'You can't even get hold of organic kale in some parts of London because it's so popular, although now they're saying broccoli leaves are the new kale. We're having both with marinated tofu and a celeriac mash.'

Sadie was a big fan of *Masterchef*.

'And there's a lovely fruit salad for dessert. All organic. Apples, bananas, kiwi and blueberries. They're all superfoods, too.'

'Can I help?' It was a disingenuous offer; it wasn't

his night for cooking, and he was watching a crucial away match. Dean was watching it online in LA, and they were exchanging comments.

'Nick and Lenny have set a date, by the way.'

Sadie pushed the celeriac mash through a ricer.

'First week in May next year.'

She stirred in a spoonful of coconut oil.

'Two hundred guests, according to Mum.'

She tasted it, added sea salt, stirred, then tasted it again.

'They don't want any wedding presents, but they're asking guests to donate to either Shelter or Save The Children.'

She placed the tofu onto warmed plates.

'Dad's all in a huff about it – asking people for money – but I agree with Mum. It's such a lovely gesture. Typical of those two.'

She wiped sploshes from the rim of the plates, gathered up a couple of knives and forks, and carried the meals to the table.

'Red card! Send him off!' Mark retreated from the television, walking backwards towards the table, transfixed at the injustice of the unacknowledged transgression.

'What do you think?'

There seemed to be enough leaves on his plate to stop a commuter train.

'Erm, I might have a bit of ketchup with this, Sade.'

A roar from the crowd made him turn his attention back to the screen.

'Taste it first. It doesn't need ketchup.'

'Why did we pay a fortune for this guy when he can't even keep the bloody, sodding ball?'

He scooped a couple of leathery ribbons into his mouth.

'Very nice,' he lied. He angled his chair carefully, to minimise annoyance to Sadie and to optimise his view of the match as he ate.

'And, instead of Easter eggs, we're all chucking in for a new racquet for Ava. Her coach has recommended one, as well as some extra lessons. She's getting a bit old for eggs now, anyway.'

'Yeah. I need ketchup with this, babe. OK?' He looked for her approval before suddenly leaping to his feet to cheer on a player who was now running into the box with the ball, onside, moving into position to score.

'OH! OH! Go on! GO ON!'

Sadie rolled her eyes and went off to the kitchen while Mark stayed glued to the television.

She plonked a jar of tomato chutney on the table, and handed him a spoon.

'One-nil! We just have to keep the ball in the second half, park the bus, and we're home. What's this?' He picked up the jar and peered at its label.

'Ketchup.'

'It's a jar of tomato chutney.'

'It's the same thing.'

'What's happened to the usual stuff? The squeezy bottle?'

'I thought we'd have this from now on. I picked it up at Mellis's.'

He spooned a blob into his mouth and grimaced. 'It tastes funny.'

'You're not supposed to eat it straight off the spoon, you idiot. Put it on your food.'

He splotched it all over his meal.

'For God's sake, what are you doing? Just put a bit on the side.'

'I don't want a bit on the side.'

'You're a beast.'

He growled and pawed her arm.

'So, what do you think? Save The Children or Shelter?'

'What?'

Sadie pulled playfully at one of his ears. 'Are these made of cloth? Nick and Lenny are getting married. As a wedding present, we're donating to charity.'

Mark hazarded a guess at the right answer.

'Both.'

He turned to face the screen where three pundits in ugly, expensive suits were bantering over the performance of various players, post-morteming the goal, and discussing the importance of keeping possession of the ball.

'And I thought we'd give a hundred towards Ava's racquets and extra coaching sessions.'

No response.

'Mark!'

He turned his chair to face the table. He could listen to the half-time discussion without watching, and he might be able to finish eating before the second half started.

'Are you even interested in what I'm saying?'

'Of course I am. What's happening?'

'When are Nick and Lenny getting married?'

'The sooner the better.'

'What are we getting Ava for Easter?'

'Is it something to do with tennis? Is it Andy Murray?'

She laughed, which was a relief. He stood up, went off to the kitchen for another beer, and typed a quick response to Dean. He managed to get through most of the kale by the time the whistle blew. Aberdeen took immediate possession of the ball. Mark pointed his beer bottle at the television.

'Come ON, get the ball off him!'

Sadie took the plates out to the kitchen.

A successful tackle saw the ball lofted down the pitch towards their goal.

'Yes, that's it! Come on! COME ON!'

The ball was heading for the Aberdeen goal. The commentator babbled excitedly, a mighty roar went up from the crowd of elated fans, some with red-painted faces. They cheered in a sea of red and white chequered flags.

'No!'

Mark froze in a crucified position, arms out, pained expression, watching the replay of a beautiful goal.

Sadie came back in, holding two superfood smoothies.

'This should cheer you up,' she said.

Just then, his phone buzzed in his pocket. It wasn't Dean.

chapter 12

IT WAS ONLY COFFEE with an old schoolfriend, but these things can go on, so Mark thought it best to say something vague to his colleagues about a dental appointment and taking an early lunch.

He scanned Caffe Centro before sitting on a sofa by the window. He switched his phone to vibrate, put it in his inside jacket pocket, retied a shoelace, glanced at the menu, fished out his phone to check it, put it back in his pocket, then ordered a cafetière of coffee. He checked his phone again — she was now late. He scanned the room, switched his phone to ring and placed it face-up on the table. He swiped a newspaper off the chair next to his and pretended to read it.

Where are you?

He jumped as the text came in, and quickly craned around to see her, before typing his response.

On sofa by window. Where are you?

What sofa? Where ARE you?

Caffe Centro George St.

We said Centotre! I'm here.

It wasn't called Centotre any more, but he knew where she meant. He scuddled the hundred or so metres to Contini, dodging in and out of traffic and bumping up against shoppers and tourists.

Half an hour later, they'd transported themselves to the golden period when they'd each been unblemished, unbruised. Awkwardness had been quickly replaced by the ease of being with someone who had shared the pain of scraped knees, acne, first love.

Back then, Ruby had seemed untouched by the common trials and insecurities of adolescence. Her sketches and paintings had graced the staff room walls, and she'd once sold a painting of Portobello beach to the headmaster for what was then a mindblowing hundred pounds. She winced when Mark reminded her about the paintbrushes she had worn like chopsticks in her hair.

'It took my mum ages to get the oil paint out of my hair.'

He took a moment to look at her hair. It was pretty much as it had been at school. Shorter, but the same colour and texture.

A car horn blared outside and they both craned to see the aftermath of a near-miss. A woman, clearly distressed, shouted and gesticulated at the car driver, and then turned to the boy at her side, vigorously pointing at the road and the zebra crossing. Her urgent expression twisted and contorted her face. The child, shocked, stared at her. For a moment, she covered her eyes with her palms, still talking, then she lifted him up and held him tightly − he was too big for it, and his feet were barely off the ground, but he didn't struggle. She was crying and the boy looked as if he might, too.

'You never know the moment,' said an old woman at the next table.

They turned their attention back to each other.

'Do you ever think about the whole thing with Fergus?' asked Ruby.

Atomic bomb. He stiffened. *Thwack.* His muscles prepared to flee.

'Sorry, I didn't mean to upset you. The kid outside reminded me…' She put her hand on his forearm. 'Sorry.'

Breathe in. Pause. Breathe out. Pause.

'Yep.' Breathe in. 'How can I not?' Breathe in. 'I've bored the arse off several therapists talking about it over the years.' Breathe in.

'I'm sorry.'

A moment.

'What do *you* remember?' He searched her face for clues, tells.

'What?'

He looked outside. The woman and the boy had moved on. 'What did you see? I only have one angle. Mine.'

Ruby shifted, and went in carefully. 'Well, I could see it wasn't your fault.'

He rolled his eyes.

'No. Seriously. You swung that bat as hard as any kid with their eye on the prize would.'

She squeezed his arm. Slowly, gently.

He softened.

'He was an only child. Did you know that?' he said, staring hard at her now, as though she might be the source of absolution, as though she might have the power to forgive him, take away the flashbacks, erase it from history, make him the man he was once destined to be.

She shook her head.

'So, that was it for his parents. Their only child, gone.'

'They won't have blamed you.'

The wine arrived. Mark uprighted, shuffled his spine backwards into his chair.

Ruby pushed Mark's glass closer to him, and lifted her own. 'You have to let it go.'

'*Let it go* is always said to people who can't let it go.'

'So what would help you move on?'

'I don't need another therapist, Ruby.'

'It's a genuine question. I'm interested.'

He opened his mouth to speak, and nothing came. Saliva flooded his mouth, his chin started to quiver, and, to his mortification, he started to cry. Not discreetly. The tears were fast and hot. His chest heaved. His hands were shaking. He grabbed at his napkin, covered his face.

By the time he returned to the office he'd formulated a story about narrowly avoided root-canal work and the need to keep an eye on his gums. So when Nisha asked, casually, how things had gone at the dentist, he launched into his elaborate tale, a section of which involved baring his teeth and running his forefinger along his gumline.

'Apparently, flossing is the key,' he said. 'Flossing and not eating sticky, sugary stuff. That...those two things – they're the key to good teeth. And those little tiny brushes for between your teeth.'

'Interdental?'

'Yeah. And don't, like, keep food in your mouth for ages, especially if it's, you know, sweet or sticky. That's to be avoided.'

'Right.'

'Has anyone been looking for me?'

'Nope.'

'Good. Good. OK,' he said. He draped his jacket over the back of his chair.

'You OK?' Nisha looked hard at his puffy face.

'Yeah,' said Mark.

'Shall I make some coffee?'

'Great.'

'Strong and black?'

'Can you put a couple of sugars in it. Please.'

●●●

'Did I ever tell you Fergus was an only child?'

'Fergus?'

He looked at her, pointedly.

Sadie muted the television. 'What's made you think of him?'

He shrugged, then, after a pause: 'Do you think bringing a child into the world in some way makes up for…'

She turned the television off, and moved back deep into the sofa. She opened her arms wide, and Mark allowed himself to be held.

'I mean, I know it doesn't help his parents, his family, but, cosmically, karmically…'

Sadie murmured in vague agreement.

'I'm talking bollocks…' he trailed off, buried his head in her lap. 'I wish you could have been there. I wish you could have seen how it all happened.'

'You told me what happened.'

'Yes, but everyone who saw it — well, you never saw the look on their faces as they looked at Fergus then back at me.'

'Nobody would have blamed you.'

'But that's just it. You can't know. You weren't *there*.'

She stroked his head as she had done so many times before.

Later, in bed, as Sadie slept, he pictured Fergus

lying on the pitch, the faces of his friends, the teachers, parents. It was a well-rehearsed vignette. But this time he scanned the crowd and, just as the sirens started up, there, in the middle, was Ruby.

Chapter 13

AVA HAD SEEN THE LARGE BOX, even though her parents had hidden it from her. She knew what was in it, and had no intention of feigning surprise. She was now spending most of her spare time developing her forearm skill and a mean backhand. She'd watched the rise and rise of Johanna Konta, creating a slipstream for girls like her. Ava knew that the box contained the Head YouTek IG Extreme MP Elite. And she knew she would swing all 275 grams of it to the court-side whoops and applause of her tennis coach come the inter-school finals.

'I might have the veggie option with Ava,' said Mark.

'Since when have you been interested in becoming a veggie?' said Sadie.

'I fancy a change, that's all,' said Mark.

There were far more interesting things Ava could be doing on Easter Sunday than sitting at home, discussing the merits of vegetarianism with Mark, but it was better than defending her stance with any of the others. The most interesting thing would be to be with Michael Deluna. His parents were having a garden party that sounded far more promising, mainly because Michael would be there, with his black hair and thick eyelashes and enormous brain. She pictured the Delunas sipping wine on the patio and discussing matters of global importance. Later, as people strayed indoors, Michael would probably adjourn to sit on the fourth or fifth step of the staircase — there was bound to be a staircase — where he would strum his guitar and pause occasionally to twist a tuning key without making the string snap. As he did so, she pictured his hair flopping over his eyes a bit. He was a god. No, actually, he was an alien super-being. She wondered what his hair smelled like. Space and rocket fuel, probably.

Last night's half-term party had been a moderate success. Most importantly, she had been hugged by Michael as the fireworks had gone off. Yes, everybody was hugging, but he seemed to single her out. That definitely meant something. She'd been so surprised by the hug that she'd forgotten to sniff him. Also, she'd been hoping for a kiss, but the fireworks had been so loud that she'd probably looked totally weird standing there with her fingers in her ears, so she couldn't blame him for not going for it. She'd been so caught up in the sight of multi-coloured starbursts and rockets that she'd jumped as he wrapped his arms around her, causing her to accidentally smack him in the eye. He fell backwards into Bryony Jones's gang, one of whom told him, in no uncertain terms, to watch what he was doing, pal. It was all a bit of a disaster, really. Still, a hug was a hug.

'Could you come and help with the salad, please, Ava?' shouted Violet from the kitchen.

'I'm sorting out my tennis lessons!' Ava shouted back.

She had two texts from Emma. One reminding her of their session time tomorrow, ending in, 'Don't eat too many Easter eggs!' and a smiley face, and another letting her know how many weeks it was to the inter-schools tournament, ending in a tense face and a thumbs-up icon. Emma liked emoticons. She also liked to be kind. Last week, when Ava had asked how likely it was that she'd play Wimbledon, Emma had steered the conversation to the schools tournament. Ava was fairly confident she was going to win, so she asked the question again. Cornered, Emma had admitted that it was rare for someone who had only taken up tennis in their teens to succeed beyond amateur status.

'Rare, but not impossible?'

'Nothing's impossible.'

'Lots of things are impossible. How much do my parents pay you?'

'I don't think that's…'

'Are we wasting their money?'

Emma had put her hands on Ava's shoulders at that point, like a coach in a movie, and had looked her dead in the eye.

'As long as you're enjoying it, improving, moving forward, we're not wasting their money.'

'But I'll never be a professional tennis player? Is it too late? Where was Coco Gauff at my age?'

'With your level of determination and skill, you could make tennis your life. You could go on to set up your own tennis academy, you could coach, there are loads of things you could do that don't involve Centre Court.'

But Centre Court was what she wanted. Centre Court and Michael Deluna.

chapter 14

'COME TO BED,' SAID SADIE, as she blinked awake in the light of the muted television. She'd fallen asleep in the middle of some dull drama, and Mark had taken the opportunity to write.

'I just need to finish something.'

'What?' She kissed his shoulder.

'A new bit of the act.'

Sadie peered at a grid of seemingly unconnected words and phrases on the laptop screen. There were star ratings against each row.

'Bowls?'

'It's a bit about — I can't really explain it. It'll kill it.'

He tried to angle the screen away from her.

'You've given it five stars. The same for hand sanitiser. What's funny about hand sanitiser?'

'Again, if I explain it...'

'What's that? Pregnant sex? What?'

He scrolled down the page quickly.

'Sade, I'm working.'

'You're talking about sex on stage? Sex with me?' She was suddenly very awake.

'No!'

'It says pregnant sex!'

Mark doubted the best comedians had anyone censoring their material before it had even been tested in front of an audience.

'It's just something...'

'No way are you using me in your material! You must be out of your mind. Nobody wants to hear about you having sex with your pregnant wife! Where's the humour in that? Delete it!'

Mark rubbed at his temples.

'Right.'

'Jesus!' she said, before finally storming out and up to bed.

He stared at the screen for a few moments, but he could feel the productive period had passed. Nothing else would come, and there hadn't been much to start with. He kicked back, opened YouTube, and watched Amy Schumer sweat it out in some comedy club. She had the audience riveted; the laughs were big, fast, often involuntary, but there didn't seem to be any ease in it. Here was a woman worth almost twenty mill, who still had to hack it at the coal face, the blank screen, to freshly mine each line, hone it, hone it some more, then deliver it to drunks and stag parties and to couples who'd paid for a babysitter and left work early to get to the gig.

Mark imagined the millions, what he'd do, how life would be so different for them, how the baby wouldn't need to grow up in a house that was falling apart. That wasn't why he wanted to do it — well, not the *only* reason — but it would certainly shut a few people up: Sadie's brother, her dad, and other people whose perception of him ranged from irrelevant to twat. Right now, he was bumping along the bottom; forty quid here and there, sometimes less, occasionally nothing; people asking how 'the comedy thing' was coming along, occasionally sneering, asking him to tell them a joke, to make them laugh. And now his material was being vetoed before he'd even written it.

He opened FaceTime. As Dean came into view, he was leaning against a palm tree, catching his breath.

'Why are you answering your phone if you're out running?' asked Mark.

Dean turned his camera to face the beach, before turning it back to his smirking face.

'Yeah, great. So. Did you know that Amy Schumer is worth nearly twenty mill?'

'Didn't she make seventeen mill last year?'

'Now I feel even better.'

'Shouldn't you be in bed?'

'As a nine-to-fiver, yes. As a comedian, nope.'

'Shouldn't you be in bed?'

'You know who I bumped into the other day?'

'Amy Schumer?'

'Ruby Suddula.'

Dean poured water over his head.

'From school?'

Mark nodded.

'Huh.' Dean took a long swig of water, looked out at the horizon.

'We went for lunch,' said Mark.

Dean rested his phone on a bench while he adjusted a fastening on his running shoe. Mark watched the people in the background; people who seemed to be having a better time than him, just walking around in the sunshine.

'I had a bit of a thing for Ruby,' said Dean.

'You had a thing for everyone.'

'So. Lunch...' Dean's grin was testament to California's unrivalled cosmetic dental services. His skin was golden and remained taut courtesy of regular visits to his aesthetician. Visible sun damage was for the poor or for those too rich to care.

'In the same cafe as a lot of other people having lunch.'

'The kind of lunch that brings on a bout of insomnia?' He laughed and rested his phone on a low wall while he stretched, so that all Mark could see was a high plane flying across a cloudless blue sky.

chapter 15

'WE'RE HAVING A THING at the gallery,' said Ruby.

Mark pressed his phone more firmly against his ear and strode out of the office.

'A portrait competition. The shortlisted artists are presenting their work. There'll be drinks and...'

'That sounds interesting,' he lied. 'When is it?'

'Next Thursday. Six.'

He'd have to give counselling the swerve.

'Great.'

He went straight from the office, arguing with himself that this would be better for his mental health than talking to Anders about the past week's manifestations of his fucked-up-ness. Anders was the man who charged sixty quid a session to listen to every one of Mark's dark thoughts, every Thursday, so that Sadie didn't have to.

As soon as he walked into the gallery, he caught sight of Ruby waving brightly at him from across the room, her smile a harbour light.

'Hello, hello!' she said, beaming.

It had been a long time since anyone had beamed at the sight of him. He wasn't the kind of man who elicited beams.

'Hi.'

'How you doing?'

'Yeah. Fine.'

'Can I get you a drink? There's champagne. Well, Prosecco. Good Prosecco, though. I've sampled it.'

'Will it have a strawberry floating in it?'

'Scottish raspberries.'

'Oh, in that case, yes.'

She caught the eye of a kilted adolescent deeply resenting the tray of Prosecco he was holding, and beckoned him over.

Once they'd clinked their glasses, Ruby launched into a witty summary of the event and cutting depictions of the various personalities involved.

'See him?'

Mark followed her gaze.

'Has his own tray of food. We've had to assign him his own waiter. Says it's unsanitary to eat from a tray that others have picked at. Says people sniff at stuff and put it back.'

'He's right.'

'Nobody would put food back on trays.'

'I would.'

'You'd take the…' she rotated her forefinger into the opposite palm.

'Excellent canapé mime.'

'…*canapé* off the tray, sniff it, and put it back again?'

'If I didn't like the smell.'

'You sniff first?'

'If it looks unfamiliar, yes.'

'And that's the test? The sniff?'

'Usually.'

'Usually?'

'Yep. But I rarely put something back on the tray if I've licked it.'

'Classy.'

And so it went on. Verbally volleying as they strolled through rooms where portraits of minor celebrities and theatrical types lined the walls to be judged.

'I've been thinking.' She made a clunky gear change in the foyer. 'Have you ever been back? To school?'

Mark peered at a portrait. 'I saw her at the Fringe last year.' He walked closer to the picture.

'To the field? The pitch?'

'She was really funny. Solid. Jayde something.'

'Because…'

'Adams. Jayde Adams.'

'I just thought it might…'

He swivelled to face her, full-on. 'What?'

'Have you heard of exposure therapy?'

'Yeah. Ruined Louis CK's career.'

'We could go together.'

He couldn't think of anything worse.

chapter 16

GETTING ONTO THE SCHOOL PITCH wasn't as straightforward as it had once been. For one thing, he'd never had to do it by moonlight. He rattled the gate.

'Locked.'

Ruby vaulted it in a oner. Mark stayed on the outside. *Thwack.*

'I'm not coming in.'

She strode off. 'I know everyone says this about stuff from their childhood, but it really is much smaller than I remember.'

He jumped the gate. 'I think this is a really bad idea.'

'And look at all this gear. We never had anything like this.'

They walked around. There were climbing frames, shooting hoops, full-sized football goal nets, a long-jump pit, a laned track, floodlights. Mark tried to orientate himself. He'd expected to be able to walk right up to the spot, but he found himself looking at the school buildings, back to the field, and back at the buildings again, trying to work out where'd he'd stood, where Fergus had stood.

'I can't figure out...'

'Here. You were here.'

He couldn't see her features. She could be anyone, standing there. He walked over to her. No thwack. He waited for it to come. For the image of Fergus to appear. Nothing.

'He was there.' Ruby pointed to the left of where they were standing. 'And I was there.' She pointed a little to the right.

Mark nodded.

'You OK?'

'I thought I'd feel...dunno. It's a different field.'

'That old field doesn't exist any more. Literally. Only in your head.'

'My head is a place.'

'Right. Yeah.'

'So it exists.'

'Well, what I mean is...'

'Don't try to...'

'Sorry.'

'Can we just be quiet here? Can I just...'

She nodded.

He crouched low, his palms flat on the grass, took some breaths, squinted into the distance.

'I'm just gonna walk back to the gate,' said Ruby.

'Give you some time.'

Once she was far enough away, he started to sing, softly. *'Today is gonna be the day, that they're gonna throw it back to you.'* No thwack. No Fergus ghost.

They sat on the gate, their legs wrapped around the metal.

'He wanted to be a sports coach.'

'Really?'

'Yeah. Not an athlete. Not a runner — and he was fast — not a cricketer or a footballer. A sports coach.' Pause. 'He had such a pragmatic approach, you know? Not like me. I wanted to be a footballer. But he knew I had a one in a million chance of making it, of jumping through every hoop, getting spotted, avoiding injury, all that malarkey. He was working towards something more realistic.'

'Clever lad.'

'His mum told my mum that he was on the autistic spectrum. I never saw that.'

Ruby shook her head in agreement.

'He was just Fergus. He could get fixated on stuff, though. He once went missing and everybody thought he'd run away from home or something — the police were out looking for him — but it turned out he was just retracing his steps over the last twenty-four hours because he'd lost his favourite pen. They found him at the bottom of Leith Walk, shivering in a shop doorway. He'd got disorientated in the end.'

'Poor Fergus.'

'He wouldn't want you to think that. He hated

anyone feeling sorry for him. Like the time he came second in the maths test, and everyone just turned to look at him when the teacher said that the new girl had come top.'

A moment of silence.

'You know what he did after that? He went to the sports block and had a shower. He was in there so long he missed half of the next lesson. He came walking into French with his hair wringing wet, sat down and just got his books out.'

Ruby let out a long breath.

'And he had a way of looking at you that meant "don't even ask" so, apart from a bit of heckling when he walked in, everyone just carried on with their work.'

'I once had a conversation with him and he spent the whole time putting all the paint tubes in number order.'

'Helpful.'

'Not really. The numbers were on the backs of the tubes so I had to turn them all round again once he'd gone so I could see the colours.'

'Brilliant.'

'It was rare to see him on his own like that. He was always with you,' she said.

'Yeah.'

'I wonder what he'd have made of you going off and getting married. It seemed like there wasn't room for anyone else between you.'

He shook his head. 'I miss talking to him. He had the best answers for anything. I could give him this really complicated scenario — I dunno, something I was going through at home — and, somehow, he'd see right through all the crap and say something like, "You just need to do this, or say this," and I'd think, "Yeah, you're right; why didn't I think of that?" There was no bullshit with him. Really straightforward. Really clever.'

'Like you.'

Hardly.'

'You know what I think your problem is?'

He turned to her.

'You give too much credit to people who don't get you.'

He smiled.

'You've done what most people are terrified of. You've taken risks.'

He laughed, gently.

'Seriously. You've turned out just how I always thought you would.'

He jumped off the gate and turned to face her. 'Fergus had this thing, if anyone put us down, he'd tilt his head towards me like this,' he channelled Fergus, 'and he'd say, out of the side of his mouth: "Fecking bobolyne".'

'Bobolyne?'

'It's fifteenth-sixteenth-century. It means fool.' He smiled and whispered it again: 'Fecking bobolyne.'

She jumped down, and they both leaned against the gate in silence for a few moments, until she stroked his arm and quietly asked him: 'Ready?'

He walked her home. And one thing led to another,

because the streets of Edinburgh have a charge, a current running through them, and there's something in the air, not just the hops. And, once most of the city's people are asleep, and the only cars on the road are cabs, even Leith Walk shimmers. So they kissed, tentatively at first, on the steps of a bookshop that also renovates old typewriters, because that's a lovely place to kiss someone for the first time. Or the second, if you count that time at the school disco. And he didn't leave her at the gate, or the stair door, but he paused at the flat door because something in him knew that once he'd crossed that line, it would be a very long walk home.

Chapter 17

'BE NICE,' SAID SADIE.

'Even if it's disgusting?' said Mark.

'*Especially* if it's disgusting. Be constructive.'

'Patronise him? You want me to lie to him?'

'I think there are positive ways of helping someone become a better cook without lying. Leave the talking to me.'

'Leave the...what?'

'About the *food*. Leave the food comments to me.'

The doorbell went. On the doorstep, Jonny held what looked like a red-checked cushion but was, in fact, a Pyrex dish of just-cooked vegetable curry, made from scratch to Sadie's recipe, wrapped in a bath towel and two tea towels to keep it hot enough to serve. His sweater was spattered with pinpricks of the sauce from when he'd transferred everything from pan to dish. In his backpack, a surprise: he'd followed Nigel Slater's chocolate beetroot cake recipe to the letter, and it had turned out spectacularly well, even if he'd said so himself, out loud, twice, to nobody in particular.

Sadie opened the door as Mark was despatched to take the warmed bowls and naan bread from the oven.

'It's still hot,' said Jonny. 'Is the rice ready?'

'Yep. Come in.'

'Especially the carrots,' said Sadie. 'Perfect. Not too soft, not too hard.'

'Carrots are fairly straightforward though, no? I'd have to be pretty crap to get those wrong.'

Mark opened his mouth to speak and Sadie shut it with a look.

'Honestly, Jonny, cooking the vegetables so they're all just the right texture is something that takes people years of practice.'

Jonny turned to Mark. 'Did *you* think everything was the right texture?'

'Yeah.' A pause. 'I'd have liked the cauliflower bits to be smaller, though. They were a bit...boulder-ish.'

Sadie shot him a look.

'Boulder-ish?' said Jonny, unable to disguise his disappointment that geological terminology was being used to describe his considerable effort at a vegetable korma.

'Well, no, to be fair, not a boulder,' said Mark. 'Smaller than a boulder. More of a pebble. A rock.'

'My cauliflower was...like rocks?'

'Small rocks.' Mark made a circle with his finger and thumb, to indicate the size.

•••

Later, as Sadie chatted with her mum on the phone, Mark scrubbed at the Pyrex dish and Jonny poked at congealed bits of rice stuck in the sieve.

'What kind of a kiss?' whispered Jonny. He put the sieve down, leaned into his friend's space.

'Full-on.'

'You dick.'

Mark scrubbed harder.

'You need to stop this, right now.'

'Yeah. I'll let it soak.'

'The kissing!'

Mark looked at the kitchen door, a warning to Jonny to keep his voice down.

'It won't happen again. It was a one-off.'

'Do you know what you have here, Mark? Really? Do you?' Jonny spread out his arms, trying to encompass everything he himself didn't have, everything his friend was about to throw away.

'Yes. And I also know —' he looked at the door, 'I also know what Ruby gives me, and they're two different things.'

Jonny checked the door before growling out his response: 'It's not all about you.'

Silence.

'What about what Sadie wants? What about the baby? What about what *Ruby* wants? Have you even thought about that?'

Silence.

'Because she's not going to just fix you, Mark, then walk away. That's not how it works.'

Mark put down the scourer and turned to face him. 'Have you ever killed anyone, Jonny? Swung a cricket bat so hard — to win, to *win* for the school — that it left your hands and hit your best mate — your *best* mate — right there?' He jabbed at his temple. 'Killed him. Stone dead.'

Jonny turned away. 'Don't even.'

'Because until you've gone through what I've —'

'You know what, Mark, if I had killed someone — and I'm really sorry it happened to you — I can't imagine the pain — but if I had, I'd do everything in my power never to hurt another soul again for as long as I lived.'

A pause.

Mark slumped. 'I'm not trying to hurt anyone.'

'No excuse.'

'You don't understand how I feel when I'm with her. I feel how I've always imagined everyone else must feel. Like I'm OK.'

'No excuse.'

Mark scraped at the last few centimetres of the stubborn baked-on ring around the dish as Jonny read down Sadie's to-do list, a rueful half-smile on his face.

When Sadie walked in, Jonny's expression shifted to a broad smile. 'Can you come over to mine and do one of these for me?'

She laughed.

'Seriously, I could do with a big list, a reminder of everything I'm not getting around to.'

'Next time we're over, you're on,' said Sadie.

He scanned up and down the list again. 'National Theatre?'

'Oh,' she looked over to Mark, who kept his back to her. She turned back to Jonny again. 'I've pitched to do some costume work for them. It's a long shot. They'll probably go for a London company.'

He nodded. 'Good luck.' He pointed to the chocolate beetroot cake. 'Ready for this?'

'Absolutely.' She turned to Mark. 'Mark? Ready to be blown away?'

Drying his hands, he gave a tight smile in response. He took out crockery and cutlery and pretended everything was fine. He thought of a beetroot joke and stored it for later.

chapter 18

THE ATTIC WAS PRISTINE. Tight-lidded, labelled boxes sat in neat rows along the shelves that lined every wall. Sadie pulled out a couple of chunky files containing several years of bank statements, revealing the wood behind.

'Anything?'

She angled her phone so Art, the second most expensive damp and condensation specialist in the region, could see the wood. He peered at it.

'Do you have the screwdriver?'

Sadie held it up to her phone.

'So, I want you to try and push it into the beam. Go steady.'

She jabbed at the wood.

'Steady! You're looking for resistance.'

'It's pretty hard.'

'That's great. Try another part. Shift along.'

Sadie moved a few centimetres to the left, and pushed hard. It was solid.

'OK. Looking good. Let's try another part of the attic.'

She walked over to the far corner. On the bottom shelf, there was a large, white metal trunk containing her wedding dress and Mark's suit. Sadie shifted it sideways and wedged her phone so Art could see the wood behind it.

'Is it dry?'

She stroked her hand across it. 'Yep. Cold but dry.'

'Good. Get in closer. Get the torch on it. Any yellow tinge?'

'Nope.'

'And are you getting any smells at all?'

She shook her head.

'Get in the corners.'

Nothing. No smell. No yellow tinge. No dry rot.

Once Art had given her the thumbs-up, the all-clear, she stayed in the attic for a while, rifling through old birthday and Valentine's cards.

'I crave your mouth, your voice, your hair...' Sadie shouted from the kitchen.

Mark closed the front door behind him and slammed it firmly shut when it bounced open again. He shrugged off his wet coat. *'I hunger for your sweet laugh.'*

'You've gone straight to the second verse!'

He appeared in the kitchen and kissed her. 'Well,

that's me all over, isn't it?'

She ran her fingers through his hair. 'Still raining.'

'*I want to eat your skin like a whole almond.*' Kiss. Kiss. Kiss.

'You'll have to make do with chilli.'

He picked up the bundle of Valentine's cards. 'Jesus. Extinction Rebellion will be after our arses. We've cleared entire forests for this lot.' He sat down and worked his way through them, smiling, occasionally laughing, reading aloud the more purple declarations, as Sadie added more spice to the chilli, stirring and tasting, stirring and tasting.

Chapter 19

WE ARE SUCH LIARS. *About ten units a week. It was a bargain. It was a one-off. Only once, and I was drunk. Everybody was doing it at the time. I preferred the novel.*

The most insidious lies are the ones we tell ourselves. *It's fine. We're doing nothing wrong. It's only coffee/lunch/ drinks/dinner. It's nothing. Really.*

'Who's Maurice Goulet?'

They were in Judy's Café on Buccleuch Street. Some time had passed, but not much; a few weeks. There had been another kiss, but his pocket had buzzed a few seconds in, and it had been Sadie so he stopped.

Ruby's mouth stayed open around the sandwich she'd been about to bite into. She put it back on her plate and brushed imaginary crumbs from her skirt.

'Ah, Google.'

'Yeah, well, slow day at the office.'

Ruby sighed deeply, and not without irritation. 'He's been my boyfriend.'

'He's *been* your boyfriend? So he was, but isn't any more?'

'I suppose he's still on the scene. Sort of.'

'The scene? There's a scene?'

She shrugged.

'You've never mentioned him.' He forced a smile, as though they were simply talking about the weather.

'Why would I?' She bit into her sandwich, and Mark watched her chew.

'How long has–'

Mouth full, she held up two fingers.

'Two days? Weeks? Months?'

She held a hand in front of her mouth as she garbled out her response, 'Years.'

'Two years?'

She nodded.

'Long time. Serious.'

She swallowed. 'It's a long time.'

'But not serious?'

'Complicated.'

Mark waited for her to elaborate.

'He wants to get married.'

'To you?'

'Well, I'm first preference. We'd been talking about maybe going travelling first. Taking a year off. Then I went off the idea.' She paused. 'And he's upset.'

'You went off the idea because..?'

She let the question hang in the air.

'Because of me?' He pressed a splayed palm across his chest.

She laughed. 'So modest!'

'I'm just checking. I don't want you to…'

The brakes were almost audible; she pulled back slightly.

'Look, Maurice is lovely, but he's not for me. And you are lovely, but you are with someone else. Married, even. So.'

She punctuated the sentence by wiping the corner of her mouth with a paper napkin. She then smiled brightly and pushed her finger into his chest. She could feel his muscle twitch. She leaned across so her face was very close to his.

'Don't worry.'

'I was just asking, that's all.'

The sunlight had reached the mirror behind him, backlighting him in such a way that his features were less distinct, and he seemed to have a halo. She had a flashback to an incident from their schooldays: she'd tripped in a chaotic school corridor, dropping her paintbrushes, tubes of paint and pencils, and he'd stopped to help her pick them up. She'd not been keen on him until that point, but now she was fourteen, and no longer immune to his easy smile, she had found herself staring at his mouth, and then she noticed he was looking at hers. Just weeks before the cricket match, before Fergus.

Chapter 20

MARK'S GRANDMOTHER HAD left her substantial Victorian house to her only child, Mark's father. Over the decades, after her husband had died, rooms had fallen into disrepair, and doors had been locked, until the old woman had confined her life to the boundaries of the ground floor: the kitchen, the pantry, the utility room, the living room, the parlour (into which her bed had been moved) and the small cloakroom with its ancient bathroom fittings and strange plumbing sounds. The house had been in such a state of disrepair when she died that Mark's parents arranged to have it boarded up until they could afford to renovate it. And then *they* died. Black ice. Car accident. So, eventually, Mark — still a teenager — inherited both the crumbling pile and the money from the sale of his parents' house, a chunk of which, initially, had kept the local pubs, fast food outlets and his dealer afloat. The pile stayed boarded up, occupied only by wildlife and stray cats, until Sadie arrived on the scene.

He wasn't unconscious, but he was sprawled out, eyes closed, at the bottom of the steps leading from George Square to Buccleuch Street. Strands of hair had stuck to his face, secured by the glue of dried dribble. A few people walked past him, and Sadie almost did, but − daughter of a teacher and a police officer that she was − she slowed to take a closer look at the man wearing one expensive shoe. He had beautiful teeth − she could see that on account of his gaping mouth. She hooked the toe of her shoe under his arm, to elicit a sign of life.

He coughed before squinting up at her. 'What time is it?'

'Nine,' she said.

'Morning or night?'

'Night.'

'Tuesday?'

'Friday.'

He rolled onto his side in an attempt to sit up. She caught his elbow, to help him.

'Have you been attacked?'

'I don't think so,' he said. He looked around and seemed confused as he took in his surroundings.

'Are you OK?'

Mark rubbed his face, exhaled loudly.

'Shall I call someone for you?'

He ignored the question. 'Have you got anything sweet on you?'

Sadie fished urgently into her bag. 'Are you diabetic?'
'No.'
She stopped fishing, and gave him a look, just as he vomited all over himself.

The first night Sadie and Mark spent together was in Accident and Emergency on a wild Friday night, surrounded by a conveyor belt of drunks and walking wounded. She spent some of it making lists on her laptop, colour-coding and prioritising, as Mark slept soundly on a plastic chair that had been designed for a shorter wait.

'You've done your duty. Leave him to the doctors. I'll come and get you.'

Sadie turned the volume down on her phone. 'I don't need you to come and get me, Mum.' She had never seen such beautiful hair on a man — apart from the bits still stuck to his face. Heavy, dark, shiny, curly at the ends. His wallet, which she'd had to look through to give his details to the desk, contained a driving licence, around two hundred pounds in cash, a photograph of him from several years ago, his arms wrapped around two people she assumed were his parents, and a donor card, on which he'd scrawled with a Sharpie: DNR. TAKE EVERYTHING.

'Sadie, your father is insisting I come and get you, or he's going to get a couple of his officers over there.'

'I'm sure they've got better things to do on a Friday night.'

'Mark Darling.' The nurse shouted his name above the din, and Sadie gently roused him, before offering her arm and accompanying him through to triage.

'It's been like that for years.'

The builder stroked his stubbly chin.

'It's never really bothered us before. But now...' Sadie pushed her belly out, by way of explanation.

'And what did you say the budget was?'

'I didn't. I just want a quote.'

'Have you got any other quotes in?'

Sadie shook her head. She knew this guy had a great reputation, but she wasn't about to be bullshitted.

'It's not a complete renovation. We've got someone coming to look at the joists next week. And we've done a lot to this place already. It's just the stuff on the list. And I can easily get three quotes if...'

The builder consulted Sadie's list. 'You're looking at seventy K. Maybe eighty. Depends on materials. That basement needs gutting, for starters.'

'And when would you be able to start?'

'Do you want to talk to your husband first?'

She mentally disembowelled him.

'If you could email me an itemised quote, that'd be great. I've chosen all the fittings, all the materials. I'll send you links to them.'

'I tend to use my own suppliers.'

Sadie folded her list. 'A lot of these things are one-offs. The kitchen floor's coming from a big house up north. The utility room shelves are made from recycled wood by a local cooperative. I'm currently bidding on eBay for the hall light — in fact that finishes in half an hour, so...' she stepped forward and just stopped short of shooing him out.

The builder checked he had the right email address, shook her hand, and left.

Chapter 21

'So, IF THE PARTNERS COULD JUST gently enfold their women — yes, very good, Hugo — and make them feel safe.'

NCT class.

'Now, ladies, when you're ready, when you feel safe and cocooned by your partner, I'd like you to guide their hands, so that they're sending their love through you to your baby.'

Mark snorted. Sadie elbowed him.

'Then I want you to place your hands on top of your partner's, and feel the warmth and love you're both sending through to the baby. That's right. Yes, that's right. Are you feeling it?'

A hipster father-to-be raised his hand. The facilitator, Ruth, smiled beatifically.

'So, our hands must have intention in this exercise,

yeah? We're not just stroking here, are we? It's, like, a bonding exercise with the foetus, yeah?'

'It's a good question, Jasper, and a very wise observation. Yes, absolutely,' she then raised her voice so everyone heard it clearly: 'Your hands are conduits of love.'

Mark choked back his laughter, causing him to cough loudly. Sadie took the opportunity to hit him very hard on the back. People stared. They both smiled — *nothing to see here* — and, once everyone had turned away, Mark blew onto each hand, rubbed them together and wiggled his fingers at Sadie's bump.

'And now I want you to sing softly to your babies — they will hear you, they already recognise your voices. Do we all remember the simple folk lullaby we learned last week? We'll try it in English first, then move to German in the second verse.'

If he could get through the lullaby, the coffee break was coming up next.

●●●

'You don't take it seriously, Mark!'

The drive home.

'Sadie, I take everything seriously, apart from the funny stuff. I can tell you the circumference of the baby's head at any given week, I know how to recognise Braxton Hicks — lovely fella — and I could probably deliver this baby single-handed if there's a bit of coconut oil to hand.'

She stared straight ahead.

'I could catch her with my conduits of love.'

She laughed.

'And I just think the pass-the-parsley thing at the end is ridiculous. *You* think the pass-the-parsley thing is ridiculous! I was tempted to throw it at Felix when he asked if it was organic!'

Sadie rolled her eyes.

'But my favourite part of the evening, and yours, too, I think, had to be...' he launched at full throttle straight into the second verse of the folk lullaby: '*Schlaf Baby, Schlaf, Dein Vater kümmert sich um die Schafe...*' and Sadie threw her head back, laughing, laughing.

●●●

'Oh it's kicking!'

The sofa. On the coffee table, a mountain of toast and two mugs of tea.

Sadie guided Mark's hands to the area.

They waited in silence, hardly daring to breathe.

Kick.

Gasp.

Kick, kick.

Kissing.

Mark wrapped himself around her. Sadie fed him toast. Right now, here on the sofa, with Sadie, toast, a cup of tea on the coffee table, and an unborn baby kicking, he felt he had all he needed.

'Woody said something lovely today...' she said, unravelling the blood pressure monitor from around her arm.

Mark kissed her shoulder, an invitation to keep talking.

'He said he thought being a dad would be the making of you.'

'That sounds more like a backhanded compliment.'

'No, he didn't mean it like that. He was talking about when he was younger — Josie got pregnant when they were not long out of school — and although they had to grow up fast when the babies came along, they loved setting up a new family unit. He said they made this loving nest that they would fly back to every night. It was very moving.'

'They had a love nest; we have a money pit.'

'Has the roofer come back with a quote?'

'Nope. Which means it's either too big a job or not worth his while.'

And so they shifted into domestic chat.

Later, after the toast, as Sadie got ready for bed, Mark padded around the house checking that the doors and the windows were locked. He put the few dirty dishes there were into the dishwasher, and wiped down the worktops with antibacterial spray. He straightened scattered newspapers and magazines into a neat pile, and put the roofer's business card on top, as a reminder to call him. He popped his head into the nursery, and made a mental list of the jobs he would do in there this weekend.

Shortly after 4am, Sadie walked into the living room where Mark was reading aloud from a list on his phone.

'What's going on?' She squinted, trying to adjust to the brightness.

Mark swivelled around to face her. 'I'm reading this track list to Dean. We were trying to remember if one of the singles was on the first album or the second.' He seemed very awake.

'Hello, Dean,' said Sadie, bending towards the laptop screen. She adjusted the lapel of her light cotton robe, drawing it over her cleavage.

Dean waved at her. 'Hi.'

She ruffled Mark's hair. 'How are you going to get up for work tomorrow? It's after four.'

'I was a bit twitchy. Didn't want to wake you.'

'You should try to get some rest, at least. I'm just going to get a glass of water and go back up.'

'OK. I'll be up in a while. We just have some stuff to sort out.'

'I can see that,' said Sadie, smiling.

'Dean's visit,' said Mark.

'I have to put a proper itinerary together or I won't get to see everyone,' said Dean.

'When do you get here?' asked Sadie.

'Soon. I'm just trying to arrange flights.'

'And where are you staying?'

Dean shrugged. 'Probably an Airb'n'b. Less hassle.'

'Well if it's before the baby arrives, you can stay here, if you like,' said Sadie. 'We have room.'

'He doesn't wanna…'

'Yeah, that'd be great, thanks,' said Dean.

'Good. OK, I'm off. Goodnight.' Sadie kissed the top of Mark's head and waved at Dean before leaving the room.

As soon as he could be sure she was out of earshot, Mark put his face up to the screen and hissed at Dean: 'Whatthefuck?'

'What?'

'You're staying here?'

'I was invited!'

Mark lowered his voice to an almost inaudible whisper. 'What if you slip up? What if you say something about Ruby?'

'Why would I?'

Mark started to breathe hard into his cupped palms.

'Listen, mate. Listen. You need to throw this thing into reverse. You are not the type who can cope with an affair.'

'It's not an affair.'

'Look at the state of you!'

Mark massaged his temples before stretching and looking up at the ceiling, at the spot where Sadie would now be trying to get comfortable in a mountain of pillows.

'Take it from one who sees his kids every other weekend, and now hates Christmas Day. You wanna end up hating Christmas?'

'There's nothing going on.'

'The first stage of an affair: nothing's going on. Except everything's going on.'

chapter 22

Bryony Jones bashed her rucksack on the back of Ava's head as she walked past her desk, causing Ava to jerk forwards, which made those watching laugh. Bryony apologised immediately, of course, profusely, in full view and earshot of Ms Henry, who accepted it as an accident and encouraged everyone to settle down and to open up their books at page sixteen. The scratch on Ava's scalp stung for the entire hour but she refused to cry, even though she was in pain, premenstrual, in love, rubbish at domestic science, and massively intimidated. She was bumped about and elbowed more than usual on the way out of class and someone stepped on her foot and, although she couldn't be entirely sure it was one of Bryony's gang, the twist on her toes felt mean.

School seemed full of people who didn't want to be there for one reason or another. The teachers were trying to cram the same information into everyone, which was an impossible task, but occasionally fun to watch, just for the sport of it. They spouted endlessly about how they wanted learners to think, but gave them so much to do that there wasn't time. And there was so much more going on than learning. Unfathomable stuff. Carrying the wrong bag, or not liking certain bands could result in merciless banter, could even make you an outcast, if you weren't already the class loner. And the threat of bullying was never far from the surface; it was like a hum pitched at a level only audible to the kids.

'Your mum's a bitch.'

They were in the corridor, at the lockers. Bryony had two idiots flanking her, and it struck Ava that they must have all got ready for school together, on account of their identical hairdos and make-up.

'You're on CCTV, Bryony,' said Ava, glancing up at the camera. Inside, her guts were churning, but she wasn't going to let this lot see the effect they were having on her, so she tried her best to smile nonchalantly.

'No mic, you dog. I'm just talking to you about homework,' said Bryony, adopting a sweet smile for the camera. 'So, have you and Deluna shagged yet?'

Ava pushed past her. The three girls made barking noises as she walked off.

She couldn't face the bus, so she walked home. As she waited at the crossing on Queen Street, a man who looked very like Mark walked past her quickly. He had his head down, and was on the phone, and she couldn't judge if it would be right to stop him. The crossing changed to walk. She looked back. The man had disappeared into the crowds. Probably not Mark anyway; this wasn't near his office.

•••

Rogerians know we're all capable of self-actualisation. Of growing. Thriving. They know that, in order to develop into our fully-functioning selves, we just need to feel loved and safe and seen and heard. We need to know that we're OK. That we're intrinsically of value. That our flaws and our mistakes are not who we are. That we're good enough.

They sat at the back of Di Giorgio's. They ordered food that they could share. They talked about Fergus — not the accident — just Fergus, the boy. Things they'd got up to. Pranks. He hadn't even done this with Anders. All these years, Fergus's name had been solely connected to the accident, the guilt. Fergus: thwack, down, dead.

An hour later, they stood on Brandon Terrace, in the glare of full sunshine, stalling as each swithered over what kind of kiss they would part on. Mark went for a conservative cheek, followed by a grateful hug. Ruby went for the classic kiss slightly to one side of his actual mouth — sexier than a cheek but not quite a full-on snog, accompanied by a squeeze of his arm.

Before going home — it was still a little early — he

stopped at Tesco to buy a bunch of flowers for Sadie.

Sadie put the flowers on the bedroom windowsill, which meant he'd bought the wrong sort. As he tried to sleep, the full moon shone through them, creating scary shadows on the ceiling and bedroom walls.

Chapter 23

THEY'D ARRANGED TO MEET at the gallery. He was early. He stood against the railings, watching people come and go. Eventually, she emerged, and the wind took her hair, causing it to flit and fly about in all directions, like wild flames. And he saw her. Saw everything he'd been filtering out. Saw that, even on this damp Edinburgh weeknight, she managed to be completely devoid of Tuesdayness. She was, in fact, a rollercoaster, a mermaid, Nell Gwyn, Marilyn. Try as it might, her rectangular plastic name badge couldn't make her ordinary; it was only there as a reminder that the universe did actually contain straight lines and corners. He clutched at the spike of a railing.

It was late. The Jazz Bar was on its third band of the night. People were dancing. He pulled her towards him, wrists up, curled her fingers into her palms, moved her diagonally to sway her right side towards him, then pulled her left side in the same way. She looked down at her feet, his feet, hers, before stumbling slightly. He released her right hand and made the two-fingered pointing gesture at his eyes, hers, his, to instruct her to maintain eye contact with him.

He pressed his palm into the small of her back and held himself taut against her. He thrust his pelvis into hers but almost immediately swivelled away before pulling her back. He brought her whole body closer by quickly moving his arm around her waist, then pressed his right palm into her left and swung her deeper into the crowd. A space opened up next to them and he twirled her into it, once, twice, three times. As he pulled her back, their bodies crashed into each other with a grunt. He angled his head, and their temples slid against each other, his sweat with hers. He pulled back and pushed her away, let her go, he dropped, grazed her belly with his nose, slid his face up her body, arched back, threw his arms in the air and swivelled his hips. She lifted her skirt, and rolled her right shoulder, her left, threw her head back. He caught her hand, twirled her, pulled her in, moved his hand down from the small of her back, but not low enough. She wiggled.

She slid her face down his neck, pushed her nose, her mouth into his shoulder and just stopped short of biting him. He dipped her on a three trombone finish and let out a 'yeah!' as she threw herself backwards into the move with great gusto. As he pulled her up, he put his face in her hair, his mouth close to her ear and, without raising his voice, said: 'Let's go.'

They emerged onto Chambers Street. He took her hand. The breeze carried a sound, an audible breath, but no chill.

They turned right onto South Bridge.

'Where are we going?'

He didn't answer her; he just picked up the pace until they were on Salisbury Crags, looking down at their twinkling city. Right then, nestled in a wee grassy catstep on the side of a beautiful dormant volcano, they joked and giggled, and most laughs were followed by a kiss and a nuzzle, until one nuzzle didn't stop and he leaned forward as she leaned back, and the only luminance on the hill came from the pale crescent moon and the rhythmic beams of four lighthouses.

She undid most of the buttons on his shirt, and he flicked open the remainder. He smoothed her dress to one side so it slipped off her shoulder, and softly bit her while looking right into her eyes, which made her breath catch in her throat. There was no smooth way to get his jeans off, but he at least did it while kissing her. The seam of her dress tore slightly as she twisted to roll on top of him. They slipped down the hill a little, then rolled towards a flat shelf, where she wrapped her legs around him. He pushed up her dress, pressed his face against her soft, empty belly, then lower, and lower. The smell was familiar yet new. She grazed her cheek against a rock. A nightjar swooped over them, silently.

●●●

He washed his face at the kitchen sink, triple-pumping the soap dispenser. He crashed on the sofa. After hardly any sleep, he made his way to the kitchen, and passed a satisfyingly productive hour cleaning taps, door handles, base boards.

'What's all this?'

It was too big, too vague a question. He buckled, sat down.

Sadie kissed the top of his head. 'Coffee?'

'Sorry!' He jumped up, dropped a pod into the coffee machine, and poured her a glass of orange juice.

She leaned back for a few moments, and rubbed her belly.

'So, what did you get up to last night, you lot?'

His stomach lurched. Dean was right — he wasn't cut out for this. He kept his back to her as he answered.

'We ended up at the Jazz Bar. You?'

'Mum's going for this promotion at work, so she was bending my ear about the politics of it all. I tuned out after the first hour. Oh, and Ava's not speaking to Nick because he's just bought a full set of leathers for this bloody big beast of a motorbike he's riding round on. She called him a murdering bastard and said she wished she'd been born into a different family. Dad grounded her for swearing loudly in the garden. Neighbours heard it all.'

He placed the glass of orange juice in front of her.

'Bless.'

'Anyone good on?'

He looked at her. Blinked.

'The Jazz Bar?'

'Oh, yeah.' He walked back to the coffee, stirred milk into it, all the time trying to stay calm. 'Yeah — Kellock, Steele, Sharkey, Kyle, you know? All unrehearsed — I don't know how they do it. Then a Cuban thing — people got up dancing, clapping, the usual after midnight stuff they do there.' He flicked the radio on.

'Is that what you did, then? Did you get up and dance?'

He was visibly shaking as he put the coffee on the table.

She reached for his hand. 'You OK?'

He held up a finger, to pause everything, then rushed to the kitchen sink, lifted out the washing up bowl and vomited.

He showed up at work on time, and snudged his way through the day. Jonny texted to ask if he was OK — Sadie says you're at work, spreading a new virus around — and he brushed him off with a half-entertaining food poisoning tale. Later, he made an effort to eat what was put in front of him at home, he responded more or less accurately in the spaces Sadie left between paragraphs, he loaded the dishwasher and put the recycling out.

Chapter 24

'I'M GOING AWAY FOR the weekend. With Maurice.'

Mark looked beyond her, at the bow-wielding cherubs that were now painted on the walls of this former banking hall, at the intricate, well-preserved cornicing and columns. He wondered where the tellers might have once sat, where the manager's office would have been.

'He has a thing...'

'Right.'

'He has to do a recce of a place for a work event, and I said I'd help because the brief is quite detailed, and...'

It had been two days since Salisbury Crags. Their texting over the past forty-eight hours had been strained and sporadic. She had sent him a New Yorker cartoon and he'd double-clicked it with a laughing emoji. He'd sent her a screenshot of an amusing email exchange he was having but he'd not cropped out the tab that revealed he was also talking to Sadie. They hadn't kissed when they'd arrived at the restaurant. He'd turned up with a head full of similes: pause, stop, consider, halt, whatarewethinking, jesusno, stop, stop. Now she'd headed him off at the pass. He pulled his attention back to her.

'Yes, right. You should go.'

'I wasn't asking permission.'

'I didn't mean…'

Ruby took a deep breath. She rolled her bottom lip between her finger and thumb. 'I think we probably had too much to drink.'

He nodded.

'And I don't want to be…some…'

'No. God. No.'

'You know? I'm just not up for that kind of life. The waiting and nothing happening, and all that shit.'

He nodded again.

'I'm assuming that you and Sadie are…'

'Yeah. Yeah, we are. So…'

'Well, there you go,' she said, picking up the menu. 'I'm gonna have the lemon sole with brown butter.'

And so they paused, they considered, they halted. But it didn't take. She went away for the weekend with Maurice and spent much of it checking her phone for messages from Mark. Once she returned, over the following few weeks, she listened, really listened, when he quietly confessed his insecurities about his act, his job, his paunch, his greys. She didn't judge him when he told her he'd taken a three-hundred gram box of jelly beans into the bathroom at work and scarfed the lot. She stroked his arm as he tried to explain, in words he hadn't ever said out loud before, his various attempts to vomit after the sugar binges. He encouraged her to paint more, to put her work online, to get out there as an artist.

Eventually, they held hands in secret gardens along the Royal Mile, on hillsides, where they were windswept, sunkissed, and drenched. Separated from the everyday tedium of life, they became the steamy back-row couple in the cinema, given a wide berth by people who had simply come in to watch the film. Sometimes, they would take unforgivable risks and meet for a sneaky drink in the library in Kay's Bar, barely a stroll away from where Sadie rubbed oil into her burgeoning belly.

Chapter 25

IF A FRIEND EXPRESSES reservations about a man or a woman one is seeing, it's probably wise to reflect on the points she raises. If more than one friend — say, a group of them, all intelligent, all on side — sit around a table and, between them, create a unified chorus that Gareth Malone would be proud of, one should, without exception, listen, making written notes where necessary.

'If you met him, you'd understand. He's funny, he's kind, he's gone through hell in his life. He's dealt with things most of us will never have to face. And I really get what he's gone through; I was there,' said Ruby.

Four blank faces.

'I've known him since we were kids. And, unlike every single man I've ever met online or in a bar, he's genuine.'

'You can't say you've known him *since* you were kids. You knew him *when* you were kids. There's a difference.' Ella. Online car tyre dealer. Absolutely loaded. All meals nutritiously balanced and delivered. Married to Rosie. Far too many cats, two of which were hairless with alarming ears that looked as though they belonged to larger animals.

'You can't say he's genuine. He's married, and having an affair. Maurice — he's genuine.' Prisha. Paralegal. Avid cyclist. Gorgeous husband. Two kids. Two greyhounds. Substantial Georgian flat.

'She can go back to Maurice when she's eighty!' Emm. Restaurant manager. Would definitely spit in an obnoxious diner's soup. On her second marriage. Stepmother to four still-grieving kids.

'You deserve better than a married man.' Nat. Teacher. Skydiver. No kids: no time. A jewel.

'His marriage is not my responsibility.'

Groans.

'Strictly speaking, she's right,' said Prisha, 'but you're going down a well-trodden path of pain, believe me.'

'Yeah, if he'll do it to her, he'll do it to you!' said Ella.

'No, that's not what I'm saying,' said Prisha. 'I've listened to enough estranged husbands and wives to be able to tell you, right now, how this could turn out. If he stays with his wife, you're wasting your time. If he leaves her, you're not much better off, because once the relationship's no longer illicit, the excitement goes.'

'Instead of summing up for the bench, Prish, could

you try being my friend?' She looked around at them all. 'Why don't I arrange for you to meet him?'

No. Nope. Nah. Sorry.

Ruby pointed her fork at each of them as she spoke: 'You know what? I've supported you all through all kinds of dramas over the years. Emm, I know for a fact you started dating Paul when his wife was still alive.'

Emm blanched. 'She was in a hospice.'

'I think the etiquette is to allow the spouse to actually *die* first.'

Emm's jaw dropped fully open.

'Nat, did I not help you when you were having all that shit with your manager? Ella, I was guarantor on your first flat! Prish, I listened to chapter and verse on your bleeding nipples after you had Riya. I sent a big order of Cook meals to you when you got out of hospital.'

'Do you have a list?' said Prisha.

'What?'

'A list. You seem to be keeping some sort of tally. I can hardly remember what I've done for any of you, but I know it will have been as much as I could at the time.'

And then they all started to talk over each other. Crossfiring, accusing, placating. The waiter arrived and took away the plates. He returned with the dessert menu, which they all waved away; the dinner was over. Ruby had never felt so alone.

chapter 26

ONE AFTERNOON, RUBY DIDN'T go straight back to work. Instead, once Mark was out of sight, she doubled back and dashed home, to take delivery of a seven-foot, stretched, fine linen pre-primed canvas. The courier was just about to push a note through her door as she approached, but she shouted (urgently, too loudly) for him to wait. She backtracked, laughed, to show she wasn't angry or mad, and he made some rather convoluted joke, but she was impatient to get back inside, to unwrap it, so she gave a noncommittal smile before manoeuvring it indoors.

Once she'd undressed it from its packaging, she found herself slightly breathless, more from excitement than effort, as she leaned it gently against the wall of her spare room. She stroked the surface of the canvas with the back of her hand, feeling its tautness and the readiness of the grain. She pushed her face close to it, inhaling the smell of fresh wood and primer, then took a few steps back to imagine the finished work. Slowly, she ran through colours in her head: white, permanent rose and cadmium yellow for the planes and jutting bones, chromium green oxide, dioxazine violet and cobalt blue for the dips, the dimples, the deep crevices. The canvas would hold her unedited confidences in daubs and strokes; a silent and reliable witness.

She decided she would have no overnight guests until it was done; nobody was to see it in progress. Her friends were now split into three distinct groups: those she'd told about Mark, those she hadn't yet told, and those she'd never tell. The first group was further subdivided: those who supported her choice to see whoever she pleased and those who pretended to. She was fast developing a language around the situation, making the truth more palatable with vague stock phrases. Mark was (cue regretful face) 'in a stagnant relationship' rather than married. He was (cue intense expression) Ruby's 'first love' rather than her schoolgirl crush. Shocking lies also sneaked into conversations; she barely knew the truth herself at times.

She also knew how these things inevitably ended; nobody escaped unscathed, all the traps had been set. So she told herself she was living in the moment, that nobody knew what lay ahead anyway, that we could all be wiped out in weeks by a super-virus, so the moment is all we can be sure of. She told herself that nobody belongs to anybody, and maybe he'd leave

Sadie, and maybe that would be the kindest thing to do anyway; he could set himself and Sadie free.

I just called you at work. You OK? Why are you not answering your phone? X

Nat. Ruby saw the missed calls notice above her text. She wondered, briefly, if she could tell her about the canvas, the paints, her coping strategy.

Throwing a sickie ☺

☺ I've got an early finish and can't face marking. I'll come over x

Ruby texted a thumbs up before shoving the canvas, its wrapping and the paints out of sight.

•••

'I thought you might be with Jay-Z.' Nat handed a bulging carrier bag to Ruby before taking off her coat and scarf. 'Crumpets, proper butter, earl grey tea, full-fat milk, cake, and Pringles and wine in case I abandon the idea of marking completely.'
    'Jay-Z?'
    'You're Becky with the good hair in this scenario.'
    'And Sadie is Beyoncé? Cheers.'
    'Put the crumpets in the toaster.'
    Ruby let out a dramatic sigh, unpacked the bag, and did as she was told.

'Emm's not speaking to you.'

'Because?'

'Because you called her out on seeing a married man, when she thought there was an unspoken agreement between us all never to call him married because his wife was dead. Nearly.'

'He was married to a woman at death's door. They could have waited.'

Nat put the kettle on and pulled two cups from a cupboard, as Ruby stood staring at the toaster. She opened the butter, took out two side plates from another cupboard, a knife from the cutlery drawer, and placed them in front of Ruby while she carried on making the tea.

'And Prish asked me to ask you not to tell the book group.'

'What?'

'She feels you'd be compromising her integrity by outing her as complicit in the affair.'

The crumpets popped up. Ruby left them where they were, but kept her back to her friend.

'And Ella said–'

'Nat,' she turned to face her. 'Can you just give me the highlights – the good stuff. Leave the shit for when we open the wine.'

'I'll butter the crumpets,' said Nat.

chapter 27

THE BLOOD. EVERY — every, every — month, the blood. Inside, a scream. Her brave face would slip for an hour as she sobbed and railed and asked unanswerable questions. Another month of circling dates on the calendar. Another month of procreative rather than recreational sex. Another few grand written off to/invested in IVF. Another month of kind, hand-holding nurses. Another month of hating big families who populated every seat and a high chair around a restaurant table. Another month of a dormant baby monitor, gathering dust, absorbing silence. A painstakingly chosen and carefully assembled empty cot. Closed cupboards filled with neat piles of clean, white nappies and folded and re-folded babygros. A large collection of sealed, boxed and shrink-wrapped this, that and the others. Still, the blood.

•••

'Venus and Serena Williams are worth over a hundred million pounds between them.' Tony stretched out the amount as though it wasn't large enough already, and made a hundred-million-pound face just to drive his point home. He'd just come in from the garden with an armful of veg, which he now started to rinse under the tap.

Ava used her forefinger as place marker in the textbook she was reading, and looked up at her father. 'You need to work on your skills if you're going to start being a pushy parent.'

'Just heard it on the radio. Venus's fastest recorded serve is a hundred and twenty-eight miles per hour.' More stretching out of the number, and a new expression that was presumably supposed to convey how fast that was. 'That's nearly twice the motorway speed limit.'

'Serena.'

'What?'

'It's Serena. She has the fastest serve.'

'Yeah, well. They're both rolling in it, either way. Tennis pays.'

'I don't care about the money.'

'But you'd like the fast serve.'

Ava pushed her laptop away. 'You're supposed to tell me all this when I'm watching TV instead of practising. Not when I'm doing homework.' She stressed the last word.

'You're still enjoying it?'

'It's domestic science. I'm writing about food safety.'

'Tennis.'

'Yep.'

'Emma says you could make a living at it.'

'Not Centre Court.'

'Nothing's impossible.'

She went back to her homework.

'We just want you to be happy.'

Oh, God. A slow day in the garden. The we-just-want-you-to-be-happy chat.

'Dad, I've got loads of homework. I'll be *happy* when I've finished it.'

'I mean–'

'Yeah, I know. But that's a lot of pressure.'

He held his hands up in surrender, and walked over to the fridge.

'I was thinking of making cheese on toast,' he said.

'That'd make me happy.'

'And a nice bit of salad from the garden.'

'There ya go. Everybody's happy.'

She watched her dad happily making her lunch, and wondered where the selflessness came from. There was nothing in it for him. He would die before the effects of a lack of vegetables could take its toll on her. What possessed people to put themselves second?

'Why do you think people have kids?'

Tony turned around.

'There doesn't seem to be anything in it for them,' said Ava.

'Can't you ask me one about domestic science?'

'Seriously.'

'OK. Well, I suppose there's a drive in a lot of us to procreate. Continuation of the species, and all that. But having children is…well, it's awesome. In the literal sense of the word. I fell in love with all three of you the moment I first held you. Nothing prepares you for the love. The strength of it. And how much there is to go around.'

'Why do you think Sadie wants a baby? Do you think she's got all this extra love to go around? She doesn't seem to have enough even for Mark. She's always moaning at him.'

'Trust me. Nobody knows what goes on in a relationship. It'll all come together. You'll see.'

She stared at the anatomical diagram of a chicken egg on her screen. Membrane, albumen, chalaza, germinal disk, air cell, yolk.

'I thought I saw Mark the other day, on Queen Street. He must have finished work early because it was only about four o'clock.'

Chapter 28

EVERYTHING WAS COMING into full bloom.

The temperature rose with each passing week. Sadie draped herself listlessly across anything that might be cooler than her body. She had taken to walking around the place almost naked. Mark would take such opportunities to gawp at the veins that were now so close to the surface, the strange markings, the tightly stretched skin, occasionally rubbing a curious finger or hand across this new and developing landscape.

Now and then, she would let out an 'Ugh!' or an 'Ouch!' and would ease her thumb under her ribcage to dislodge a tiny foot or elbow or fist. He always stopped whatever he was doing when that happened. He'd rush over and lay his hand gently on the spot, feeling the kicks and punches in his palm.

Whenever she fell asleep, which was often, he'd go upstairs and consult the Ruby phone. More often than not, there would be a message, and he'd judge if there was time to respond before Sadie woke up. It would take him longer than normal to jab in his message because he'd disabled predictive text — many of the words he used were not in the standard dictionary, and it had become a right old faff having to keep retyping the ins and outs of his urgent passion.

Normal life was now anything but. The intrusive thoughts and images that had once dogged him — the ones in which Fergus would appear — were now rare, more benign. He'd talked them through with Ruby, and she'd been able to stand in Fergus's shoes sometimes, say what she thought Fergus might do, might think. She'd support her remarks with examples of things Fergus had done in school, causing Mark to rewrite deep old scripts. His panic attacks had subsided. Daily life was bearable now. Jelly-bean scarfing incidents were rare. Occasionally, though, he had dreams in which Ruby would burst into the house, see Sadie's pregnant bump, and tell her everything, causing a huge clash in which they would grab alarming weapons — bread knives, heavy books, the big Dyson — and attack him. He'd wake from these dreams with a shout, drenched in sweat.

•••

'And the intrusive thoughts?'

Mark's GP seemed genuinely pleased to hear that

her patient was making progress.

'The Fergus flashbacks have gone,' said Mark.

'Good. Very good. That must be such a relief.' The doctor looked at her screen.

'I met someone who was there. Someone who saw the whole thing.'

She turned to face him.

'It could have happened to anyone. It was just an accident,' he said.

She nodded.

'She made me see that. Just a random, tragic accident.'

'Absolutely.'

'I've stopped taking the meds.'

'When?'

'I started cutting them in half when I picked up the last lot, then taking half every other day, then...' he shrugged.

'And the counselling?'

Mark looked sheepish. 'I binned it off. I got bored with hearing myself go on and on about the same shit. Also, we needed the money to pay the IVF instalments, so...'

The doctor nodded.

'I think I'm nearly fixed,' said Mark, laughing.

'That's wonderful. Often, the prospect of a new life, a new baby coming into the family, can put things into perspective.'

He walked through reception without stopping to make his next appointment, and mentally waved goodbye to the repeat prescription box.

Chapter 29

AVA HAD WORKED OUT THAT the standard double-decker bus comprised six distinct zones, excluding the driver's cabin and luggage rack. Zone One: standing room at the front — for people travelling for one or two stops, or for those wishing to closely guard their luggage. Zone Two: the first few seats on the lower deck — for the infirm, people with prams or in wheelchairs, and the headphoned oblivious. Zone Three was the belly of the lower deck, for the shoppers, the chatters, the day trippers. Zone Four: the back seat — reserved solely for those who like to chew their gum open-mouthed and ignore signs to keep their feet off the seats. Zone Five: the upper deck — for adventurers, for those whose children have run on ahead as they bought tickets, and those who prefer not to be observed. The back seat of the upper deck was Zone Six.

There were rules, too. Choose your zone, and head for the emptiest area within it (an empty double seat in front of and behind other empty double seats was a rare luxury). Never sit directly next to anyone if a double seat is available in one's zone; it was preferable to take an empty seat in an adjacent zone, to avoid disconcerting fellow passengers (and oneself) with unwarranted close physical contact.

Ava sat in Zone Three next to the steamed-up window. A substantially built man wedged next to her, pushing her up against the bus shell, taking up two-thirds of the seat. Ava tucked her hand into her sleeve, and rubbed a tiny porthole with her cuff. She could see umbrellas, a man running holding a newspaper over his head, tourists in plastic capes, and people craning at bus stops, willing the next bus to hurry.

Bryony held court in Zone Six. She was singing. Ava couldn't detect lyrics that included her name, so today was a good day. She had also been put into a maths project group with Michael earlier, which made it more than a good day. He'd asked her opinion on a particularly thorny problem they were struggling with and, although she didn't have the answer, she gave a coherent, intelligent response, despite feeling her face burning as she spoke. At one point he'd said something slightly funny and Ava had let out a disproportionate laugh which then turned into a cough, which resulted in one of the group thumping her on the back. It was a friendly thump, though. At Michael's suggestion, they'd all swapped mobile numbers, ostensibly to text each other their progress.

Ava looked at his number. She opened his contact and scrolled down to the notes field, and started to type.

Maths
Space/Astronomy
Guitar

The substantially built man leaned over her, and peered through the porthole. Ava held her breath.

'Sorry. Need to see.' He had a heavy accent. 'Botanical Gardens?'

Ava suspected he was German. She'd had a pretty good German lesson today, and had come top in the test.

'Ja,' said Ava, 'dort drüben.'

'Merci,' said the man, who smiled kindly, stood up and got off.

Why did people set so much store by taking risks? This was where risk-taking led: acute social embarrassment. Life seemed to be one carefully negotiated social situation after another, and Ava felt she got it wrong far more often than not. Earlier today, before the test results had been handed back to the class, the girl sitting next to her had wittered on about how hard the test had been, and asked Ava how she thought she'd done. Ava had answered honestly that she thought she'd come top of the class, and that the test hadn't been hard at all. Her answer had led to whispers and sniggers all around the table, which then spread to other tables. Honesty wasn't always the best policy, but the rules around when one should be honest and when one should lie weren't written down anywhere. She'd even tried googling it, but had ended up trawling through a load of sexist drivel about how to answer questions about women's bums looking big in certain clothes.

She jumped off at Goldenacre. As the bus rounded the corner, Bryony and her friends shouted out of the windows and made rude gestures at her from Zone Six. One of the boys had his mouth up against the window. Ava hoped that at least some of the twelve hundred bacteria he was ingesting would make him sick.

'Ava! Ava!' A voice from behind her. She turned to see Sadie waving frantically, a pile of shopping bags at her feet.

'What?' said Ava, not moving towards her.

'Well, hello, first of all. And, secondly, can you come over here and help me carry these bags, please.'

'That would mean my enabling your shopping habit,' said Ava.

Sadie put her hand on her bump.

Ava stayed put.

'I'll give you a fiver.'

'I'll do it, but I don't want the money. I just want you to know that I resent doing it, and I think your consumerist habits are terrible for the environment and for those who work in unacceptable conditions.' She was walking towards Sadie as she was saying all this, oblivious to the glances from passers-by.

'Just grab a couple of these bags.' Sadie handed two

bulky but not heavy bags to her sister.

'Why are you here, anyway?'

'Dad's got some veg for me.'

'How are you going to carry all of this *and* a load of vegetables home?'

'Dad'll drop me.'

'So you're coming for the veg and for a lift home.'

They were walking side by side now, down South Trinity Road. Ava scraped her heel along the pavement every sixth step.

'You're wrecking your shoes,' said Sadie.

'How do you know you'll have enough love to give to the baby?'

Sadie stopped, shuffled the bags into a more comfortable position, and started walking again.

'You just do.'

'No, I'm asking *you*. How do *you* know?'

'I suppose I just trust what other people, other parents, say. Some people have loads of kids, and they're all loved.'

'I don't think so.'

Sadie laughed.

A pair of whippets on long leads nuzzled up to them, their owner panting an apology a few metres way. Ava unceremoniously dropped the bags, crouched down and petted them.

'Watch they don't bite,' said Sadie, nervously. Ava gave her a teenage look.

'Oh, they don't bite,' said the owner, a ruddy-faced woman in a tweed skirt, who was now level with them, 'but they might lick you to death.' She smiled at Sadie before turning her attention to the dogs. 'Ena! Albert! Leave the girl alone!' She gently yanked them away and continued her walk.

Ava pulled out a hand sanitiser and rubbed it thoroughly into her hands.

'Will you have a vaginal birth?'

After a moment, Sadie answered. 'It depends.'

'On what?'

'Well, ideally, but–'

'Do you think you can take the pain?'

'There are all sorts of ways of relieving–'

'Because babies have massive heads. I've looked at my vagina with a mirror and I just know I could never get a baby out of that.'

'It stretches,' said Sadie.

'Do you remember the time I tried to eat a whole satsuma at once?' said Ava.

'It's not the same.'

'You can have an elective Caesarean.'

They were at the garden gate now. Sadie gently kicked it open.

'You just end up with a small scar. They make the incision, pull the baby out, then stitch you back up. You don't feel anything. No pushing. Nothing.'

Sadie rang the doorbell.

'And, if you decide to have more babies, they'll just do the same. It's like they make this opening that's there for your convenience,' Ava fished her keys out of her bag and opened the door just as Tony got to it, 'which saves you trying to push them all out of your vagina.'

Tony took their bags and walked ahead into the kitchen.

'Also, it's better for your sex life,' said Ava.

'I've just made a smoothie,' said Tony. 'Anyone want one?'

•••

Nisha approached Mark's desk.

'Zivile's brought cake in. Want some?'

Cake. Great.

She held a selection out to him. He picked the biggest, stickiest-looking of the lot. Nisha handed him a napkin.

His phone buzzed in his pocket.

Hi! Ring me!

Sadie.

In a mtg. Text me.

He put the phone on his desk, and gave himself a cake break.

'Can I have a word, please, Mark?' His boss, Holly, loomed over him. He quickly wiped cream and cake crumbs from his face and turned his phone face down.

'Your PDR's due soon; have you filled in your prep document yet? I have a month to get this through HR.'

Mark nodded, and surreptitiously tried to clear cake

from between his teeth. He'd forgotten all about his professional development review. He hadn't filled in the prep form. He didn't know where the prep form was.

'Good. Send me the document when you have a minute. We need to set a date to go through it.'

He picked up his phone, and dismissed Sadie's messages before opening his diary. He scrolled through the week ahead. 'Sometime next week would be good.'

'I'm away. How about two weeks' time?'

As they settled on a date, his phone started to buzz again.

'OK, I'll leave you to it. You'd better get that.' Holly walked away.

Mark scuttled towards the meeting room. 'Just hang on, Sade...'

Sadie was shouting. The words were fast, garbled.

He closed the meeting room door behind him, and stood leaning against it. He made out a word: London.

'Sadie, slow down, babe.'

'They want me to go down to London for a meeting! They just rang me, while I was here at Mum and Dad's!'

'Who?'

'The National Theatre! They want to meet me next week!' She started to laugh. He could imagine how she looked right now, huge grin, eyes crinkled.

'I need to do a test — so...' he could hear her scrabbling about: '...yeah, I need to repair something that they supply on the day — that could be anything at all, I guess — and I have to make something simple from scratch with materials they will supply. Then there's a panel interview. They don't call it an interview, but that's what it is.'

'That's brilliant! They'll love you.' They would; he knew she'd dazzle them.

A knock at the door. Nisha.

'Hang on a sec, Sade.' He opened the door slightly, and held the phone against his chest.

'Don's booked this room for a sales team meeting,' said Nisha. 'He's getting a bit edgy. He said they're coming in at three on the dot.'

Mark pointed to his phone, outraged, pretending he was on an important call.

Nisha looked at him, evenly, then said, sotto voce, 'You have icing sugar on your nose.'

● ● ●

'Oi! You're supposed to book ahead if you want that room,' said Don, as Mark emerged back into the office.

'It's all yours.'

'What were you doin' in there, anyway? Going for a new job, are we? Setting up an interview?'

'You wish.'

Don approached him.

'Yeah. Yeah, I do. Because my lads are not making their bonuses. And when they don't make their bonuses…'

Mark rolled his eyes.

'You need to pull your finger out, and get people flooding in here at the weekend, sonny boy. You should be out there, offering 'em all sorts to come in. Once they're in, you can leave 'em to us.'

'Lucky them.'

Don dropped the month end figures and future projections file. It scraped hard along Mark's shin before landing, corner down, on his foot.

'Oh, sorry, mate!' said Don, for everyone's ears. He bent down to pick it up. As he rose to Mark's ear level, he grinned like a mad ventriloquist and said, through gritted teeth: 'You better watch it, sunshine,' before patting him menacingly on the face.

chapter 30

RUBY SAVOURED THE MOMENTS before she picked up her paintbrush: the blast of linseed oil as she lifted the dustsheet, the squeezing of raw sienna, white, raw umber and alizarin onto her palette, the peering from all angles at what she had already painted and what would be needed today. Time stood still as this happened. Then, as she approached the canvas and tentatively began, time accelerated until it flew like a war-jet.

She made Mark's hair slightly longer than it was now, more like it had been when he was younger. And, as she remembered his lashes being long and thick back then, she painted them that way. But everything else was faithful to how he was now. His lines, bumps, scars, open pores and wrinkles. His ugly feet.

It was her first life-sized portrait. After cleaning her brushes, after she locked the studio door, her eyes would take time to adjust to three dimensions again. She would turn on lamps, light candles, then pour wine, shove something in the oven, and tip salad leaves onto a plate. If she was feeling lazy, she'd fish salad dressing from the deep recesses of the fridge and pour it generously over the rocket, butterhead and radicchio. On other days, she'd use a tiny whisk to blend mustard, oil, vinegar and seasoning. She imagined a child holding such a whisk, perhaps standing on a stool to reach the kitchen worktop, just as she had once done with her own mummy.

•••

Sadie was invisible to Mark. The way the light bounced off the train window prevented him from seeing her waving and smiling. He waved in her general direction, just in case, but his timing was all off; she mouthed 'Love you,' as he looked at his watch. It was only once the train started to move away that he saw her clearly.

Their goodbye kiss on the platform had been perfunctory — nothing unusual in that — yet he'd felt the urge to run his hand down her spine and pause at the curve of her bottom, as if to remind himself of something.

As he left the station and headed for the car, he kicked a pebble and watched it skim to its intended target, a small depression in the pavement. He caught up with it, hooked his toe underneath and kicked it again, this time to the car. His aim was excellent. He picked up the pebble and turned it like soap in his hand before dropping it down a storm grid, where it made a satisfying splash.

As he carefully snipped away at his pubic hair in the shower, he consoled himself with the thought that he wasn't as hackneyed a cliché as most men in his position. The problem wasn't that his wife didn't understand him; it was just that Sadie only understood who he was now, but Ruby understood who he used to be, who he still could be — she had seen him in his glory days, she'd cheered as he'd scored a much-needed crucial goal for the school football team, she had seen him hoisted in the air and carried off the pitch by others in their heyday, she'd watched girls — and boys — gather around him and make excuses to touch him, to have his magic rub off on them. Ruby reminded him, two decades on, that he was a man worthy of being carried on the shoulders of others.

•••

Ruby was uneasy about Mark's imminent arrival. He'd asked her outright if they could meet at her place — it would be more private — and he'd not noticed (or had ignored) her lack of enthusiasm for the idea. So here she was, lighting candles, wearing uncomfortable lingerie under a dress that suggested she was wearing uncomfortable lingerie. She'd chilled two bottles of Prosecco and a six-pack of beer, and had stocked up on olives and other food that had no need for cutlery.

'Hello?'

'Hi, it's me.'

She hesitated for a moment, leaving him standing there for a few seconds longer than strictly necessary. She imagined him looking around furtively as she buzzed him in.

'Nice place.'

'You like it?'

'Yeah. Great.'

It would have to do. She knew there wasn't much to speak of architecturally and it was too dimly lit to expect him to comment on the book spines or the artwork.

She wrapped herself around him, ignoring his physical hesitancy, which she put down to his being nervous.

'Listen…' he said.

Nothing good ever starts with 'listen'. She knew that. Everyone knows that.

'You look amazing,' he stroked down her arms and caught her fingertips; it was a strangely asexual gesture that she recognised for exactly what it was: a prelude to an announcement. She leaned over to kiss him, as though she knew subsequent kisses would be different. He tasted delicious, smelled gorgeous; there was something fruity about him.

'First of all, I want you to know that I am…well, that you have made me so…'

She planted small kisses on his shoulder.

'I think this is the right time to tell you that things

are probably a bit more complicated than I've had the chance to explain. I should probably have brought this up sooner, actually.' He gestured for her to sit down and she did. He perched on the edge of the coffee table.

She folded her arms into a self-hug. It had been pretty complicated up until now, anyway. What could be more complicated than being married to someone else but running around town with her?

'Neither of us meant for this — *this* — to happen, right?'

She adjusted her dress, pushed a bra strap back into position.

'I love you to bits, right?'

To bits? Shit, this was going to be horrible.

'Sadie had IVF.'

A pause, as she tried to remember how to form words.

'Did she?' It was all she could manage, as she tried to make sense of what he was telling her.

'And she got pregnant.'

'Sadie's pregnant?'

'She is. Yes.'

Another pause.

'How long?' She didn't know if a lower or a higher figure would be easier to handle.

'What?'

'How long has she been pregnant?'

'Well, with IVF, you count from the, erm…'

'How long, roughly?'

'About seven months.'

She stared at him. He reached for her hand and she

let it be taken because all the energy she had in her body was now being used to keep her breath flowing in and out.

'Seven months?'

'Give or take.'

'It's not yours, though?'

'What?'

'The baby. It's not yours? You said it was IVF. It's donor sperm? It's not your sperm?'

'Well, technically...'

'Oh, Christ.' She put her hands to her face. She was having an affair with a man who was not only married but was married to a woman who was pregnant, a woman who was pregnant not by accident, not as a result of a careless night, but intentionally, and as a result of struggling through a series of difficult and probably unimaginable hurdles.

'I meant to tell you. But, after we...'

'You *meant* to tell me?' Her voice quivered with anger. She pushed him away. 'What, you couldn't put a two-word phrase together? *Sadie's pregnant.*'

'I didn't know how to...'

'*Sadie's pregnant!* That's all you had to say! Two words!' She was shouting now, and she stood up to loom over him. 'Two words!'

He bowed his head and answered quietly: 'I know.'

'Seven months?'

'Give or take.' He lifted his head and looked straight at her. 'I didn't realise we'd get in so deep. This was never my intention.'

She held his gaze. 'Get out.'

He stood up, slowly, reluctantly, and knocked over a lit candle that continued to burn. He fumbled to prevent the flame catching on anything else; something in him couldn't blow it out — it was too slight a gesture for the moment — so he stubbed it out with a hardback, causing Ruby to reach over and snatch the book from him, which knocked over a vase of flowers, sending water everywhere.

'I'm sorry,' he said, as water trickled onto his shoes.

She didn't attempt to pick up the flowers. She didn't rush for a cloth or a towel. She just stood there, holding a signed copy of *Queenie* that now had a daub of candle wax on its cover. 'For Sadie being pregnant? Or for not telling me? For stringing me along like an idiot?'

'I'm truly,' he stretched out the word: *truuuuly*, 'sorry for everything. You're not an idiot, obviously. I'm the idiot.'

As he left, she glanced at the clock. He'd been there for less than ten minutes. She necked the Prosecco straight from the bottle, and rang Nat.

•••

'Seven months?'

'Give or take.'

'Twat.'

'I think I'm going to be sick.'

'I'll be there in half an hour.'

•••

'Twat,' said Nat.

'Yeah,' said Ruby, who was now enveloped in a bear hug.

'She's about to drop it. That's the only reason he's told you now.'

'I know.'

'It's the most deceitful, cruel…'

'I know.'

'You can't carry on, not now you know there's a baby.'

'I know. I know all that. But the love… I feel like I've swallowed a rock.' She rubbed her fist against her chest.

'That's not love.' Nat pulled away, looked at her, eyeball to eyeball, and shook her head.

'No, it is. It *really* is.'

Nat sighed.

'Look, I need you to be on my side here. I need you to understand.'

'I *am* on your side.'

'So listen to what I'm saying!'

'OK.'

A silence, as Ruby gathered her thoughts. 'Whenever I'm with him, the only way I can describe it is that everything feels right. I feel like I've come home. And I know he feels the same.'

'Right. OK. But, even if he does feel the same way—'

'He does!'

'Yes, OK, but he already has a home. With a wife and a baby on the way.'

Ruby dropped down to a sobbing crouch, and Nat

quickly followed her, taking hold of her hands.

'I'm not saying he doesn't love you.'

'He does.'

'Right. I'm just saying that the baby…'

Ruby let out a loud sob.

'The baby complicates things.'

Still crouching, Nat stroked Ruby's forearms and started taking deep encouraging breaths, which Ruby eventually mirrored. They stayed that way for some time, settling to quieter breaths, fewer punctuating sobs.

•••

On his way to work the next day, Mark shunned the bus in favour of a fast uphill walk to clear his head, to feel some physical pain, and to give him time to think. He loved who he was when he was with Ruby. He loved Sadie; he just didn't like who he was when he was with her. But that was his fault. Because when he was with her, he hated that he was an unfaithful husband. Even before he was a cheating piece of shit, he knew he wasn't good enough. And when he was alone, like now, mostly, he hated himself. Not just for killing Fergus. He hated himself for the long-term damage he'd inflicted on his body years earlier, with drugs and drink and general abuse. He hated himself when he was shoving sugar, in all its forms, into his mouth so fast that he often swallowed things whole. He hated himself for sometimes trying to make Anders side against Sadie with him. He hated himself for sometimes letting Nisha take the burden of a day's work, even though she was keen. He hated the way his hair looked, he hated his dry, eczema-prone skin, his hairy toes, his inconsequential voice, his bitten fingernails. He hated his hatred of hearing people laugh at someone else's joke, quip, sharp comment.

Halfway up Broughton Street, a woman gently hosed large pots of flowers outside Narcissus, to prepare them for the heat of the day ahead. As Mark approached, she haunched down and nipped off a couple of browning petals.

'Morning,' said Mark.

The florist looked up and smiled, curling the petals into her palm.

'Hi.'

'Do you deliver?'

'Sure, sure. Come in.'

Once inside, she discarded the petals into a bucket and wiped her hands on her apron. Her smile was natural, easy, as though she hadn't had to hide much.

'I'm looking for something that says, "I've been an absolute arse and I'm sorry".' He laughed as an invitation for her to join in with the joke, which she did.

'Ah, we do a roaring trade in those!' she said, moving towards the most expensive blooms.

'Did you have anything specific in mind?'

He looked around the shop, clueless. 'Maybe a bunch of red roses?'

The florist screwed up her nose slightly and walked

back towards him.

'The thing is, in a situation like this, I'm guessing you want to make a statement. To do that solely with long-stemmed roses you'd probably need a couple of dozen.'

'Right.'

'They're four pounds fifty per stem,' she said.

Mark, suddenly aware of his scuffed shoes, pretended to take the information in his stride.

'And, to be honest, roses are more...' she paused and scratched gently at her head. 'Well, they're very romantic — probably better saved for special occasions rather than apologies. Beautiful, of course, especially these,' she stroked the head of a stunning red Grand Prix.

'Well, I do want them to be romantic but they also have to say sorry...'

'For being an arse. Yes. Absolutely.'

She reached into one of the highest vases and pulled out a single stem.

'Peony. Huge impact.'

'OK. Yeah. Looks nice.'

'Now, they would look stunning in a bouquet with,' she took a couple of steps to the right, 'these delphiniums and stocks' she said, grabbing a stem of each and pushing them together, 'and a couple of snapdragons.'

'And we could put some roses in, of course, if you like,' she said, swiping a stem of white spray roses. She inhaled and pushed the flowers towards him to do likewise.

Mark sniffed, and nodded in silent approval.

'Gorgeous, yes?'

Mark eyed a vase of tall, delicate-looking, pink flowers.

'They're sweet peas. Misnomer, really, because they're poisonous. Beautiful, though. Shall I?'

She pulled a couple out of the vase and positioned them in the expanding bouquet.

'So, would you like me to make up something like that for you? Quite dramatic, very romantic and bold?'

'Yeah, dramatic and romantic and bold, yeah, great.'

'It looks like you've really thought about it, like you've not just gone for the obvious. Makes a statement.'

She pushed the flowers to arms' length and scrutinised them, twisting and rearranging them slightly.

'Do you think they say sorry? *Really* sorry?'

She pushed another couple of stocks in. 'Yep.'

'OK, that's…yeah, that's great.'

'What size would you like?'

Mark started to make a size with his hands and arms, not immediately realising that the question was to be answered in pounds rather than centimetres.

'I could do something very impressive for about seventy-five pounds, including local delivery.'

He swallowed hard, and made a mental note not to do anything that required this level of apology again.

'Great.'

'They'll bowl her over!'

The florist beamed as she swished the flowers in a

dramatic gesture before placing them on the counter.

'OK. Now, would you like to choose a card for your message?'

She pointed to a display of small cards, as though any of them might be able to convey what Mark had to say.

'No message,' said Mark, as he fished out his wallet. 'Of course.'

He didn't have the exact address of the gallery, but the florist knew it and reassured him that the flowers would be delivered to Ms Suddula that morning.

The welcome vibration of the phone shortly after lunchtime caused him to make an involuntary whimper in the office. He scrabbled to pull it out of his trouser pocket.

Stop sending me things.

A chink of light. It didn't say leave me alone. It didn't say never try to contact me again. He texted her back.

Sorry. X

She didn't respond to the apology and he hadn't expected her to. He'd give her at least a few days before getting back in touch, partly not to seem desperate or stalkerish, but mainly to allow himself a short break from being an unfaithful shit.

He indulged in the crosstalk of the office more

enthusiastically that afternoon, relieved and undistracted. His colleagues might have observed that he was on top form. He didn't do much work but he'd make up for that another day. Re:Klein was the type of workplace in which one could occasionally coast.

Chapter 31

'YOU'RE FALLING SHORT ON three of your five key performance indicators.' Holly took a sip of water.

Mark could hear his own pulse.

'And Don is concerned that the sales team isn't receiving appropriate marketing support. I forwarded his email to you for action, but you didn't get back to me,' said Holly. 'Did you deal with him direct about it?'

Mark shuffled some papers around, pretending he was looking for a hard copy of his response. In truth, he couldn't even remember receiving the complaint.

'I think we sorted it out between us.'

'OK,' she sighed as she scrolled through Mark's record, 'just looking at your performance overall, it's been quite erratic — absences, non-delivery, a number of missed deadlines.' She looked up. 'I wondered what you might put that down to.'

Mark pretended to consider the question.

'You know my wife's pregnant?'

Holly nodded.

'Well, things have been quite difficult. We went through IVF, and there have been some very dark times, scary moments, you know?'

'Sure,' she said, evenly.

It occurred to him that Holly could probably smell bullshit from three postcodes away.

'And you like it here?'

Shit. 'Love it here, yeah,' he lied.

'How far did you get with the neuromarketing stuff I sent you?'

He tried to make an appropriate face, as she clicked onto the email she'd sent.

'Copenhagen Neuromarketing Conference delivered to Mark Darling's Inbox on the ninth. Unread.'

'I'll look at it as soon as —'

'That was three weeks ago. I imagine it'll be booked up by now.' She sighed and rubbed at her temples. 'I've also been made aware you've arrived at work drunk on at least one occasion. If that's true, we would have grounds for dismissal.'

Mark put his hand on his heart. 'I was *not* drunk. Hung over, maybe, but *not* drunk.'

She gathered up a sheaf of papers and tapped them on the desk like a newsreader at the end of a bulletin. 'You have three months to turn everything around. Do you understand, Mark?'

Three months. OK, he could do this.

'Absolutely,' he said. 'And, Holly, thanks. I've been distracted. Personal problems. But I'll sort it.'

Less than an hour later, he'd booked his place on the Copenhagen conference.

Chapter 32

THE TRAIN FROM EUSTON to Waverley was delayed. Over the tannoy, a man unable to pronounce his Rs informed passengers that the seat reservation system was down and, unfortunately, the train was operating with a reduced range of refreshments. There would be no hot drinks, and no trolley service, but Ruth and Rory were ready to serve customers in the buffet car at the rear of the train.

Sadie was negotiating herself into a seat when a woman approached her.

'Hi, I think that's my seat.'

Sadie sighed. 'Sorry, the system's down,' she said, looking up at the blank display. 'Mine's an open return, so...' She struggled to her feet.

'Look, I'll sit here,' said the woman, indicating the

seat opposite, 'and we'll see if anyone else comes along.' She smiled, took a flask and a plastic container out of her hold-all, before pushing her luggage into the overhead racks.

'Wish I'd thought of that,' said Sadie. 'No trolley service.'

'Par for the course. I do this route twice a week.' She put her hand out to shake Sadie's. 'I'm Ali.'

The box contained plenty of stuff for sharing: samosas, bhajis, stoned cherries. The flask had two cups, one small, the other tiny, and contained enough strong coffee to fill both twice. By the time they passed through the green, green, green Lake District, life stories had been sketched out, some intimacies shared. Sadie embellished what was already a pretty exciting anecdote about the meeting she'd just had, and portrayed Mark as a comedian and writer without mentioning his day job. She liked this version of their life, and it wasn't a million miles away from the truth.

'So is it just theatrical costumes you do?' asked Ali.

Sadie stepped off the train at Waverley with an invitation to pitch to design and make capsule outfits for staff in Ali's three shops. As she crossed the concourse at Waverley, heading for a taxi, she was taller than she'd been two days earlier, and she led with her chin rather than her bump.

Chapter 33

I'M SO SORRY. HOPE YOU'RE OK.☺

The text arrived just after midnight, as Ruby was finishing a funding application that had to be submitted the next day. She stared at the stupid sad face as she thought of potential responses.

Later, as she slept, another pinged in.

You're not OK obvs. All my fault. Sorry. M x

•••

A couple of days later, they sat on a low wall in St Andrew Square and talked about work. The new exhibition was going well, great reviews, national media interest, she'd done a radio interview that morning. He was in the middle of a big marketing campaign, the sales figures were down on last year so the pressure was on, they'd brought in a new head of sales and marketing, everyone was a bit worried about jobs, did she want to buy a sofa, just joking, hahaha.

'How's Sadie?'

'She's fine. Yeah. Yep. Fine, She's, erm, going for another scan tomorrow.'

'On her own?'

'No.'

'I read the reason they like fathers to attend them is so they can start the bonding process as early as possible,' she said.

They sipped their flat whites. A family walked past; two dads, one pushing a baby in a pushchair, the other holding the hand of his toddler who mis-kicked a ball that rolled in their direction.

Mark threw it back. 'Good shot!' he said, laughing.

'Anyway. I'm a bit late. I should go,' said Ruby.

'Yeah. Yeah. Me, too.'

'Loads on.'

'Same.'

They walked to the gate slowly.

'See you tomorrow?' said Mark. 'We could have lunch at–'

'If I'd known she was pregnant...' As she blurted it out, a woman from Re:Klein's accounts department walked past them and said hi to Mark. He let her get a safe distance away before he spoke.

'Can we talk about this somewhere else?' he said.

Ruby continued. If anything, her voice was now louder. 'You know when you went swimming as a kid, and you'd get a coloured wristband, and the pool attendant would call out your wristband colour after a while, and everyone with that colour had to get out because their time was up?'

He steered them down towards the Portrait Gallery where the crowds thinned out.

'Well, I thought you were about to have your colour shouted out, but it turns out you've only just got in the pool. Your marriage is only just starting properly.'

He looked beyond the Botanics across to Fife. It glowed above the bluest strip of water. They turned into North St Andrew Lane. It was deserted, and he had an urge to lie down on the cobbles.

'I know what you mean about the armbands,' he said.

'Wristbands.'

'Wristbands.'

She folded her arms across her chest.

'When I first met Sadie, I was lost. Completely lost. Off my head every day, every night. I wouldn't be here today — literally — I wouldn't be alive today. You know?'

She waited.

'And this,' he made a back and forth movement between them both with his hands. 'I never expected...'

A cyclist zoomed past, causing them both to jump.

'Most people live really easy, uncomplicated lives. They live in nice places — no dry rot, they spend weekends enjoying themselves... I've no idea how they do it, how they run their lives so seamlessly. I'm an absolute fuck-up most of the time.'

She stared hard at him. 'You couldn't live that life.'

'Try me.'

'You'd be happy to ditch the stand-up?'

'No.'

'You want to live in a semi, next door to the guy who barbecues every weekend? Or a terrace with noisy neighbours either side? You want to work hard, get in early, stay late, go for promotion?'

'No.'

'No.'

A pause.

'Everybody thinks I'm...'

She interjected. 'Doesn't matter. Doesn't matter what anyone else thinks.'

He nodded slowly. 'What do *you* think?'

'I think you're complicated. I think you sometimes get things wrong — like most people do. I think your heart's in the right place. I think you need to stop listening to people who try to put you down.'

'Do you mean Sadie?'

She didn't answer right away.

'We all love in different ways,' she said, eventually.

Chapter 34

'Do you like this?' Mark asked Sadie one Saturday morning, as he stroked her belly.

'The bump?'

'No! This! The stroking.'

'Do I like the stroking?'

'Yeah.'

'Yeah, it's nice. Feels like you're stroking the baby.'

They hadn't got up yet. The blinds were still drawn, the light soft on their skin.

'I think we should look at prams this weekend,' said Sadie. 'We might need to order the one we want. We can't leave it till the last minute.'

He stayed focused, ignoring the unwelcome prospect of a pram shopping expedition, cutting short any discussion of frames, fabrics, colours.

'Shall I give you a massage? A back massage?'

'What?'

'You sit up, I'll sit behind you...'

'What for?'

'You might like it. You used to like it.'

'Did I?'

He nodded and wiggled his fingers in the air. 'Magic hands. You said I had magic hands.'

She laughed. 'Craig said you had magic hands when you stood in goal for Ben that time. I've never said it!' She rolled on her side to upright herself out of bed. 'Come on, get up! Prams!'

'You definitely, definitely did! You said it in the back of the cab after some party we went to.' He pursued her, reached for her waist. 'Come back to bed for an hour. The shops will still have prams this afternoon.'

'OK, but I need the loo first,' she said, before disappearing into the bathroom for a pee, a wash, and a quick brush of her teeth.

In the fifteen minutes it took her, Mark googled the most exciting sexual positions suitable for women in their third trimester of pregnancy. It made for an interesting subsequent hour, even if the pillow talk wasn't up to much.

'What are you doing?'

'It's fine, I googled it. Just relax.'

chapter 35

AT THE SIDE OF RUBY'S BED, there was a small box that looked like it had been painted by a child. It was aqua blue with white clouds; he could see the brush strokes if he looked closely enough. The box contained a considerable number of assorted condoms. He felt conflicted. On one hand, it showed initiative. And on the other — well, it showed initiative. The sight of the box, the magic box, the box of tricks with its poorly fitting lid had the power to reduce his erection to something less than impressive.

'Did you paint it?'

'No.'

'Who did?'

'A friend.'

'A friend gave you a box of condoms?'

'A friend gave me the box containing a certificate of membership of a cloud appreciation society.'

'Nice gift.'

'I didn't appreciate it at the time.' Sad face.

Wilt.

They lay on their backs, side by side, intertwined at the legs. They had been silent for a couple of minutes, alone with their thoughts of cloud appreciation and lost opportunities.

'Best day and worst day of your life?'

'Best: scoring the winning goal in the regional championship.' His answer was fast, as though it had always been there, ready to come out.

'Of course.'

'You?'

'Best: I was once left alone for a whole day in the art room at school. I'd missed the coach for a school trip, and one of the art teachers said she'd keep an eye on me. Anyway, it was really sunny and warm outside, so the windows were open, and this bird landed on the windowsill and stayed there for ages. When it flew off, I put some crumbs from my packed lunch on all of the sills, and it attracted more birds. It was amazing. I felt like I was in a fairytale. Also, I had all the paper and art supplies, and clay and collage materials I could want, and the teacher left me with a little radio from the staffroom, so I even had music, too. I just felt like I was free. I imagined this is what it would be like to be a grown-up.'

They returned to silence for a few moments.

'Worst?' she asked.

'The night the police arrived at the door, to tell me Mum and Dad had been killed.'

'Fuck.'

'Or,' he covered his face with his palms, 'the day of the funeral, when the music started and I realised they were being cremated to 'Come Together' by Primal Scream instead of 'Come Rain Or Come Shine' by Chet Baker.'

Ruby's eyes widened.

Mark rubbed his face and shrugged. 'I was off my head on grief. Everyone tried to help, but I was determined to arrange as much of their funeral as I could. At some point, I must've given the wrong song to the funeral director, or to Auntie Lil who was trying her best to help.'

'What happened?'

'People sang along. It was probably as close to a rave as the crematorium's had.'

She laughed, cautiously, then rolled onto him, kissed him, and he rolled her over, and she never got to tell him that the worst days of her life were the days she didn't see him, the days he spent with Sadie.

chapter 36

IT WASN'T REALLY A DATE. It was just two people meeting up to work on tablature homework from guitar club. The aim of the assignment was to improve speed and accuracy. They were in Michael Deluna's dining room. Alone.

'Can I get you anything to drink?' asked Michael.

Ava grinned. 'Is that what you say to all your customers?'

'At the new place I do, yeah. We have to get them to order a drink while they look at the menu, then offer them more drinks when their food comes, and coffee afterwards. We have a target of three drinks per person.'

'Really?'

'Yeah! We get a bonus for every extra drink they

have once they've had the three minimum.'

'I'll have a vodka, please,' said Ava, deadpan.

'I don't think…' He looked slightly thrown until Ava smiled and he visibly relaxed. 'Yeah, vodka's off, sorry. We have a coffee machine that only my mum and dad can work. You're welcome to have a go at it. Or there's orange juice, Coke…'

'Does the juice have bits in it?'

'Bits?'

'Yeah, you know, like, bits of orange?'

'I don't think so. I can check.' He opened the enormous fridge and crouched down to peer at the juice carton slotted in the door. Ava could see the waistband of his boxers and a couple of inches of pattern below that. Blue check. Probably bought by his mum. Cute. And hair in the small of his back. Dark. Downy.

'Smooth. It says "smooth".'

'Great. I'll have a smooth orange juice, then, please. To sit in. No ice.'

So, here she was, in his dining room, parents out, like someone had waved a wand and granted wish number one. The place wasn't as glamorous as she'd imagined — no imposing columns at the front door or leopard-skin rugs in the hall, a kitchen table pretty much like the one back at home. There were, however, shelves everywhere, crammed with books, spine out, spine in, vertical, horizontal, precarious; she doubted anything was in alphabetical order.

Michael put the glass of juice in front of her and picked up his guitar.

'I'm working on the E shape, and trying to make that

transition from G to B faster.'

He positioned his fingers to play G and sang in a lo-fi kind of way:

'Whatever makes you happy…'

He stuck out his tongue slightly at the corner of his mouth, to help him with B. His hair flopped forward and he leaned over the guitar and sang the next line:

'Whatever you want…'

He glanced up at her.

· 'See? It's getting from G to B that I need to get right by next week's class. What about you?'

She pretended that he hadn't just serenaded her, and was trying her hardest not to be too distracted by his tongue or his fingers.

'I think my finger positioning is OK, but I can't get the tension right,' she said.

He held his plectrum up to her, between his finger and thumb.

'You need to find a natural hold, not too tight, not too loose, and you should position it at about twenty degrees to the strings, like this.'

He strummed to demonstrate.

'You're aiming for a smooth tone, no separate notes. You have to try and iron out the staccato sound.'

He pushed his hair out of his eyes before continuing.

'And there are other techniques we can work on once you get the hang of it.'

Ava picked up her guitar.

'No, you see, you need to get the right starting position.'

He stood up and walked behind her where he leaned

across and moved her arms into position.

'Your left arm needs to be looser, drop your shoulder.'

She could feel his breath on her neck.

'Now, try that.'

She strummed, as he pushed down slightly on her shoulder.

'Relax this shoulder a bit more. Yeah. That's right.'

He gently pulled back, watching her technique, then walked around to face her.

'That's great, Ava. You have it. Just keep the rhythm going.'

As she looked up, she felt his breath on her face, her eyelashes, lips. She leaned forward to kiss him.

'I think you should know that I plan to go to Mars.'

Ava nodded, as though he'd just announced he was about to get a glass of water.

'I know some people might think that's a bit...'

'Not me. I think you're...'

'I just don't want to string you along.'

Ava nodded again, although this time she wasn't sure why.

'Your shoulder's tightened up again,' he said.

Ava looked at it but made no attempt to drop it. She looked back at him.

'When are you planning on going?'

'Eight to ten years' time.'

'And you're not going to, like, you're not planning on getting involved with anyone unless they live on Mars?'

'I just think I have to let people know that I'm going to be off the planet at some point, 128 million miles away. And that I might not come back.'

'But someone could come with you?'

'Yes.'

She leaned forward again.

'Could I come to Mars with you?'

He leaned forward, kissed her gently, 'Yeah.'

As he pulled away, she thought it best to share her own plans for the future, just in case he had an abundance of love he needed to share with any future offspring. 'I've decided I don't want children. I hope that's OK.'

He nodded. 'I suspect Mars would be a difficult place to bring them up, anyway,' he said. 'There'll be no infrastructure in place when we get there. No hospitals or schools. No theme parks or anything.'

And then they got on with the business of snogging the faces off each other.

Chapter 37

'KATE AND NANCY ARE throwing a baby shower for me.' Sadie coiled her hair into a twist.

'A baby shower?' Mark hoped he could swerve this.

'It's an event where everyone drinks except me. I have to be satisfied with Kate's home-made macarons.'

'Macarons.'

'You know, the wee…' she drew a macaron shape in the air. 'She does a gin and tonic flavour.'

'I think you're allowed one of those, at least. When is it?'

'The twelfth.'

Ruby's birthday. 'I think Ben from work is having his stag on the twelfth.'

'Perfect. Keeps you out of the way.' And she kissed him. A light, playful kiss. And it took all he had not to crumble. He felt a powerful physical urge to wrap his arms around her and tell her that the stag was off, that she was amazing, that he loved her, even though he didn't deserve to be loved by her. If there was any such place as hell, he knew he'd just bought himself a fast-track, one-way ticket.

'I wondered if we should go public on the sex?' said Sadie.

It was a startling phrase that made no sense. He gawped at her.

'The sex. Of the baby.'

'Oh, right! Ha! Right! Yeah. If you think so.'

'What do you think?'

'Well,' he paused as though he was having relevant thoughts; he furrowed his brow a little and stroked his chin. 'I think it's a good idea to let people know now, because it means you don't have to worry about keeping the secret. Yeah. It seems like a good opportunity to make an announcement.'

She kissed him and he kissed her right back, passionately, gratefully, guiltily.

Chapter 38

IT WAS A THURSDAY EVENING. Sadie was in the bath, and Mark was loading the dishwasher when the comedy club manager's number flashed up on his phone.

'Eddie…'

'Mark, this benefit gig tonight — there's fifteen on the bill, and two have gone AWOL. I can stretch it out, but the third slot's yours if you want it.'

Mark was silent.

'Nobody's getting paid, but it's a big gig. Two thousand seats. Sold out. You never know who's in.'

The dishwasher gel tab burst in his hand.

'Mark? You there?'

The sticky liquid oozed into a gloopy puddle at his feet.

'Yeah, er, what…what time?'

'I need you to be here in an hour.'

He walked on stage to the loudest applause he'd ever heard. It startled him. He couldn't gauge where to come in, whether to cut them short or stand there and take it in. He couldn't remember his opener, so he shouted, 'Hello, Edinburgh!' as though he'd arrived at the venue on a tour bus rather than the Number 8. He wasn't the worst on the bill, but his nerves got the better of him; he stumbled over his words a couple of times, and murdered a big punchline. The best, the very best on the bill, seemed special, somehow. It wasn't that she was funnier, exactly — one comic was cheered and whooped as he walked onto the stage, simply for putting one foot in front of another — but she had an ease about her, as though she categorically knew she could do this. Her arms didn't let her down by dangling awkwardly. Her fingers wrapped around the microphone without any constant adjusting for palm sweat or cramp. She didn't kick her glass over, or go onstage with the zip of her jeans slightly undone.

It was over in a flash. He felt intense relief that his legs had held out long enough to get him off stage. Someone in the wings said *good job*, but he couldn't make out a face. He stopped walking when he saw an ice bucket on the end of a long table; he plunged his hands into it.

By the time he was two beers down, his back sweat had evaporated to a dry itch. From where he stood, he could see at least six household-name comedians. He grabbed a third beer and scanned the room, saying the names to himself. He caught the eye of Dara Ó Briain, who was mid-chat with Frank Skinner. Mark walked over.

'All right', said Mark, putting his free hand out to be shaken.

Dara shook it first. As Frank did the same, Mark started to speak again.

'So, what did you think?'

'Yeah, great craic,' said Dara, who took a side step so Mark could join them.

'Good crowd,' said Mark.

'Well, Edinburgh,' said Dara, as though that explained it.

'Yeah. Home turf for me,' said Mark.

'Oh, you live here?' said Frank.

Mark nodded. 'And I gig here.'

'Grand,' said Dara. 'Great place.'

'So, how do you think I did? Tonight?'

Although not everyone in the room stopped speaking at that precise moment, things certainly dropped to a definite hush, as though someone had just introduced the topic of syphilis at afternoon tea. They stammered encouraging platitudes. There was no mistaking what was happening: they were being kind. He hastily tried to change the subject.

'So, arenas. They must be hard, right? Your O2s and all that? It must be weird if you can't see the audience's faces. You know, you're just speaking into a void, yeah?' And he closed his eyes, stretched out his arms in front of him, waved his hands about and wiggled his fingers.

●●●

He splashed very cold water onto his face.

There was some sort of commotion going on in one of the cubicles. A man from one of the benefit's charities stood at the next washbasin, carefully lathering then rinsing his hands.

'Thank you for taking the time to come tonight. We really appreciate it.'

Mark nodded.

'I liked that bit you did about supermarket olives. Made me smile.'

'Cheers.'

'And the bit you did at the end, about sending the parcel at the post office and being sold other services. That's happened to me, actually. They tried to sell me travel insurance, but since the incident with the llama I don't tend to travel so far and wide.'

Mark gave him a tight smile. He wasn't going to ask about the llama.

'Do you carry a little notepad around with you?'

'Notepad?'

'To jot down your observations.'

'No.'

'You must have an extraordinary memory. I mean I'd forgotten all about the post office thing until you mentioned it.'

Mark turned to face him.

'It didn't happen.'

The man looked at him, nonplussed.

'I made it up. I wrote it.'

'How clever! Well done!' said the man, before turning to leave. 'Well. Better scoot. Dara Ó Briain gets a little fractious if his rider's not to the letter. Comedians! Such divas!'

As the man left, it became apparent that the commotion in the cubicle was either people engaging in a highly charged sexual activity, or someone enthusiastically packing a rucksack for a family of six.

The light above the mirrors picked out silver specks in his stubble.

His phone vibrated in his pocket. A text from Ruby.

OMG AMAZING! CU in bar XXX

Two dishevelled men emerged from the cubicle brushing past him as they left. One mumbled something and they both burst into laughter.

He stared into the washbasin and wondered what it would be like to be small and narrow enough to slither down the plughole, to negotiate the drains, to emerge eventually at sea, free to roam the planet unjudged, perhaps to dock briefly at pink or pebble or white beaches, to watch people dance around bonfires. He glanced sideways at the door. Out there was embarrassment, lust, love, imminent fatherhood and the bar.

As he walked into the bar, Ruby flung her arms wide open, as though welcoming him home from war. A few people glanced around to see who'd walked in, then immediately went back to their drinks and chat. Mark signalled for her to join him in a quieter corner.

'The olives thing – omigod, my ribs were aching laughing with it. And I thought you LIKED olives, so I was laughing even more because I've fed you them! I said to the woman next to me: *I've fed him olives! I had no idea!*'

Ruby's voice bounced off the walls. It didn't seem to occur to her that he was feeling somewhat less than the man of the moment.

He spoke quietly, in the hope it would prompt her to turn down the volume: 'Shall we go back to your place?'

'Yeah, superstar!'

Mark put his finger on her lips and tried to keep things light.

'Let's see if we can dodge the paparazzi,' he said.

They upped and left. Nobody noticed.

●●●

By the time he arrived home, Sadie was in bed. He showered, ate a heap of toast, then softly snuck under the duvet next to her.

'Hey,' she whisper-drawled.

'Hey.'

'How was it?'

'Yeah, OK.'

She turned towards him, smiled.

'Did you make 'em laugh?'

'I think I did, yeah.'

chapter 39

RULE NUMBER ONE IN THE comedian's handbook: If you're not on top form on stage, if you kick over a glass, leave your flies slightly undone, murder a punchline, and you're in any way neurotic, it's best to avoid social media for a day or so.

Hardly anybody had mentioned him but the most mortifying aspect of it was that Ava had responded to those who had. Rule number two is: Don't let your fifteen-year-old sister-in-law handle your hecklers.

He rang her.

'Ava, hi.'

She rushed straight in: 'Mark, I know someone who was there last night, someone from the maths club, and he said you were OK, so, you know, those people on Twitter are just haters. So, anyway, we're going to try and get you to come and do something at our prom. We've started a petition. I said you'd write some material about our teachers and stuff. There's a magician and a covers band, but you'd be the only comedian.'

Don West's staff had briefed him on finer details of the Twitter fallout.

'Here he is: our very own Jimmy Carr!'

Mark walked directly to his desk and switched on his computer.

'Come on, then, let's hear a joke.'

The sales staff started braying. He handled it good-naturedly, initially, pretending to clutch his ribs laughing, smirking at the funnier remarks. It went on for a while, the jockeying and squeals. Then, someone threw a scrunched-up KitKat wrapper. It hit him in the face. There may have been a nanosecond of silence before everyone roared with laughter. A rush of adrenaline surged through him and, before he knew what he was doing, he ran at them all.

'You're all pointless twats, the lot of you! Pointless, pointless twats.'

They fell silent.

He strode right up to Don, nose to nose, and said: 'Fucking no marks.'

●●●

At the disciplinary meeting, Mark glazed over while some human resources bod read aloud from a densely typed sheet, and rotated east-west-east in her swivel chair.

He allowed himself a brief fantasy in which he threw the swivel chair out of the window.

'An apology would be appropriate under the circumstances. Don is very upset and offended at such language being used in the department, and he'd also like your personal assurance that it will never happen again.'

Mark laughed.

'I want to remind you, Mark, a formal warning is a very serious matter.'

She was maybe late-twenties. Wedding ring. Steady. In five years' time, she'd probably be senior management.

'Don is happy for this to be taken no further, as long as you are willing to apologise to him face-to-face and give him your word that this won't happen again.'

●●●

'You're gonna have to do it.'

'Sade, the man's a…' He pushed his dinner away.

'I know,' she said, pushing the plate back towards him.

You're bigger than this. Tell them there's no way you're apologising to this knobhead. Speak to Eddie. See if he can get you more regular gigs. See you tomoz. Love you. R xxx

'Bite the bullet,' said Dean.

•••

'Are you going to get fired?'

Ava had been asked to drop off an excess of strawberries and courgettes. They'd been in her school bag all day, and the strawberries were showing definite signs of fatigue. Mark started to eat them straight from the carrier bag.

'Next door's cat pees in our garden, so Dad says you should wash everything first, especially if Sadie's going to be eating them.'

'So it's OK if I eat fruit covered in cat pee, as long as your sister doesn't? Is that what you're saying?'

'No. It's what Dad's saying.'

Mark fished around for a colander.

'So is it true? Are you going to get fired?'

'Who says I am?'

'Dad. Mum. Nick and Lenny.'

'Well, you can tell them from me that it's not true.'

'Sadie rang Mum and said she was worried about you. She said you'd shouted at one of the bosses and called him a no-mark, and if you didn't apologise you'd be sacked.'

She opened the fridge and started to pick up various things and sniff them.

'OK, first of all, he's not my boss…'

'Dad said if you can't control yourself in a work situation, you need to be seeing more of your therapist.'

Mark clenched his jaw, further wearing down the

enamel on his already stress-damaged back teeth.

'Dad said if you lose your job, he's gonna have to have a word with some people he knows.'

'What people?'

'Police people, I think, from his old job. I dunno.'

Mark rinsed the strawberries and made another start on them.

'I think he was gonna get you another job, but Nick said you'd be rubbish at it and that he should leave well alone. Lenny thinks you should retrain, go back to evening classes or something.'

'It might have escaped everyone's notice, but I am busy in the evenings. That's when I gig.'

'Yeah, Dad said you're gonna need to knock all that on the head once the baby comes along.'

Mark took a deep breath and changed the subject. 'You want me to set up the Wii and the tennis games for you in the spare room?'

'Nah, I can do it.'

Mark looked at her pointedly.

'You want me to go up there now?' she said.

'Yup.'

'Is it because you're annoyed that you're gonna get sacked and have to give up the gigging?'

'I want to have something good in the oven for when Sadie gets back.'

'Dad said you should ribbon the courgettes. He said you probably wouldn't know what that was, but I said there'd be videos on YouTube.'

'Thanks.'

Tomorrow, he would apologise to Don West, get Nisha to search for names and contact details of comedy managers, and he'd stop off at Lakeland for a bloody ribboning tool.

Chapter 40

VIOLET POURED TWO VERY large glasses of red wine, put one on the worktop next to Tony, and knocked back a good third of the other.

'Deputy head?' said Tony.

'Yes.'

'You never said you were going for it.'

'It never came up before. If I got it — and it's a big *if* — I'd probably be able to do more of the kind of thing I've been working on recently.'

Tony carried a frittata and a bowl of salad to the table.

'The project to re-engage disenfranchised students,' she said.

'Right.'

She sighed, put down her fork and, after a moment,

pointed her knife towards the window: 'I could tell you exactly what crops you've got growing in that garden, where they're planted and how they're doing. I could even tell you what station your shed radio will be tuned to at any given time.'

'Crops?'

'I take an interest, Tony.'

'Well, it's very nice to know you take such a keen interest in my *crops*. I had no idea. I'll get you some gloves, so you can help me do some *harvesting* at the weekend.'

'Very funny.'

'You know I'm growing peas because you eat them,' he speared salad leaves and a chunk of frittata onto his fork. 'But you don't have a clue what variety they are or why I chose them.'

'My point is...'

'Knowing stuff isn't the same as taking an interest, Vi. I know water comes out of the tap when I turn it on, but I'm not interested in how it got there.'

'Yes, well maybe you should be.'

'Are you suggesting I take up plumbing?'

'I'm suggesting you should take more of an interest in stuff, that's all.'

'What stuff?'

'Like...I don't know...like theatre, or music. Just... new things.'

He took a long swig of wine, allowing the gear change to settle. As he placed the glass back on the table he looked at her, evenly.

'You know what, Tony?' She quickly edited most of

what threatened to come out of her mouth. 'I wanted to talk about this job. I was hoping we could have a discussion.'

'Of course we can have a discussion!'

She rolled her eyes and immediately hated herself for doing so. He seemed to be closing down, coming to a standstill just as she was getting her second wind. She was reminded of it every day, when he stroked her too gently with his garden-weathered hands, or when, on hearing a door slam after dark, he wondered out loud where on earth a neighbour might have been till this time of night.

They both pushed overloaded forkfuls of food into their mouths to excuse themselves from speaking; the mastication and swallows were perfectly audible.

'Sadie rang,' said Tony, eventually.

Neutral ground. A joint concern.

'Is she OK?'

'She was saying something about...Higgs Boson, I think.'

'Higgs Boson?'

'They're like contractions, but they're not.'

'Braxton Hicks.'

'That's the fella.'

'Well, Mark'll be home now. I might call her later, see how she is.'

'Mark's at a conference, apparently. A weekend thing.'

'Is there any of this left?' she asked, glancing down at her plate.

'Plenty.'

'I'll take it over to her.'

Violet packaged up the remaining frittata, various items of garden produce and a few indulgent toiletries she'd been saving to give to Sadie after the baby was born.

●●●

Sadie balanced the plate on her belly, and picked at the frittata.

'All I want is oranges. I'm obsessed by oranges.'

'They'll keep your bowels moving.'

'I'm gutted they're not actually on menus. I would tip really well for a good orange, especially a peeled one.'

'Your dad's not quite got to grips with growing citrus fruit yet.' She stroked Sadie's hair and adopted a breezy tone. 'So, what's this conference Mark's at?'

'Copenhagen. Neuromarketing. All about how people make buying decisions. Do you know that Coca...' She flinched and grabbed Violet's hand, placing it quickly on her belly. They looked at each other open-mouthed as they felt the baby kick and kick.

After a while, Violet broke the silence. 'Neuromarketing?'

Sadie waved a patronising hand at her mother. 'It's the current–'

'I know what it is. I'm just wondering what it's got to do with Mark.'

'He was banging on about it last time we were over

at yours, after Dad had a go at him about giving up the comedy. He was telling you how making people laugh can get them to buy things.' A beat. 'He was really trying hard to impress you both.'

'Oh, I never know if anything Mark's saying is a joke or not. I can't take him seriously.'

'You know that's really offensive?'

'It's a compliment. He's a comedian. Shall I peel you an orange?'

'No.'

Violet let her hand remain on her daughter's belly, as she braved questions that would've been more difficult without the gesture. *Is everything ready? Is Mark looking forward to it? Is he doing his bit? Could you ease off things? Put your feet up? Is there anything you need? Can we be doing any more for you? Could Dad help with the garden? Or with the electrics and all the other stuff? He could project-manage, give the workmen a kick up the backside.*

Sadie volleyed the offers back. She embroidered tales. The words came out of her mouth, fast and sure. She talked about her work for the National, the plays, the intricate costumes that were due to arrive any day, her plans to move more into design, do less mending and fixing. Perhaps she'd do a kids' line; she'd already spotted gaps in the market for organic fabrics that had high antibacterial qualities. She'd reserved some domain names and social media handles, just as placeholders for now.

As she spoke, Violet reached into the bag and pulled out a facial oil. She held it up to Sadie's nose. 'I'm just worried about you over-stretching yourself. This is a time when you should be taking care of yourself. And Mark should be here, not in Denmark.'

Sadie dabbed a drop of the oil onto the back of her hand, and rubbed it in gently, before bringing it back up to her nose and inhaling deeply. 'There's nothing to worry about. I'm ready for this, for all of it,' she said. And she stroked her mother's hand to reassure them both.

•••

It takes just an hour and forty-five minutes to fly from Edinburgh to Copenhagen. Mark and Ruby stayed at Hotel d'Angleterre, a stone's throw from Kunsthal Charlottenborg. They walked everywhere hand in hand, kissed openly on the streets, in cafés, in front of beautiful paintings. They ate ice cream on public benches, relaxed on sofas in the hotel lounge, strolled into the bar together dressed for dinner, ordered cocktails and, later, champagne and oysters. They talked at a volume audible to those on the next table and beyond. They reminisced — of course they did — and racked their brains to remember the name of the music teacher. Was it Mr Dixon? And who was the girl who started half way through the first year who never quite fitted in? Who threw the best party? Who wore the weirdest outfit at the school disco? Favourite school meal? Worst teacher?

At one point, he glimpsed Sadie in the reflection of a shop window, except it wasn't her, of course, but he thought about how much she'd have loved the outfit on the mannequin, and he momentarily considered how he might give Ruby the slip so he could zip in quickly to ask the shop assistant to wrap it, ship it.

The smell of the eucalyptus soap in the wet room and the thought of the dirt and the germs going down the drain helped him feel less bad, less shitty, less of a cheating bastard. He was mid-cleanse when he heard a sharp knock at the hotel room door. Ruby was on the bed picking out key words from a Danish newspaper. She opened the door to an outrageously beautiful young man standing next to a trolley.

'Erm…yes?'

'Your food.'

'Sorry?'

The man consulted a tiny notepad. 'Two club sandwiches, a bowl of potato wedges, a pot of Earl Grey and a pot of Darjeeling.' He pronounced it darsheeling.

'We haven't ordered any food.'

'Oh. Just the tea?'

'No, no, we haven't ordered anything.'

He looked at her, confused, and checked his notepad again. 'I have two club sandwiches, wedges and tea for Frey.'

'Free?'

'Frey. Mr and Mrs Frey.'

'No, we're Suddu…Darling! Darling.'

'Oh, OK. This is my mistake. Sorry to disturb you.'

'No, that's fine. That's OK.'

He backed away from her, grinning, before turning

the trolley around and trundling off. As she closed the door, Mark edged out of the bathroom, a towel around his waist.

'I can smell chips,' he said.

'Not for us. Wrong room.'

'Was it chips?'

'Wedges.' She plonked down onto the bed.

'Yeah, wedges, I can smell them. Should we order some food, d'you think?' He picked up the room service menu, stretched out beside her and started to read out the highlights.

'You used to eat a lot of meat,' said Ruby. 'At school. You and the rest of the team. Chicken, beef, everything. You shovelled it in like cavemen.'

He laughed. 'I still can't believe you noticed me, let alone took the slightest interest in what I ate!'

'Well, I was veggie back then. I was on a crusade to convert everyone. I even managed to get Mr Kendrick on side.'

'I bet you did!'

She laughed indulgently, secretly enjoying the reminder of her powers of persuasion back then.

'I used to watch you eat all that meat at lunchtime and part of me would be disgusted — "Oh, that Mark Darling! He's such a carnivorous beast".'

She laughed as she nuzzled up to him, trying to recapture the mood. 'You seemed so different from me. You know, all that meat-eating and running about the football pitch.'

'Yeah. And you surrounded yourself with grungy Nirvana fans and cardi boys with books under their arms!'

'Cardi boys?'

'Boys who wore their grandads' cardigans. And cords. And glasses.'

'I didn't surround myself with anyone!'

'No, well, they surrounded you, all the same.'

'And all the time I was looking at you.'

He let the menu go.

'And all the time you were looking at me.' He pulled her closer. 'And I was looking at you, Ruby Suddula. Like everyone else, I was looking at you.'

They kissed. She pulled his towel open. She remembered how she had felt all those years ago, when men had fallen at her feet — sometimes literally — and she shrugged and wiggled out of her clothes, slowly, sexily. She tossed her hair about, made little moaning sounds. They kept their eyes open most of the time, scanning each other, fascinated with the combination of familiarity and newness. Ruby gathered dozens of mental snapshots: the little black spot in the pale brown mole on his neck just below his right ear, his lopsided hairline and the golden downy hairs at his temple, his wide, flat feet and the toenail that had been ruined by years of kicking as hard as he could to score. There was no talk of IVF, or dry rot, no to-do list. The sheets felt new and pressed, the pillows plump and yielding. They didn't fall into a familiar post-coital entwinement, but Mark's body made a Sadie-shaped gap that Ruby nestled into. He fell asleep wondering if the builders doing the basement renovation could sort out the plasterwork in the utility room.

•••

At the dizzy stomach-churning height of an affair, at the point where one is led by hedonistic risk-taking, lovers leave tiny clues for friends and colleagues to pick up and puzzle over. Those who have strayed, who have broken their own vows, broken hearts, will know how to join up the pieces and see past the gaps. As they spot the signs, the cellular memory of the thrill will throb, causing them to google a name they haven't said out loud for months, years, maybe decades. They know all the tricks the lovers are learning because they, too, have returned from lunch flushed, a little breathless, then explained it away while they glowed and glowed. They, too, have crowbarred their lover's first name, street name or workplace into conversations, for the thrill of hearing it, of making it exist in the real world.

Kaiser Chiefs, Springsteen, The Stones, BB King, The Drifters, Tom Waits, Bjork, Donald Fagen, Carl Perkins and Foxboro Hot Tubs — Mark's humming playlist grew. He would hum around the office and, predictably, unforgivably, at home, the songs with Ruby in their titles. She was leaking out of him.

'You shouldn't have taken her,' Jonny leaned with one arm up against a tree trunk while he gripped his foot behind him, stretching out his quads.

Mark sipped from his water bottle as he looked across Inverleith Park, scanning Edinburgh's distinctive skyline, punctuated by cranes. He didn't respond.

'You've crossed a line.'

'Yep.'

'Was that the plan?'

'There was no plan.'

'You just fancied a cheeky weekend away with her?'

Mark sighed. It wasn't the sex, or the excitement; it was the way she looked at him, as though she could see what his insides were made of, like she could pick out his heart in a line-up.

'What message do you think you gave her when you took her *to a different country* for the weekend?'

'I didn't *take* her. *We went*. She had free will.'

'You're full of shit, Mark.'

'Cheers.'

They started running again. Once they reached the swans, Jonny peeled off to the right and Mark to the left.

Chapter 41

RUBY DIDN'T SEE ANYONE on Tuesday or Wednesday evenings. Instead, she would throw open her windows, and set to work on the portrait. She had photos of Mark now, of course, sorted into an album on her phone, backed up to the iCloud, but she preferred to rely on what she remembered, what she had touched. Each time she saw him naked, she would secretly home in on something — a spattering of freckles, a tiny scar — and commit it to memory. Sometimes, she would go straight to her paints after they'd been together, and dab at the canvas, honing the shape of the scar a bike handlebar had left on his knee, or a more or less faithful constellation of freckles on his shoulder. Other times, she would arrive home after an evening with him and extend it by sitting in front of the portrait, looking, saying the unsayable, imagining.

The smell of turpentine and oils was enough to conjure up a naked image — her naked image — of him and occasionally, when nobody was looking, she would nose up to the newer paintings at work, close her eyes and inhale deeply. The merest aromatic trace could do it.

She struggled to remember the exact shade of his old football shirt, and wondered if she had the skill to paint it crumpled into multiple folds at his feet. Cadmium seemed too blue-red and quinacridone too pink.

'Do you still have your old football shirt?'

'From school?'

They were on Calton Hill, at Café Milk. It was lunchtime; they had half an hour.

'Yeah. I thought you might – you know – keep it. You were captain, after all.'

'Blimey, I dunno. I doubt it.'

From a distance, they could have been colleagues. Each was wearing sober work attire, there was no touching. Only the most observant viewer could see the sparks flying across the table.

'Why would you want it, anyway?'

'Secret.' She held her sandwich out to him. 'Taste this.'

He looked around, swivelling his head left and right, like a comedy spy, and back at her.

'Break a piece off for me.'

'Just take a bite!' She pushed the sandwich further towards him.

'Someone might see us, Ruby. Break a piece off and pass it to me.'

She tore a corner off and handed it to him, huffily. He put the entire piece in his mouth.

'Yeah, lovely.'

Ruby looked into the middle distance. She scanned around.

'They say this is the highest café in Edinburgh, although some say Harvey Nics is. I think this is the highest outdoor café, perhaps.'

'Balcony. Harvey Nics has a balcony. That would count as outdoor.'

He glanced at his watch.

'It's nearly quarter-to. I'd better be heading back.'

They both stood up to leave.

'Come for dinner on Friday. To mine.'

'I don't think I can get away.'

'Saturday, then.'

He looked around at all the people who seemed to have less complicated lives. 'Tricky. Leave it with me. I'll see what I can do.'

'It's dinner, Mark. Not a week in Paris.'

'Listen, there's a guy over there I think I recognise, so I'm just going to shake your hand, but I don't want you to get upset about it, OK?'

'Shake my hand?'

He nodded.

She sighed.

'That's ridiculous. Even colleagues hug.'

'Not at Re:Klein, they don't. The arts world is very different from that of soft furnishings, Ms Suddula.

There's nae hugging in my world. And that's a bonus when you look at the people who work in it.'

He shook her hand and put a couple of pound coins on the table. They walked away, their shoulders just millimetres apart, looking exactly like two people who'd just had an illicit assignation on a beautiful Scottish hill.

Chapter 42

LATER THAT EVENING, Mark arrived home to find scary masks scattered around the place.

'Everything OK?'

'Oh, it's just part of the consignment from London,' said Sadie.

She was unravelling richly coloured satin bolts. A roll of padding was at her feet. Mark held one of the masks in front of his face.

'It doesn't end well for him,' she said.

He whisked it off.

'Can you just wash your hands before you touch this stuff?'

Mark looked at his hands.

'It's the oils. In your skin. Some of these fabrics are…'

'Loud.'

She laughed.

'Yeah, they are a bit!'

'Why's it here?'

'I've decided to do more from home until the baby comes.'

'Right,' he said distractedly.

He couldn't smell anything cooking.

'Shall I order a takeaway?'

'God, no! Not until this lot's upstairs!'

'We'll eat in the kitchen.'

'The smell, Mark! I can't send costumes back reeking of pizza!'

He spent the next hour hauling the consignment upstairs. Sadie made a chicken salad, and Mark resigned himself to eating low-odour food for the foreseeable future. Later, he half-listened to Sadie running through the cast list and plot of two operas.

After she went to bed, he scrolled through the TV channels, pausing on an old episode of *First Dates*.

'Where's this from?' Sadie was standing in the doorway, holding a two-tone Engesvik-designed toothbrush that wasn't his.

His jaw dropped open, as though he was about to use it. It was Ruby's. She'd bought it in Copenhagen. He tried to control his breathing.

'Cos I'm thinking it'd be good for around the taps in the utility room.' She splayed the bristles with her thumb. 'It's just the right size for getting behind them.'

She threw it to him, but not as hard as she might

have done had she known whose mouth it had been in.

He bounced up. 'I'll do it now.' And off he went, to clean the ingrained gunk from behind the utility room taps with his mistress's toothbrush.

chapter 43

'You.'

'No. Really, what would you like? I want to get you something special.'

'OK. Stay at mine for an extra night. Two nights instead of one. That way, we can wake up together on my birthday, too.'

Mark was suddenly aware of a familiar feeling: the unmistakable realisation that he was about to fall short, about to disappoint.

'I can't.'

There it was. That face. He'd let her down, just as he'd let everyone else down. After all she'd done. After she'd listened. Seen and heard him. Held him. Championed him.

'I saw a necklace in Annie Smith's the other day. It

was silver — I know you like silver — hand-made, and it had a heart, and —'

She looked down at her shoes. 'Just do me a drawing or something.'

'A what?'

'One of your funny drawings. I liked them.'

The lost memory popped into his mind so clearly that he expected it to be accompanied by a sound. How had he forgotten the drawings? The cartoons? He and Fergus had spent ages drawing stick figures in various situations, passing them around class. Some preceded a detention, of course, but one clever teacher had rolled with it and allowed them to submit their physics homework in the form of a cartoon strip. She'd framed it, put it up on the science lab wall. How had he forgotten all that?

'Right. Yeah. Course.'

Chapter 44

Sadie didn't need a ruler to draw straight lines. Using a white marker, she made a line the length of the large kitchen chalkboard, twisted her hand ninety degrees, and made a vertical line to the top of her reach. Retracing her steps, she made a perfect oblong. Once she had her outline, she worked quickly to make a grid. She entered 'week commencing' dates along the top row, and populated the left-hand column with various tasks and key words. Although much had been done in advance of the baby's imminent arrival, there were still incomplete jobs and new ideas she wanted to action.

'A steam clean of the oven?'

Sadie uh-huh-ed in response to Mark's question. He was standing somewhat slack-jawed, scanning left to right and back again, his head moving from side to side as though he was watching a Wimbledon rally.

'What does that have to do with the baby?'

'Nothing,' she said, polishing the taps vigorously.

'Why have we got steam-cleaning the oven on the list, but not repairing the hole in the roof?'

'I've got someone onto the roof. By the way, the water will be off all day next Tuesday.'

Mark sighed. 'And haven't we had the radiators bled recently? Didn't your dad do it?'

Sadie rubbed hard at a stubborn stain. 'Yup. Needs doing again, just in case. Apparently, we're in for a harsh winter.'

'What do the asterisks mean?'

'There's a key at the bottom. The green asterisks are for tradespeople: builders, plumbers, sparks. Everything with a red exclamation mark is yours. I'm the yellow circle.'

There seemed to be a disproportionate amount of red exclamation marks. He picked up a pen.

'Don't use the markers! Use the chalks,' she said, without turning around. 'And don't draw anything stupid.'

He put down the pen before turning his attention to the fruit bowl. He took out a banana.

'Tea will be half an hour,' said Sadie. 'Sea bass.'

'What does "clothes" mean?' he asked, pointing the banana at one of the rows.

Sadie nodded towards a notebook on the kitchen table. 'There's an index at the front of that. I think the clothes list is on page 6. It's divided into three sections:

you, me and the baby. So, you need a completely new wardrobe of socks — I've thrown a lot away just lately — and new work shirts — I've given a lot of your old ones to the charity shop. I need new underwear — bigger. And—'

'All this stuff for the baby?' He looked up from the notebook. 'We already have loads.'

'Yes, I know. They're the things we don't have.'

'Do babies *need* shoes?'

'Why don't you go up for a shower, or help me prep some veg?'

He'd hoped that, now she was finally pregnant, now the gruelling rounds of IVF were a distant memory, she might relax a little. In some ways, she had. There was no need for the strict fertility-boosting dietary regime, although she had retained the ability to accurately keep track of his fruit and vegetable intake as well as her own. He sensed that, just lately, she ran out of steam long before she stopped. And, often, she fell asleep quickly. When she finally, literally, put her feet up, he knew it wouldn't be long before her head lolled back. Within moments, the minute twitching of her fingers and toes would stop, and her breathing would be punctuated with occasional snorts. Now and then, a shiny slow stream of saliva would edge down towards her jawline. She'd once accused him of loving her most when she was asleep, and he'd corrected her: his love was constant, but his affection was more fickle, and, yes, he had to admit, the unguarded, snoring, dribbling Sadie was utterly glorious.

He closed the notebook, put it back on the table,

kissed her head, pulled his jumper off and dropped it on a chair before disappearing to forget the lists under a hot stream of water. As he left the room, he hummed, absently, dangerously.

Chapter 45

OVER THE YEARS, RUBY HAD experienced terrible trouble with men's hands. It was only when she tried to paint Mark's that she realised it wasn't men's hands per se, but unfamiliar hands that had caused her the most trouble. She knew Mark's almost as well as her own. She had watched his deft thumbs as he sent quick texts before selecting the little crescent moon icon on his phone. She'd seen his fingers glide slowly over her skin, and had felt tiny scratches when he'd clipped but not filed his fingernails. She knew the position, shape and orientation of each scar and was happy to humour his extravagant tales of how each had been made: the wild dog he fought off with a stick, the dirty tackle unnoticed by the ref, the near-death plunge in a canoe.

She spent hours with her face barely a nose away

from the canvas, painstakingly rendering irregular freckles and sunspots, creating sparse knuckle hairs with swipes of her knife. One evening, she spent almost two hours painting and perfecting a protruding vein on the back of his left hand, playing around with chroma orange before giving up and opening the indigo. She knew the colour and texture of every millimetre of him, apart from the band of flesh beneath his wedding ring.

'Are you bringing anyone to the Christmas party, Ruby?' It was the time of year for Pari, the gallery's social media executive, to do the rounds with her clipboard.

Ruby dreaded the event, with its enforced jollity, tooth-rotting fizz, the damned-if-you-do/damned-if-you-don't paper hats. She hated the banquet-style seating, being trapped between the likes of Sal from Accounts on one side and Felix from Marketing on the other. She hated mistletoe — the universal harbinger of bad breath and cold sores. She hated turkey and cranberry and mince pies and hated herself for eating them every year, just to be sociable, just to feel the same awful bloating as everyone else. But most of all, she hated going to it alone — the unarticulated wisecracks to a kindred spirit, the unsmirked smirks. She ached to make a secret sign for 'let's get out of here' and, moments later, to do a runner, hand in hand with someone else.

'It's August.'

'All the best places have been booked for months,'

said Pari.

'Surely that's a good reason not to bother,' said Ruby. She knew, of course, that Pari would push until she gave in.

'Shall I put you down for one or two places?' Pari clicked her pen ready for action.

'Two,' said Ruby.

'And is he or she a vegetarian?'

'He,' said Ruby, 'he is a carnivore. Mark.'

'Ruby and Mark the carnivore,' said Pari, as she jotted down the booking.

Ruby imagined walking into the Christmas party with him. She visualised giving the secret sign once the pudding dishes had been cleared — a wink, perhaps, or a code word — and taking his hand to leave the party, laughing as they hit the fresh night air.

•••

'I don't think it's a good idea to–'

'Why not? Are you saying that, come Christmas, we'll still be sneaking around?'

'No,' he glanced around, to make sure there was nobody he recognised — they were on a bench overlooking Wardie beach – 'of course not.'

She waited for him to continue.

'I thought we'd perhaps go away for a few days.'

She imagined Christmas together in a ski lodge.

'Manchester has one of the best Christmas markets in Europe,' he said, twisting her hair up into Princess

Leia headphones.

'Manchester?'

'With your hair like this, you've got a look of—'

'A holiday? In Manchester?'

'Well, more of a break than a holiday. I was speaking to a comic who had a great gig at The Frog and Bucket. We could make it into a mini tour! There's a Comedy Store just off Deansgate. I've always wanted to say I've gigged at The Comedy Store.'

'I thought it was in London.'

'I could try to get into the London one next year.'

Chapter 46

'EVERYBODY'S GOING ON about Mum's new job,' said Ava. 'Someone even asked me was I proud of her today!'

'You should be proud of her,' said Tony. 'We're all proud of her. Deputy head's a big deal.'

'How can I be proud of her? It's got nothing to do with me. It's her achievement. It's not my place to be proud.'

'You know what they mean!'

Ava swiped at her phone, frowning. 'People should say what they mean.'

'Well, sometimes it's easier to just go along with things, you know...'

Ava jumped up. 'I need to go out.'

'It's twenty to nine.'

'I know what time it is.'

'Where are you going at twenty to nine?'

'It'll be ten-to by the time I'm ready to go.'

'Where will you be going at ten to nine?'

'When I'm sixteen, will I still have to tell you where I'm going? When does this stop?'

'Where are you going?'

'...because I can't take further years of this interrogation.'

She walked out of the living room before breaking into a run up the stairs.

'Ava!' Tony walked to the foot of the stairs and shouted. 'Ava, you are not leaving this house unless you tell me where you're going.'

'Out.'

'Not if you're grounded.'

Ava reappeared at the top of the stairs. 'You can't just ground me like that! You can't.'

'I want to know where you're going.'

'Nowhere, if I'm grounded.'

'And if you're not?'

'The Filmhouse.'

'To see what?'

'A film.'

'You're grounded,' he said, walking off.

Ava dashed down the stairs, taking them two at a time. 'Dad! Dad!' She caught up with him. 'Why am I grounded?'

'You're being deliberately elusive.'

'I'm right in front of you. I think you mean evasive.'

Tony took a deep breath. 'What film are you going to see? Who are you going with? How are you getting back? It'll be dark.'

'*The Absence*. Michael. Bus. I can't control the movement of the sun.'

'*The Absence?*'

She nodded.

'What's it about?'

She looked him dead in the eye. Tony sighed. 'OK, well, as it's the weekend, and now I'm fully conscious of the facts…'

'I think you mean "cognisant".'

'Quit while you're ahead.'

Michael's face broke into an involuntary grin when he spotted her standing on the bus, waiting to get off.

'Are we going to be late?' she asked, as she approached him.

'The film won't start for another fifteen minutes.'

'I need to be in there before the lights go down. Will the lights have gone down yet?'

'I don't know. Come on!' They ran across the road and into the Filmhouse foyer. All three members of staff behind the counter looked up as they dashed in.

'Erm, *The Absence*… Two tickets, please. Students. Two student tickets,' said Michael.

'Smooth,' said Ava, smiling.

The cashier handed over the tickets. 'Cinema Two.'

The lights dimmed just moments after they took their seats.

Moments later, Mark and Ruby bustled in in the darkness, and took their seats just six rows behind them.

'It was a film about nothing, really,' said Michael. He was walking Ava home. He was holding her hand. 'That's a hard thing to do, when you think about it. Make a whole film about nothing, set in an exciting city like New York.'

'It wasn't really about nothing. Absence is not nothing. Absence is a thing.'

'Hmm.'

'The clue's in the title: *The Absence*. Not just Absence. *The* Absence. The. Pronoun.'

'You're the cleverest person I know,' said Michael.

'Thanks.'

He dropped her hand and slipped his arm around her waist. It was more awkward to walk that way but neither minded.

'I'd love to go to New York,' said Ava. 'It always looks so cool in films.'

'I've been!'

'Oh, wow. What was it like?'

'Weird. It was something to do with Dad's work — like checking out how the city catered for kids or something. Anyway, we went to some musical with a load of other families, but I got really scared a few minutes in — it was all so loud — so we had to leave. And then I vomited when we got outside. It was quite windy so it went all over us all.'

'Gross.'

'We just trawled around galleries and museums after that.'

'That sounds OK.'

Michael shook his head. 'We'd be all cultural and shit in the daytimes, and then we'd have to spend the evenings with all these other families in the hotel. My mum hated the other kids. She was so blatant. We ate in this big dining room and she'd just give them these filthy looks if they made a noise or anything.'

'Wow.'

'And my dad would go — he'd be like: "Suze, darling, your expectations are far outweighing the reality." It's one of my dad's sayings. He's always saying it.'

She laughed and looked across at him as he did an impression of his parents.

'"Your expectations are faaaar outweighing the reality, Susannah." "Oh, fuck off, Simon. The problem is you are under-delivering. That's the issue here."'

'They sound hilarious. I think my parents are too tired to fight.'

'We should really go to New York, just the two of us,' said Michael. He stopped walking, but Ava continued, causing him to lose his balance.

'Oh, sorry!'

'Would you like to go to New York, Ava?' he said, in a serious tone more fitting to a marriage proposal.

'Yeah! Definitely! Let's go! Just book it and go!'

They laughed.

Michael put his free hand on her shoulder. 'Your teeth are so nice since you got your brace removed.'

'Thanks. It hurt like shit, that brace. Agony. Proper agony.'

'You always smell good, too. Like really nice shampoo or something.'

'Thanks. We change shampoos all the time, so it won't be the same one you've been smelling. And it's probably the conditioner you can smell; I can't imagine there'd be much residual scent of the shampoo after conditioning. I stopped using shampoo a while ago, but now we buy paraben-free stuff, so I've started using it again.'

He stood there, scanning every detail of her face, smiling unguardedly at her.

'I think we should, like, kiss now, because I should be getting in,' she said.

Ten minutes later, she nuzzled into his neck, and inhaled. He smelt of something unique and otherly. Space dust. Rocket fuel.

chapter 47

RUBY OPENED THE DOOR to Mark with a grand sweeping gesture. She wasn't exactly drunk, but she'd made a valiant start. Her face was slightly flushed, her hair was tousled, and her underarms prickled with urgent beads of perspiration. The deluxe edition of *Back to Black* blared out from a powerful speaker. She had done a lot of thinking that afternoon, egged on by Ms Winehouse, and probably more cooking than any one person should attempt in a domestic setting. Over the course of several hours, she had followed recipes to the letter, sought help from YouTube when things had gone awry, and had ultimately prepared a gastronomic feast, after which she slipped into a dress that she only half-buttoned up. Somehow, she felt taller, more statuesque than her usual self.

'Hey! Happy birthday.' He thrust a gift bag at her.

She kissed him, knocking him backwards slightly and causing him to hold onto the door frame for balance. As he shrugged off his jacket, she dashed off to the kitchen, placing the gift bag on the coffee table en route, and quickly reappeared with a heavy ceramic mixing bowl of ice in which a bottle of Chablis listed awkwardly. She deposited the bowl into. his arms and scooted off again, returning holding two slightly bloomed wine glasses upside down between the fingers of her left hand and a basic corkscrew somewhat menacingly in her right. 'You can pour, while I just plate up the starters.' She leaned across the bowl to kiss him again.

'Scallops,' she said, as she pulled away.

'Ooh! Yum.' He widened his eyes and stretched out the word so it ended on a closed-mouth smile.

'Two minutes.'

'Two minutes.'

She shimmied back to the kitchen. When she heard the cork popping out of the bottle, she let out a whoop.

He spilled a little of the wine as he poured, and fought the urge to rush for a cloth. He didn't need to do that here. A spill was just a spill.

'This. Is gorgeous.' Mark was halfway through his scallops. Ruby had run her wrists under the cold tap and was now sitting opposite him at the tiny table, looking less pink and almost composed.

'What's the sauce?'

'Secret recipe.'

'Secret, huh? Very nice. Verrry nice.'

Her stomach did a little forward roll. She wanted to seem on top of things tonight. He was more relaxed. Sprawling, almost. At one point, he put down his knife, switched his fork to his right hand and started scooping food up from his plate. He'd never done that in a restaurant and, she suspected, he'd never dare at home.

'My grandma used to eat a lot of sherbet fruits. Do you know what they are?' It was a non sequitur kind of evening.

Mark had a mouthful of scallop, so he nodded.

'You know, little coloured sweets of all flavours with sherbet inside. So the red ones were, I don't know, strawberry or raspberry flavour, and the yellow ones were lemon, and the green ones...'

'Lime.'

'Lime. Exactly.' She touched the tip of her nose with her left forefinger and pointed at him with her right; she was categorically squiffy. 'Anyway, she used to have two jars — one full of sherbet limes and another with all the other flavours.'

Mark smiled.

'And I noticed that the jar of coloured sweets — all the different flavours — would go down more quickly than the jar of sherbet limes. She hardly touched the sherbet limes, and I wondered what this was about, so I asked her.'

'What's with the sherbet limes, Grandma!' he laughed.

'Yes! That's what I said, or something like that. I said: "Grandma, why do you keep the jar of sherbet limes separate?" And do you know what she said?'

Mark shook his head. He'd finished his starter, and he put down his cutlery gently.

'She said: "Sweetheart" — she always called me sweetheart — "Sweetheart, I don't like sherbet limes but when there's nothing else, I don't mind the odd one or two".'

Mark looked at her with an expectant smile.

'And I've thought about how that's a lot like life — we sometimes pick at the chocolate limes...'

'Sherbet limes.'

'Sherbet limes, yes. We sometimes pick at the sherbet limes when there's nothing else available.' She stretched out her arms, as though she had just delivered an illuminating manifesto. It was her turn to look at him with an expectant smile now.

'That,' he glanced down at his empty plate, 'was delicious.'

Ruby shook her head and held her palms out in a suspended shrug.

'What?' said Mark.

'The sherbet limes?'

'What?'

'Well, that's you.'

'That's me? The sherbet limes? I'm the sherbet limes?'

'You,' she twirled a finger at him, 'are eating sherbet limes when there's a jar of all the other colours here. I am the jar of all the nice flavours.'

He smiled. 'I don't like sherbet. It makes me burp.'

'Don't be obtuse. You know what I'm saying. I am the raspberry and the strawberry and the...the lemon.'

'Shall I help you with the lamb?'

'No.' She scraped her chair away from the table and gathered up the plates and cutlery. 'You can sit here and think of a confectionery-related metaphor for our relationship by the time I get back.'

'Very tender.' He was talking about the slow-roasted lamb.

'Isn't it?'

'Turns out you're a culinary genius!' He kissed his fingertips like a gastronome. 'On top of everything else.'

'I *am* a culinary genius. Dead right. I am.'

'And our love is like a Curly Wurly: sweet and never-ending.'

'Ah, I like it.' She smiled. 'Very good. Like a Curly Wurly.'

'Or...or, like a bag of Revels with all the orange ones taken out.'

She laughed.

'Or,' he was on a roll. 'like a selection box, but only if the Milky Way has been replaced with...'

'Flake!'

He shook his head. 'Nope. A Mars bar.'

'Hmm, not so much the Mars bar.'

'Ruby, the Mars bar is the greatest chocolate bar known to humankind.'

'Nah.' She wasn't convinced.

'You have the thick chocolate…'

'Too thick.'

'…the malted base…'

'Ugh. Claggy.'

'…and the soft layer of caramel.'

'I'll give you the caramel. The caramel is good.'

He forked another chunk of lamb into his mouth. 'Oh. This is so tender.'

By the time they were onto pudding — a mascarpone and passion-fruit trifle — they were well into a second bottle of wine, elevating half-baked ideas to the status of strategic planning.

'I know you don't want to hurt Sadie, and I hate to think of her hurt, but you're living a half life.'

Mark spooned in more trifle. His facial muscles tightened. He took a swig of wine. And another.

'It's not doing you any good, all this sneaking around.' She stood up and scooshed onto his knee. She raked through his hair, and noticed he hadn't eaten much of the trifle. 'You don't like the trifle?'

He poked at the pudding with his spoon. 'What are these bits?'

'Passion fruit.'

'Hmm.'

'It took me ages to find a recipe for this trifle. I ordered it once, at The Witchery. Oh, it was divine!' She threw her head back, shaking her hair so it swung against her back and over her shoulders. He caught a tendril, twirled it.

'Not keen.'

'Not keen on The Witchery? It's gorgeous!' she said, in mock protest.

'No, the passion fruit! Yeah, The Witchery is gorgeous. We...'

That tiny, two-letter word, stuffed with ambiguity, almost meaningless without context and tense, hung in the air. A moment.

'I once went, a couple of years ago. Stayed over.' He let the tendril drop.

The singular pronoun seemed odd now. 'On your own?'

'No.'

A long moment.

'We should go,' he said, taking her hands in his. 'They have rooms. You wouldn't believe the rooms...'

'Mark,' she took a breath. 'Mark, I don't want to revisit the places you went to with Sadie. They were your places. I want us to have our places. Salisbury Crags. Copenhagen. That's how we make the moments.'

He looked faintly puzzled.

'I read somewhere that, when we look back, all we really remember are little flashes of life — moments. Just like you remember your first time in the rooms at The Witchery. Only that memory belongs to you and Sadie. We'll have our own.'

'It wasn't Sadie.' He paused. 'It was before Sadie. It was someone else.'

It hadn't occurred to her that there had been others. It was obvious — of course it was — but, somehow, it hadn't occurred to her to consider them.

'Passion fruit is full of zinc,' she said. 'Good for your

sex life.'

It served no purpose to be aggrieved over what had gone past. He would slip, occasionally, and she would deal with such slips as gracefully as she could. She never doubted for a moment that, one day, soon, when Mark said 'we', she would be included. We're spending Christmas at home this year. We don't like blockbuster films; we prefer arthouse. We plan to go to Biarritz this summer.

She was glad of the distracting gift bag, and the atmosphere brightened as she opened her presents. The stick-figure drawing, captioned with an Oasis lyric, was professionally mounted and framed. And the Annie Smith box contained a hand-made heart necklace.

Later, they loaded the dishwasher together and he wiped down the surfaces, like children playing house. She made stovetop coffee that they sipped but didn't finish; instead, there were clothes to be removed, slowly, slowly. They strewed them about the flat, marking the places where they paused: the sofa, the rug, at the bedroom door.

Chapter 48

MARK COULDN'T GO straight home. His skin didn't seem to fit the way it had on Friday; it felt tighter, hypersensitive to the slightest touch.

He jumped the number 23 bus to the Botanics and walked through the gardens. It was a route he occasionally took home from the office, if he knew Sadie was out and there was nothing to be back for. He sat on the only empty bench he could find, close to the exit, and started to formulate his alibi. He googled Newcastle stag nights on his phone, and a wealth of material was suddenly in his palm — club names, photos of various landmarks, videos of actual stag nights in Newcastle — it was all there. He memorised a few key facts and took a couple of screenshots. A couple walked past, the mother carrying a tiny baby in a papoose. He wondered how the baby shower had gone, if he should have called. No. Sadie would have loved being the centre of attention all weekend; he had no doubts she'd have had a great time without him.

His mind flashed back to Ruby taking a towel from around his waist and slowly unbuttoning, unhooking and sliding out of her clothes. He closed his eyes, took a moment, and positioned his bag over his crotch. He pictured her as she had fallen asleep in breaking daylight, how the pale golden hairs on her face had given her an ethereal, angelic quality.

He approached the street twice; turning into it was tricky. He had his story, all the key facts, back-up photos of strangers and landmarks, he had creased his clothes to a believable degree, now all he had to do was walk and talk normally. He tested his opening line: 'Hello. Hullo. Allo. Hi. Hiya.' He tried to seem normal, tried to imagine how he might be had he been returning from a stag weekend in Newcastle; he shook his limbs about, trying to relax into a normal gait.

'A'right, mate!' Archie, Nancy's husband, shouted from his open car window. He came to a halt outside Mark and Sadie's front door and stepped out of the car. Mark scanned him up and down — here was a man without a care in the world. Bed head, slightly crumpled weekend clothes, and no doubt the whiff of a mown lawn if he got close enough.

'I've just come to get Nancy. How was Newcastle?' he winked.

Mark hated the wink, even though it was more than well-deserved.

'Oh, it was a riot, mate. Full of stags and hens!' He pulled an exaggerated disapproving face.

'Ooh, hens, hey? Cluck, cluck!'

'Nah, nah, none of that. We were too busy drinking!' He did the hangover headshake and put his hand on his stomach for extra effect. 'And last night's curry is still, you know...ooof!'

Archie laughed and patted him on the shoulder. Nancy and Sadie appeared at the door. They looked clean and bright. Sadie appeared positively scrubbed.

'Oh, dear me!' said Sadie, as she looked at Mark.

'He's suffering!' shouted Archie, slapping him on the back. They all laughed. 'He's had a little drink and a bit of food that didn't agree with him. He needs a couple of paracetamol and a pint of orange juice, Sade! And probably a shower!' More laughter.

Mark walked towards the door, grateful for the company, however irritating. Archie stayed put, smirking.

'Come on then,' said Mark, 'who's putting the kettle on?'

'We're going home!' said Nancy, stepping off the doorstep.

'You can't go home. I've only just got here. And Archie's driven across town in tourist traffic — the least you can give him is a cup of tea!'

So, Archie was rewarded with tea and leftover macarons, and Mark was saved the high-pressure arrival of walking into a quiet house to face his wife alone. He entertained them with funny little tales he'd remembered from previous nights out, updating them by dropping in stag-related references. At one point, he stood up, folded his arms across his chest, and did an impression of a Geordie bouncer: 'Are yers all sober, lads? Nah drugs an all? Are yers gonna behave yerselfs?'

When he and Sadie slid into bed later that night, he rolled towards her and half-convinced himself that his erection was for her — or a general one, at least — and that it was, therefore, OK to slide under her, to lift her onto him, to have sex with her quietly and suspiciously quickly. The only time he felt the stone of guilt was when he took his wife's hands and laid them over his eyes, to block out what he could see in the half light. Afterwards, as they lay there, he considered the prospect of reinvention.

'I may grow a beard.'

'What?'

'A beard. I quite fancy one.'

'Really?'

'Yeah. You know, a neat one. Trimmed.'

Sadie narrowed her eyes and surveyed him. 'You've never mentioned growing a beard before. What's brought this on?'

'I just fancy a change.'

'Huh.'

He scratched his chin with both hands, feeling the start of metamorphosis. He wondered if he'd gone too far already; if she suspected.

'I hear they are very ticklish.'

She giggled and rubbed his face. He was in the clear.

'Yep,' he said, 'very ticklish. I think you'd like it. You never know what you might like until you try it.'

She laughed, and wrapped herself around him as much as her pregnant belly would allow, and he demonstrated how a beard might, indeed, tickle.

Chapter 49

'WHO'S BEEN A NAUGHTY BOY then?' said Don West as he undid his fly and aimed his penis at the urinal.

Mark finished peeing and gave Don a contemptuous look. He'd been expecting him to kick off about his latest piece of marketing material, which had put the most visually appealing sofa front-and-centre of a campaign, rather than the range which had the biggest bonus structure attached to it. Nobody was going to be attracted by the Provence range.

'My job's to get them in, Don. Yours is to sell them.' He zipped up his fly.

Don grinned hard, revealing two loose crowns. 'Is that right?'

'Yeah. That *is* right,' Mark said, as he washed his hands.

'Thing is, my figures are looking very dodgy for this month, Mark,' he glanced down and shook his penis. 'And that concerns me.'

Mark jerked at the looped towel, trying to get the mechanism to release an unused section. Don zipped up, wiped his hands on his trousers, and walked towards the door to block Mark's exit. Mark tried to dodge past him. 'If you don't mind, Don, I've got a few things on this afternoon.'

Don placed the splayed fingertips of his right hand on Mark's chest. 'You know what, Mark?'

Mark looked down at Don's hand.

'I would like a little favour from you.' He started to jab at Mark's chest with all five fingers every few words, pushing him backwards slightly each time: 'I would like YOU to help my LADS down in the showroom SELL some fucking SOFAS, so that we can ALL KEEP our JOBS.' He took his hand away from Mark's chest. 'Now, what can you do for me?' he said, putting both palms out, ready to receive whatever Mark was about to give him.

'First of all, Don, the campaign has launched. It's out there. And, second, don't you ever...'

Don put his nicotine-stained forefinger on Mark's lips and moved in even closer, so their noses were almost touching. He spoke slowly, quietly: 'You listen to me, lover boy. You put something out, and you put it out this afternoon, or you will leave me with no option but to blow your tiny fucking world apart. Got me?' He made a quiet pow sound as he hand-mimed a bomb going off.

Mark stared at him.

Don pulled out his phone, thumbprinted into it, and brought up a photo. He held it up for Mark to see.

'A very nice bit of skirt you have there, Marky-boy.'

The photo had been taken earlier that day in a lane that was evidently not as deserted as he and Ruby had believed. It was as incriminating and unambiguous a shot as he could imagine, considering both parties were fully clothed.

Mark grabbed for the phone but Don had anticipated it and snatched it away as soon as he raised his arm.

'Now, then! Let's stay nice and calm.' Those loose crowns again. He put the phone in his inside jacket pocket and reached for Mark's tie knot, tightening it slightly. 'I just need your help — what do you call it? — your *expertise* — in moving some of those bastard-ugly sofas. You can start with a fifteen per cent discount from the marketing budget...'

'I can't give...'

'Please. Mark. Didn't your mummy ever tell you it's rude to interrupt? A fifteen per cent discount from the marketing budget, and a £50 cashback voucher also from — can you guess?'

'Don...'

'Can you guess?'

Mark dropped his head. 'Marketing.'

'Clever boy. A £50 cashback voucher from the marketing budget on the...'

'Don...'

'On the..?'

'The Provence.'

'Bingo! On the bastard-ugly, uncomfortable-as-fuck Provence. Bang on!' said Don, and he smacked Mark hard on both cheeks before walking away.

Mark didn't have the authority to issue discounts, much less vouchers, but he did it all the same. He sent the copy to the designers, ignoring Nisha's offer to proofread it, before he headed for the boardroom to call Ruby.

'Someone took a photo of us.'

'What?'

'Someone — Don at work — saw us and took a photo. At lunchtime.'

Ruby was silent.

'Are you still there?'

'Yes.'

'He threatened me.'

'He threatened you? How?'

'He said…he wanted a discount and a £50 voucher…'

'He wanted what?'

'I'm not supposed to…'

'A voucher for what?'

'Never mind that! He said that if I didn't…' He pinched the bridge of his nose and closed his eyes.

'Are you still there?'

'He's blackmailing me. He has a photo of us from lunchtime today. It's… well, you were there. He saw us. And he took a photo, the bastard.'

'You could go to the police. Blackmail is…'

'I'm not going to the police, am I?' He sighed and then groaned. 'What a fucking mess. What an absolute fucking mess.'

'Perhaps this is the right time, Mark. Perhaps this is the right time to tell Sadie.'

Silence.

'Because it would be horrible if she heard from someone else, wouldn't it? You wouldn't want her to have some lunatic from work telling her, would you?'

Silence.

'It's better coming from you. And it gives her time to plan what she's going to do before the baby's born. Once the baby's here, it'll be…'

'What, you want me to go home and say: "Oh, sorry, Sade, I know you're almost ready to give birth and all that, and I know we have to be careful with your blood pressure, but I just thought I'd let you know, before Don West does, that I'm having an affair." Really, is that what I'm supposed to do?'

'I didn't know she had high blood pressure.'

'What?'

'You never said.'

'It's not something that would come up in the course of our conversations, Ruby, is it?'

'And you call her Sade?'

'What?'

'Is that what you call her, to her face? Sade? You call her Sadie to me.'

'Ruby.'

'I've got to go now. I'm late for a meeting.'

She hung up.

Chapter 50

DEAN'S VISIT TO THE UK included 'a three-day window of opportunity' — that's how he spoke these days — during which he was free to do whatever he pleased. He would drop off his kids with their grandparents then catch up with old friends, including Mark. He'd scheduled 'a twenty-four hour pit-stop' in Edinburgh, which would include an overnight stay at Mark and Sadie's place.

Mark met him off the train at Waverley. They immediately locked into a bear hug, slapping each other hard on the back.

'Great to see you, man. Great to see you!' said Dean, with a faint Californian twang.

They made their way onto Princes Street, exchanging

small talk as they walked. At one point, Dean laughed hard at something and Mark was astounded to see a mouth full of pure white teeth — not a filling in sight.

'My God, you've had the back ones done, too?' said Mark, who had stopped walking for a moment and turned to face Dean full-on. People stopped to look.

'You have to, mate. No choice. Can't sell real estate with British teeth.'

'I thought you'd just had the...' he spanned his thumb and finger across his own six front uppers. 'So, are they false or what?'

'They're all attached.'

Mark peered at them again.

Dean grinned. 'You like 'em?'

'They're a bit...'

'White?'

'Yeah. And big. I hadn't really noticed on FaceTime.'

Mark ran his tongue over his own teeth. They felt strangely inadequate. Perhaps he'd pick up a tube of Blanx at the weekend.

'So,' Dean resumed walking at full pace. 'How's Sadie?'

'Big. Even bigger than your enormous teeth.'

'Yeah. Thought so. Getting close, huh? Another month to go, is it?'

'Three weeks.'

'And Ruby?'

Mark grimaced and looked straight ahead. 'Let's jump the bus down to our place. You can drop your stuff off, then we'll head for the hills.'

Dean looked right at him.

'She's great. But, you know…'

Dean nodded, and they headed for the bus stop.

The two men sat on a flat rock at the top of Arthur's Seat, eating sandwiches.

'And Sadie has no clue?'

He took a bite of his sandwich and chewed on a mouthful of wholegrain bread, coleslaw and Crombie's roast beef. 'I can understand how men commit bigamy. Really, I can.'

'Don't even think about it.'

Mark laughed. 'No, seriously. That feeling of wanting to be married to two different people… If I could clone myself, I think both versions of me would be happy. Sadie makes me happy, Ruby makes me happy. I make them happy, but only because Ruby thinks I'm leaving Sadie and Sadie doesn't know about Ruby.

'Thinks?'

'What?'

'You said "Ruby thinks I'm leaving Sadie".'

'Did I?' Mark took a sip of apple juice.

'You know what you are, man?'

Mark sighed.

'You're lucky, but you're not brave. And you need to be both to survive an affair. You need to be lucky enough not to get caught, but also brave enough to stand in front of one of them, at some point, and say…' Dean made a cutting motion at his neck, 'Finito.'

'Or I need to be lucky enough to keep all the balls in the air.'

'Can't be done, mate. Not indefinitely. In the end,

you'll drop one.'

They gazed across the city, sitting in silence for a few moments.

'Bass Rock, yeah?' Dean pointed eastwards.

'Yep. Did you know there's an old chapel there, too, and a lighthouse?'

Dean shook his head.

'Ruby told me that.'

'Clever.'

There were brief stretches of silence, but they were comfortable, companionable.

A gull screeched past their heads, dipping close to what remained of their sandwiches.

'So. What's the plan? You gonna tell her before the baby's born, or after?'

Mark exhaled and brought his knees up to his chin. 'No idea. Before seems cruel. Afterwards seems…well, it all seems cruel. I don't know.' He turned to face Dean. 'What do you think?'

'Fuck, mate! Don't ask me! I'm the one whose wife is currently skiing in Squaw Valley with a guy called Julio.' He pronounced it correctly, for effect. '*Julio!* I'm the last person you should ask. Whatever I think, you should do the opposite.'

Mark plucked a piece of grass and started to chew on it.

'Ugh, that's full of rabbit piss, at best,' said Dean.

Mark spat it out and laughed. 'I was always chewing on grass as a kid.'

'We were hungrier than today's generation.'

Mark laughed. 'Yeah. Yeah, we were. Ruby said she

remembers us all in the school canteen — the team — eating like mad, chowing down on burgers and big hunks of meat!'

'God, I barely touch red meat these days! That sandwich was my first taste for months. It's all alfalfa and organic chicken over there. A lot of them get by on smoothies for almost every meal, but they go right through me — I stick mainly to solids and throw spinach in with more or less every meal.'

Mark puffed out his cheeks and blew out a stream of air as he shook his head. 'Sadie's got us on the kale and broccoli leaves.'

Dean nodded. 'And running — out there, you have to run if you want to stay in the game! And you gotta have all the gear; I swear it takes me longer to get ready for a run than it does to dress for the office. And when you're not running, it's yoga — sun salutations, downward dog.' He made approximations of the poses with his arms. 'Oh, and meditation instead of beer! I've never been so fucking healthy.' He lifted his t-shirt to reveal a six-pack.

'Whoah!'

Dean covered up again. 'I know. I know. That's what it takes to get a date, or to sell condos to kids barely out of college. They walk around the place with their iPhones pinging, shooting video — video! — like they're making a movie. And every room, it's: "Awesome", "Awesome", "Oh, awesome". And I'm like: "Yeah, awesome". And then they ask if I'm Australian.' He grimaced and rubbed his face with his palms. 'It's a tough gig.'

'The weather, though, mate. I mean, look at you. You wouldn't get that colour over here.'

Dean dipped his chin close into his chest and ran his hand over the crown of his head. 'See that?'

'What?'

'Exactly.' He brought his head back up and patted his crown. 'No more egg in the nest. You have two options over there when that happens: you either shave the whole lot off or get plugs.'

'Plugs?'

'Or a system. I could'a got a system.'

Mark adjusted his position so he could look at Dean full-on. 'What?'

'A hair transplant or a wig. I went for the transplant.'

Mark ran his knuckles roughly over the top of Dean's head. 'Seriously? A hair transplant? Why've you not mentioned this before?'

'Oh, it was when I was going through all that shit with the divorce.'

'Did it hurt?'

'Not as much as the divorce.' A glance, a moment. 'You just have to ride it out. You take a couple of weeks off work, wear a baseball cap when you go out — to cover the scabs, nobody wants to see the scabs — then you're all set. A new man. The time you take off work, you hit the gym hard, you go back and tell everyone you had a great vacation. Standard. No questions asked.'

'Bloody hell.'

'Have it tinted every four weeks, too.'

Mark did a double-take.

'More for the gloss than the colour. Maintenance! Little and often. If you let anything slip, it's tougher to get it back. I tried Botox a coupl'a times, too, but it wasn't for me, so now I have these electric shock facials every month.' He put his fingertips on his temples and made a buzzing sound.

'Botox? Electric shocks? You're forty!'

'Except in California — I'm permanently thirty-two over there. Everyone is.' Dean reached over to grab at the soft paunch Mark had developed. 'You have to start doing the plank, now. Really. Every day. Trust me.'

Mark had read about the multiple benefits of the plank, and had even seen pictures of people doing it, but his belief that there wasn't much to it had led to complete inertia. Ditto yoga — those poses looked so easy that it seemed pointless to waste time doing them. It occurred to him that, although Dean didn't look much younger than him, despite all the intervention, he certainly looked as though he'd last longer — almost as though he might well be perfectly capable of giving death the swerve.

The sun emerged from behind a cloud. Two young women appeared at the summit, scarcely breathless and laughing. The men had the best seats, and Dean immediately stood and tilted his head towards the rock to indicate they could have it. Mark followed suit.

'Gorgeous day,' said one of the women.

'Yeah,' said Mark. 'Enjoy the view.'

The prospect of Dean and Sadie being in the same room for several hours brought Mark out in a profuse sweat. As he made his way down the hill, with Dean scrambling a couple of steps ahead, he could feel his clothes sticking to him, in the small of his back and his inner thighs, in the crooks of his elbows and knees.

'So, just steer clear of school stuff. Focus on life in California — you know, the sunshine and all that.'

'I'm not gonna spend the whole time talking about the weather! I'm perfectly capable of talking about school without mentioning Ruby — it'll seem weird if I don't talk about old times.'

Mark flinched at the sound of Ruby's name being said out loud, albeit on a hillside by someone who was also once at school with her.

'OK, OK. Just…just try to limit it to football.'

'Jeez, relax! What, you think I'm just gonna blurt out that you're having an affair? Give me credit.'

'Hey, Dean, just tell the bloody world, why don't you? Stop shouting your mouth off!'

Dean laughed. 'The world is not on this hill. Hardly anybody is on this hill. Chill out!'

Mark took a couple of audible deep breaths. Just lately, he'd felt as though the air was thinner. He lost his footing slightly and stumbled.

Dean looked back. 'You OK?'

He shook his head. 'What do you reckon the altitude is up here?'

Dean laughed. '*The altitude?* Here?'

Mark stopped walking and bent over, putting his hands on his knees.

'Hey, seriously, are you OK?'

Mark straightened up. They stood in silence for a

few moments.

'Take a few deep breaths.' They breathed in sync. 'You can't carry on like this.'

Mark pressed the water bottle against his forehead. 'It's just so bloody complicated. I spend most of my time on edge, I'm sneaking around, I'm eating two lunches most days — a packed one as well as another in a cafe with Ruby, and I've got three fucking mobiles!'

'Three mobiles?'

'Work, personal and the Ruby phone,' he patted his trouser pocket. 'And the house — it's a bottomless money pit. Workmen there most days, drilling, banging. If I lose my job, we're fucked.'

'You could lose your job?'

'I'm on a final warning...'

Dean winced. 'Mark, man. You need to find a way of dealing with the stress. It's a killer.'

They started walking again. Mark felt his chest tighten. 'I think I'm having panic attacks. I looked up my symptoms the other day. Either that or pre-eclampsia. I keep getting these waves of...this kind of...' He positioned his hands over his stomach.

'Could it be indigestion? I mean, two lunches a day...'

They approached a bench and Mark slumped onto it as though he'd walked for miles. Dean perched alongside him.

'Panic attacks, indigestion, always on edge, no exercise. Oof! You gotta do something.'

'I might go see the doc again. Get some pills.'

'Mate, pills are not the answer. You have to make

a decision — Sadie or Ruby. You can't go on like this. You're a wreck!'

Mark rubbed his face. 'I know. Yeah, I know. Just try to stay on neutral topics tonight, OK?'

Chapter 51

Ruby squeezed the last of her supply of quinacridone red onto her palette, adding a small amount of yellow ochre and white. A whole evening of focusing on Mark's beautiful mouth. She knew every plane and curve, how deep his cupid's bow was, where the stubble started, where the outer lip became softer, damp flesh. She could picture the tiny swelling – imperceptible to those not obsessed with his mouth – where one of his teeth protruded slightly and pushed against his upper lip.

She'd drawn his lips slightly parted, as though he was mildly exerted. She struggled somewhat to suggest gleaming teeth in the dark hole that was his mouth, but she persevered. The level of focus required meant she didn't need to think about him playing happy families at home.

'Sadie, this is gorgeous!' Dean twirled strands of spaghetti expertly with his spoon and fork, making intermittent appreciative noises. 'I can't remember the last time I ate like this.'

'It's my sauce,' said Mark. 'I made it yesterday. It's always better the day after.'

Sadie leaned back from the table. Dean glanced at her with a concerned expression, and she smiled. 'Heartburn,' she said, rubbing at the bump.

'It's minced beef,' said Mark, 'but you need to ask the butcher not to make it too lean – the flavour is in the fat. I read that; I think it was Jay Rayner said it: "Eat fat!" And onions — you cut them small, but not too small. Then there's the herbs — chives, parsley, thyme, oregano — or,' he put on a vague American accent, 'orEGano, as you might say, these days! And to-may-to. Lotsa to-may-toes.' He took a quick breath, then bubbled out a high-pitched laugh. Dean and Sadie smiled good-naturedly.

'Plenty of seasoning, too. No holding back on the salt and black pepper.'

'Excuse me.' Sadie stood up.

'Can I get you anything?' asked Dean.

Sadie waved for him to relax. 'No, I'm fine. I just need a glass of water.'

'Here,' Dean jumped up, 'please, let me get that for you. Really. Sit down.'

She sat, and looked at Mark pointedly.

'Hey, Deano,' laughed Mark, 'you come over here

with your American manners, making us Brits look bad!' He emitted another involuntarily high-pitched laugh. He was feeling hot again. His scalp tingled.

Dean took a glass off the draining board, rinsed it and dried it to a polish. 'Ice?'

'No, thanks,' said Sadie. 'Just tap water, please.'

'So, Dean. Do you have a lot of ice in California?' asked Mark.

'Do I..? Do I have a lot of ice?'

'Yeah! You know? Ice with everything? It's quite hot, isn't it?' His crotch felt damp.

'Yeah, it's hot. Yeah, I have ice with things, usually.' He strolled back to the table and placed the glass of water in front of Sadie.

'Do you have one of those, you know, ice dispenser things?' Mark attempted to make the sound of an ice dispenser.

'Well, right now, I don't have an ice dispenser, but I guess I've been thinking of maybe getting one.'

'You should. You definitely should. Because the heat must be…phew!' The tiny vibration of the Ruby phone quivered in his trouser pocket. He pulled at the neck of his t-shirt and blew down onto his damp chest.

'Yeah, yeah, it can get pretty hot,' said Dean.

'You must have acclimatised by now, though,' said Sadie. 'How long have you been out there?'

'Ten years. Yeah, you get used to it. After growing up with British weather, playing football in the freezing cold, it seems churlish to complain, you know?'

'Oh, yeah, you were on the school team with Mark, weren't you? Now, I can find out if everything he's told me is true.'

Mark stopped his fork mid-air. A spaghetti strand hit him in the chin, depositing a blob of Bolognese sauce.

'Was he really the record goal scorer he claims to be?'

'What's it like playing in the heat?' asked Mark.

Dean looked at Sadie, then Mark, then back to Sadie. 'Yeah, we were both forces to be reckoned with in our day!' He looked at Mark, 'Yeah, you have to stay hydrated in the heat. That's the secret. That, and not growing old!'

Mark pushed his plate away and took a deep breath. 'I think I must be coming down with something.' He pulled at the neck of his t-shirt again, stretching it with both hands.

'Your face looks very red,' said Sadie, and she placed her hand on his forehead, as Dean had done earlier. 'I think you're running a temperature.'

Dean got up again, walked over to the sink, held the tea towel under a gush of cold water, wrung it out and took it back over to Mark. 'Here,' he said, 'put this on your head. Do you feel dizzy?'

'Yeah. Yeah, I do.'

'Take some deep breaths.' Dean placed his hand on Mark's shoulder. 'This is soaked through, take it off,' he said, pulling at Mark's t-shirt. Mark pulled it off quickly. His white flesh glistened, and sweat oozed from the little rolls of fat around his waist.

'I think I should call a doctor,' said Sadie.

Mark started to pant.

'It's a panic attack,' said Dean.

'Are you panicking, Mark? What are you panicking

about?' Her voice rose. 'What's he panicking about? Is it work?'

Mark waved for her to shut up. He struggled for breath and started to moan. Sadie swiped and jabbed at her phone, then stroked Mark's head as she waited for a doctor to answer.

'My chest feels very tight. Like a...'

'Hello, yes. My husband is having some sort of attack or a reaction to something. He's very red and... erm, yes. No. Darling, Mark Darling. Yes. Yes. In his chest.' She turned to Mark. 'Where exactly is the pain in your chest?'

'My heart.'

'Your heart? His heart! What? What?' She thrust the phone at him. 'She wants to speak to you. Can you speak?'

He nodded and took the phone. His voice was strained, as though he was being held firmly by the testicles. 'Yes. Yeah. About half an hour, but it's happened before. It happened earlier today, just after I'd been walking up a hill. Yeah. No, not that high. Lunchtime. Yeah. No. A couple of months ago, but they've been getting more frequent. No. Yeah. OK, thanks.' He handed the phone back to Sadie. 'They're sending an ambulance.'

Two paramedics arrived a few minutes later. They calmly asked him a host of questions, gave him a low-dose aspirin, and hooked him up to a heart-rate machine. They corroborated the details of the walk with Dean. After ten minutes or so they categorically concluded that Mark was not having a heart attack.

'Are you under any stress?' asked one.

'Yes,' said Mark. 'I'm under a lot of stress.' He glanced over at Dean who was now clearing the table.

'Well, I think you might have had a panic attack, fella,' she said, as she peeled the sticky pads off his chest and wrapped the wire around her hand. She turned to Sadie, and eyed the bump. 'Are you OK?'

Sadie nodded. 'Just worried about him.'

'He'll be fine.' She turned back to Mark. 'You need to find ways of dealing with stress. Do you do yoga or meditation?'

He shook his head.

'He does a breathing exercise sometimes,' said Sadie.

The paramedic nodded. 'Well, anything like that can help.' She turned to Mark. 'Do you do any exercise?'

He sucked his gut in. 'A bit.'

'That's good for stress, too. Moderate exercise. Walking, that kind of stuff. You should talk to your GP.'

'I'll make him an appointment,' said Sadie.

'She looks after you, doesn't she?' said the paramedic.

He nodded and started to cry. No longer in the throes of panic, he now felt embarrassed and weepy. 'Sorry to have brought you out for nothing.'

'Not at all. We get called out to panic attacks a lot. It's great you're OK. That's the main thing.'

Dean placed a tray of tea and biscuits on the coffee table.

'You're a lucky man,' said the paramedic, 'but take it easy on those custard creams.'

Chapter 52

Take Waverley Station — almost any station — on any weekday morning; subtract anyone with a suitcase or backpack, anyone kissing, anyone wearing feathers or leathers, and you'll be left with commuters. Professionals. They know exactly where to stand to be in with the best chance of bagging a seat. They also know which platform to run to if the 7:36 is delayed or cancelled; if they leg it, they might just catch the 7:41, which is slower, but will get them to work on time if they walk briskly at the other end.

Some are on their way to a job they love; most are not. For the latter, their journeys are made less traumatic with books, playlists, podcasts, and coffee just the way they like it. Thirty-six percent will have an affair with a co-worker. That can make the days fly by. Eighty percent reckon it's fine to steal stationery from work. That leaves twenty percent handing over actual cash for paperclips. Over half will fantasise about killing their bosses, but almost none will carry the fantasy to its conclusion. Most, however, will benefit from a brush with death.

When Mark was in the care of the paramedics, his life did not flash before him. He didn't even think about Fergus. Mark was consumed with what can only be described as an overwhelming sense of 'Oh, fuck.'

'Oh fuck' can be an excellent springboard. It can lead to change, a new lease of life; it can act as a metaphorical slap across the face. People have scaled mountains after heart attacks, run marathons after the death of a child, walked out of dead-end jobs to become entrepreneurs.

Half of them will just be glad to put the moment behind them.

chapter 53

'DID YOU EVER SEE *Un Coeur en Hiver*?' asked Mark. They
had taken refuge from a sudden rainstorm in a small
café. The howl and scat of the wind and rain rattled at
the windows. Mark shook his sodden coat and placed
it inside out on the back of his chair. Ruby pushed her
half-collapsed umbrella under the table.

'There's a scene like this,' he continued, 'where
she leaves a music rehearsal and bumps into...can't
remember his name...Daniel something...and they get
soaked in the rain...rain like this...before they run into
this Parisian café. Or was it a bar? Anyway–'

'We're not in Paris.'

'No, I know...'

'And I haven't been rehearsing music. I've spent
the morning dealing with insurers over carriage

arrangements for twelve fragile canvases.'

'I know, but…' He tried again: 'It's pouring down. And we're both wet. We're like the couple in the film because we're meeting like this, like they did.'

She had seen the film, but she tried not to remember the ending.

'Emmanuelle Béart is a violinist and Daniel what-his-name…'

'Auteuil. Violin-maker.' She adjusted her clinging, damp clothes and twisted her drenched hair into a pretzel.

'Yeah, that's right. He repairs hers because…'

'How was Dean?'

'Dean?'

She held his gaze expectantly.

'Erm, he was fine. It was good to see him, you know. Hey, by rights, he should be nearly bald by now but he's had plugs.'

'And how was dinner?' She poured herself a glass of water from the pitcher on the table. From where she sat, she could see rose petals dashed from bushes and plastered to the pavement.

'Yeah, it was fine. I said in my text: Bolognese followed by a panic attack for dessert. Do you know what plugs are?'

'Does he like Sadie?'

'Oh, you know…' He waved the question away.

'No. No I don't. Tell me.'

Mark felt a rising sense of unease. After quickly glancing around to ensure there was nobody he knew in the café, he put his hand on her knee. 'Is something the matter?'

She folded her arms across her chest. 'This is not a film, Mark. I'm not Emmanuelle Béart.'

'No, I know.'

'And you're not Daniel Auteuil.'

'No.'

'So, what are we doing here?'

He felt it was a trick question; he had no idea how to respond. 'Erm, lunch?'

'No, Mark! No! I'm not meeting you for lunch. I'm meeting you so that we can get lunch eaten and I get to kiss you at the end. I'm meeting you to kiss you again, to hold you, to be held by you. I could eat *lunch* at my desk!'

People on the next table stopped talking and exchanged meaningful glances between themselves. Ruby lowered her voice slightly. 'I don't think we should be sitting here, pretending we're in a French film, when you have a pregnant wife at home whom you need to be honest with so we can all get on with our lives.'

Someone dropped a fork.

'Er...'

'Did Dean not want to see me?'

'Well...I just thought...you don't know each other that well. I mean, did you ever talk to each other at school?'

'It's not about school, Mark!' The pretzel came undone, releasing coils of her hair onto her damp neck and collarbone.

'I know.' He had no idea what she was talking about.

'Dinner at your place gives the wrong message.'

He nodded.

'I don't know why you'd do that.'

'It just seemed easier, as he was staying at our place.'

'This is not about what's easy, Mark, is it?'

'No.'

'It's about stating your intentions.'

A waitress hovered close to the table. Mark looked at her and smiled in anticipation of an easier exchange about sandwich fillings. He turned to Ruby. 'Do you know what you want?'

'Yes, Mark. Do you?'

'I'll have the hummus and falafel wrap, please.'

The waitress made a note.

'A hummus and falafel wrap? Is that all you can say? That's what you want? Hummus? Falafel?'

'No.' He looked up at the waitress. She had a wonderfully simple and open face. 'Can I have a flat white, too, please.' He looked back at Ruby, who seemed very serious, so he turned back to the waitress again, for comfort.

'Nothing for me,' said Ruby. She passed the menu to the waitress and gave her a go-away-right-now look, sending her scurrying off to the kitchen.

'Why didn't you invite Dean to eat with us, as a couple? To stay overnight at my place?'

'I, erm...you don't have a spare room.'

'Yes I do.'

'You keep it locked.'

'I have a key, Mark. I could have unlocked it.'

'Is there a spare bed in there?'

'No.'

'So, where would he sleep?'

'That's not the point. This is not about a comfortable night's sleep!'

'I know that.' He still had no clue what was going on.

'It's about status. My status in your life, as your partner.'

'I know. I know.' He made a mental note: status.

'Can you imagine how I felt, thinking of you three cosying it up around the table, chatting about old times?'

'Well, it was mainly the panic attack, to be honest. I barely ate a thing. We spent most of the time with a couple of paramedics in the room.'

'It's not about how much you ate or the fucking paramedics!'

'No.' Mark caught the eye of a family sitting nearby, and tried to arrange the half of his face closest to them into an apologetic expression.

'It's about the signals you're sending.'

'I know that. I know.' He stroked her knee. 'And I know I was really stupid.'

'Do you?'

'Yes, of course. And I'm sorry. I wasn't thinking. It all happened so fast. Sadie invited him and he just said yes. I was very uncomfortable with the whole situation, and I told him that. I said: "Mate, I'm very uncomfortable".'

The waitress arrived with the wrap and coffee. Mark was looking forward to having his mouth full of food so he could avoid any further speaking. He took an enormous bite.

'I just want everyone to know that we are together, Mark.'

He nodded and chewed furiously.

'We need to sit down and make a plan.'

He'd spent his entire marriage sitting down and making plans, and had learned that such sessions invariably ended with his being handed a spreadsheet detailing a range of unappealing tasks he was going to have to do.

'Yup,' he said.

'Thursday?'

He nodded.

She let out a long sigh of relief and ran her fingers through her hair. 'Do you want all of that wrap?'

Mark pushed the plate over to her and smiled. He'd lost his appetite, anyway.

•••

Mark stared at the email and, without turning around, he hissed for Nisha to come and read it.

'What do you think she's asking me to do?'

'She's asking you to share what you learned at the neuromarketing conference with other relevant staff. You have to write and present a report. Can I sit in on that?'

He looked up from his screen at Nisha's open, honest face.

'I *am* supposed to be getting some sort of training

while I'm here. This sounds interesting,' she said.

He was silent.

'What?'

He shook his head.

'I can't sit in on it?'

'I didn't go.'

'What?'

'To the conference. I didn't go.'

'You didn't go to Copenhagen?'

'I went to Copenhagen.'

Nisha's hand shot in front of her wide-open mouth, so all he could see were her bulging, disbelieving eyes.

'Seriously?'

He stared at her, wild-eyed, nodding.

She started to laugh and shake her head. Mark frantically waved his hands to try and quieten her down.

'How did you get this job?'

'Listen.' He took a deep breath. 'OK, right. I have a plan. I'll start on the report, and you google everything you can on neuromarketing. Do me some bullet points, quotations, graphs, that kind of shit.'

'What?'

'Fifty quid. I'll give you fifty quid. I'll give you a hundred if you'll write the whole report.'

'One-fifty. Cash.'

'Mercenary. I want it emailed to me by first thing tomorrow morning.'

'I want a hundred upfront,' said Nisha.

'What?'

She held her hand out. He pulled his wallet from

his bag, and counted eighty-five pounds in notes and another six pounds and fifty-four pence in coins. She gathered it up.

'You owe me fifty-eight pounds and forty-six pence.'

'You get the balance on completion to my satisfaction.'

'I want the balance at nine. I get the balance, you get the report.'

'OK, OK. And make it funny. She'll be expecting it to have some humour in there as it's from me.'

'You're unbelievable.'

'And you're a hundred-and-fifty-quid richer, so win-win.'

Chapter 54

MICHAEL SAW AVA'S MUM enter the classroom and whisper to the teacher. There was muttering among the students, speculating and dramatic face-pulling, but he went back to what he was doing.

'Michael,' Violet was looking at him. 'Could you come with me, please?'

He quickly looked left and right, half-expecting another Michael to have appeared in class. He put his palm on his chest and gave her a quizzical look — *me?*

She nodded, 'And please bring your belongings.'

She walked out slowly. He followed her, through the stupid noises people were making, through the catcalls and laughter.

He noticed, as they walked along the corridor, that he was taller than her.

'I just want to let you know that your parents are here.'

'My parents?'

'And Mr Salter. We need to ask you a few questions.'

'What about?'

She held her arm out for him to continue walking. As soon as he did so, once he fell into step with her, she delivered another bombshell: 'There are also a couple of police officers here, but I don't want you to worry. I just want you to tell the truth. Is that clear, Michael?'

He stopped, terrified. 'The police?'

'As long as you tell the truth, we'll be able to sort things out.'

'Is it Ava? Is Ava OK?'

'It's nothing to do with Ava. Ava's fine.'

His mum had been crying but she smiled as he walked in. His dad was stroking his mum's hand. Mr Salter was the first to speak. He was calm, reassuring, and introduced the police officers to him.

'Michael is one of our most talented students. He helps out at the after-school maths club, and works very hard at his studies.'

The police officers nodded and smiled.

'Michael,' said the one on the left, 'we understand that you recently received a picture message from another student.'

'A girl called Bryony?' said the one on the right.

Michael struggled to speak.

'You just need to tell the truth, Michael,' said his dad.

And, right there, in front of Ava's mum, his parents,

the headmaster and the two officers, he started to shake and cry.

Once things calmed down, the one on the left started talking again.

'Do you have your phone with you?'

Michael nodded.

'We'd like to take it away with us today.' Both officers looked at his parents, who nodded.

Michael fished about in his bag.

'Will I get a criminal record?'

The officers looked at each other.

'No,' said his father.

'We need to look at your phone back at the station, then we might have more questions for you,' said the officer on the right.

Michael stood up. 'She just sent it to me! I don't know why!' Panic-stricken now, he turned to his parents. 'What's going to happen?' He started to cry.

Violet stood up, and put her arm on his shoulder. 'At this stage…'

'You're ten steps ahead, Michael,' said the one on the left. 'You need to calm down. Nobody's talking about criminal records at this stage. Let's take things one step at a time.'

His parents had always told him to avoid taking things just one step at a time. 'That's how bad things happen,' he said. 'Taking things one step at a time means you get left behind. You have to think ahead. Ten steps ahead if you can.'

Ava heard the story from Violet later that evening; she explained that Michael would be out of school for the rest of the week, and without access to his phone or laptop.

•••

'I think I'm being bullied.'

Sadie placed a hot chocolate in front of Ava.

'Who by?'

Ava let out a long sigh. 'Bryony.'

'Have you told Mum or Dad?'

She shook her head before sipping at the hot chocolate.

'You definitely need to tell Mum. She can deal with it in school.'

'She sent a naked photo to Michael.'

Sadie was non-plussed.

'I know that sounds weird, and Mum knows about the photo, but there's loads of other stuff, too. Stuff I can't prove.'

'Like what?'

'This is pointless. Everything on its own sounds like nothing, and even when you say them all together…'

Mark walked into the living room at that point, late home from work.

'You know Bryony Jones' dad, don't you?' said Sadie.

Mark flinched.

'Can you have a word with him? Bryony's been

picking on Ava.'

'Voldemort's not really the kind of person you have a conversation with.'

Sadie put her arm around Ava. 'Mark will sort it out.' She turned back to him. 'Yeah?'

Mark shifted uncomfortably. 'Yeah, of course.'

'Voldemort will kill you,' said Ava.

An hour later, Mark dodged copious mounds of dog shit as he made his way up the stairs that led to Bryony's dad's flat. He knocked gingerly. No reply. He took a photo of the door, texted it to Sadie, as proof he had been there, and turned to walk away.

'Why are you taking a photo of my door?' asked Bryony's dad, as he and his even more terrifying dog approached. The dog sniffed aggressively at Mark's crotch before looking back at its owner as if to seek permission to sink its teeth in.

'Angus, hi. Mark. Five-a-side?'

'You here for drugs?'

'No.'

'Drugs,' he pointed upwards, 'Spike. Top floor.'

'Good to know, but I'm not...'

The dog started to drool and push its nose forcefully against Mark, rearranging his genitals. He tried to create a barrier with his hands, and it nipped his thumb. Mark jumped and the dog growled menacingly.

'He's just playing with you. C'mon, Crush, leave him alone.'

The dog loped over to its owner.

'Angus, I wonder if I could have a word with you

about your daughter?'

'Bryony?' The dog started to bark.

'Yes.'

'What about her?' He turned his attention to the dog. 'Shut it, Crush.' The dog toned it down to a growl.

'Well, you know she's at school with Ava.'

'Tennis girl.'

'Yeah.'

Mark looked over the balcony and estimated the drop. 'Thing is, Angus, she's been — well she's been bullying Ava. And I wonder if you could possibly speak to her about...about stopping.'

Angus put his keys into the various locks without saying a word.

'I realise this is a difficult time for them all, they're all under pressure with exams, and they all deal with pressure differently...'

Angus opened the door and stepped aside. 'You'd better come in. Watch your step, the snake's on the loose again.'

Chapter 55

SOMETIMES, WHEN IT ALL felt too much, Mark turned his work phone, his private phone and the Ruby phone to silent, and placed them all in his desk drawer before going for a walk. He'd lied to Sadie on countless occasions, lied to Ruby about Sadie, lied to colleagues about how he'd spent lunchtimes and weekends, lied about Copenhagen to everyone, and now there was the financial impropriety of authorising funds from the marketing budget. Most days, he woke up from very little sleep, with a tight, hard knot in his stomach. Most nights, he'd struggle to fall asleep.

'Voldemort's actual flat?' said Jonny.

They were running, and Mark was struggling to keep up.

'I know. Madness.'

'You know he's got a snake?'

'Yeah,' panted Mark. He slowed.

Jonny adjusted his pace. 'Voldemort *and* blackmail. Tough week.'

'I've not had a proper night's sleep for months.'

'That's the life of an unfaithful, blackmailed comedian.'

Mark stopped, doubled over.

Jonny kept running on the spot, facing Mark. 'Oh, I meant to say, someone from work went to your gig. She wondered if you could get Frank Skinner's autograph for her mum…'

Mark straightened up, and looked across Princes Street Gardens at people who seemed to be living simple, unblackmailed lives.

'I said you might not have access to him,' said Jonny, running backwards.

'It's all a big joke to everyone, isn't it? Me trying to carve out a life.'

Jonny grinned in response, and launched into star jumps. Mark turned around, headed off in the opposite direction. While he was still within earshot, Jonny called after him. 'Don't be a dick!'

Mark turned back, then strode up to him. Before he could speak, Jonny got in first. 'Mate, seriously, be careful. You're turning into an arsehole.'

'Because I'm trying to do something with my life?' Spots of Mark's saliva landed on Jonny's face.

'You want some advice?'

'No.'

'You can't run two paths at once. Family or Ruby. Choose one. Do it fast. Get on with the rest of your life. Be grateful.'

Mark laughed. 'Yeah, thanks for that, Oprah.'

'Grow up, Mark,' said Jonny, breaking into a run.

Mark stood magnetised to the spot as Jonny disappeared into the distance, seamlessly weaving around couples and groups, with long, effortless strides. His breathing would be steady, no sweat.

chapter 56

IT WAS TOO RISKY TO MEET in their usual places; this conversation wasn't going to be café-appropriate, so he asked her to meet him in a small pub in Leith. Ruby invented an afternoon meeting to get out of work and, as he was convinced he was about to lose his job anyway, Mark took the afternoon off.

He waited for her in the lounge bar, grappling with words and phrases, mumbling to himself between urgent swigs of beer.

'Is everything OK? Has something happened? Has Don..?'

Mark shook his head.

'What? What's happened?'

He took a deep breath before starting to explain

how everything was not OK, and how many things were actually pretty far from OK. He riffed on various themes: the IVF debt, Sadie's blood pressure, Sadie's family, Don, the house falling apart, the panic attacks. As he oscillated, spewing out the litany of non sequiturs, Ruby sat perfectly still, in silence. In the end, he realised he couldn't deliver the crucial line without a qualifier, to soften the blow.

'So I just think that putting the brakes on things, *for a while*, would be the right thing to do.'

She opened her mouth, but no sound came out.

'It doesn't mean I don't love you. You know that… you know that, don't you?' He rubbed her shoulders. 'Hey? You know that.'

'You're not leaving?' She started to blow her outbreaths audibly between pursed lips. 'Everybody said…' Her shoulders started to rise dramatically with each breath. She spoke quietly, while looking at the floor. 'Everybody said this would happen. They said you wouldn't leave.' She shook her head.

'I'm not saying…'

'And I defended you.' She looked straight at him. 'I DEFENDED you!'

The pub's large Alsatian dog barked, and the barman looked over, pointedly.

Ruby bowed her head. She wiped at fast tears. 'I said to them all, I said: You don't know him. I've known him since he was a boy. I know him. I really, really know him. I have always known him. I knew him when he was…' She was speaking quickly now, almost chanting and becoming incoherent as she started to sob between words. Mark stroked the back of her left hand. She used her right to wallop him hard across the face. She stood up, grabbed her coat.

'You spineless, shitting…spineless, fucking…'

The dog really kicked off now, growling between each sharp bark, as the barman tried to pacify it.

Mark nervously looked at the dog. Its front paws were on the bar, and its saliva dripped onto the brewery towels.

'You've wasted my time…' She started off quietly but Mark could sense this was going to build in volume. He reached for her hands but not so suddenly that it might aggravate the dog.

'Listen. Sshh, listen. I love you, right? I. Love you. And…' He dropped down onto one knee. He bowed his head into her legs, partly to hide his own shocked expression at being on one knee. He had no clue as to what he was going to say next; all he knew was that he was now in the universally accepted pose that accompanied a marriage proposal, which was pretty much the absolute opposite of his intention.

Ruby shook him off.

'No! Ruby! No! Don't go.' He was walking on his knees now, shuffling along like a toddler being left at playschool for the first time. His face was stinging from the slap and, this low down, he could smell the carpet. It was rank. He looked up just as the dog approached him, growling. It jumped on him and barked.

'Joan!' shouted the barman. 'Get off him!' Joan barked harder, and opened her jaw around Mark's arm. 'She's only playing!' shouted the barman, rushing over to the scene.

As Mark jumped up, glad of the air five-feet-nine inches above carpet level, Joan rose up on her hind legs, growling, her paws heavy on his shoulders.

'Ruby…' said Mark, the dog now like a sack of coal on his back. 'Please…'

'Joan!' The barman took hold of the dog's collar, and pulled her to his side. 'OK, enough, you two. Take it outside.'

As the door closed behind Ruby, Mark's phone pinged.

He ran hard, dodging pedestrians and chained up bikes. His throat was on fire. Every time he heard the diesel engine of a cab, he would try to flag it down. Once he reached Glenogle Road, he paused and put his hands on his knees. He felt sick. As soon as he had the thought, the vomit came up, splashing over his shoes and trousers. And again. Three times. Then a dry heave. He started to stagger. A few more yards, and he'd be home. He ran the back of his hand across his forehead as he walked up the path. He reached into his pocket. No keys. The other pocket. No keys. Inside pocket. No keys.

He pulled out his phone. Three new missed calls from Sadie. He rang her. Tony answered.

'This had better be good, because my daughter — your wife —'

He heard Violet wresting the phone from Tony.

'Mark? Mark, we're at the hospital.'

And then a scream in the background. Bloodcurdling.

He started to run again, and rang a taxi at the same time.

'I'm running along Glenogle Road, my wife's in labour...' He dropped the phone. He dropped the fuckingfuckingbastard phone. As he picked it up, he grazed his knuckles along the pavement. The screen wasn't cracked but the cab firm had rung off. He ran as fast as he could to the main road, stood in the middle of it, and frantically waved at every cab he saw, whichever direction they were coming in. Eventually one stopped.

•••

'Mark Darling, my wife, Sadie Darling... she's in labour... I'm late!'

The receptionist looked him up and down. There was still vomit on his trousers and shoes, blood on his knuckles, and his hair was plastered to his head with sweat. The Ruby phone pinged. He'd forgotten to switch it off. He pulled the phone out and dropped the other one. This time, the screen did crack.

'Sir, you need to change.'

'I will. I definitely will.'

'You need to change out of *those clothes* into something more...hygienic.'

'I can't. I have no house keys. I have no access to my clothes!'

'Then we'll have to put you into some scrubs, because you cannot go in like that.'

An auxiliary took him to a cubicle and handed him a flimsy cotton top and pair of trousers and a plastic bag for his own clothes. Once he'd changed, she led him to where Sadie was. He entered the room as she was mid-scream. Her face was scarlet with effort. Violet was holding a damp flannel.

'Where have you BEEEEN?'

Bizarrely, his brain started to perform a search for the name and address of the pub in Leith.

'I'm really sorry, babe. My phone was...'

' A a a a a a a a a a a a a r g h ! AAAAAAAAAAAAAAAAAAAARGH!!'

Saved by a contraction.

Tony glowered at him. He sensed that this would not be the end of the matter with his father-in-law.

Forty minutes, numerous screams, several inhalations of Entonox and many impressive pushes later, Mia Emmeline Darling emerged, five weeks early and quite jaundiced. Six pounds nine and a half ounces. She was indubitably her mother's daughter, protesting from the off: *Too bright! Too cold! Not womb-like enough!* What lungs for such a tiny package!

As the baby snuggled into her mother's arms, Mark looked at her tiny fingernails. Smaller than shirt buttons, thin as rose petals.

Chapter 57

As EDINBURGH FRINGE'S performers pack up and leave town, the International Festival's grand finale gets under way. Opera singers reach their highest, clearest notes; big movie stars wipe off their stage make-up in battered old dressing rooms; and the world's best pyrotechnicians calibrate the brightness, colour and patterns of the choreographed firework display. Tourists and residents stop walking, lean out of sash windows, and emerge from pubs and restaurants, all of them looking at the sky, the beautiful sky.

Mia was sick. Not life-threateningly so, but sick enough to be kept in a phototherapy incubator, her eyes covered by a gauze mask, as Sadie squinted at her daughter's charts, trying to work out if the zigzagged lines were going in the right direction.

'The doctors are thinking she might be home by the weekend,' said Mark.

Ruby smiled, and tried not to ask what this now meant. 'I'm glad she's on the up,' she said.

'Can I get you something to drink?'

They were in his kitchen. Ruby stood up from the table and perused the unfamiliar selection of teas, picking up and sniffing at some of the boxes.

'Nettle.'

She started opening cupboards to find cups.

'I'll do it,' said Mark, too quickly.

'Oh, sorry, I was just…'

'No, honestly, just sit down. I'll do it.'

She prowled around a little more, checking out the fruit bowl, the spices, everything on display.

'I didn't think people actually ate these.' She picked up a physalis.

'We have them in fruit salads,' said Mark.

We. We have them in fruit salads.

'Can I have a tour?'

'A what?'

'A tour. I'd just like to look around.'

He looked hesitant. She moved towards him, put her arms around him.

'I just want to see how you live. What I can expect. Do you leave your socks on the bedroom floor?'

He didn't leave his socks on the floor. Not any more. Not since Sadie had drilled it into him to put dirty socks – dirty anything – into the washing basket.

She browsed through a small pile of books. 'Ooh, *The Hidden Tools of Comedy*.' A smile. '*Digital Marketing*?' She picked one up. '*The Conscious Parent*?'

'Brushing up on stuff. You know?'

She nodded, squinted at a page. 'Unconditional acceptance...'

He gently took the book from her. 'I didn't get enough time with my own mum and dad. I just want some guidance. On how to do it right.'

She picked up the digital marketing textbook, frowning. 'Do you need this? Because,' she tapped the comedy book, 'surely this is the one you want to focus on?'

'I need to be better at both.'

'Says who?'

'Says me.'

He kissed her forehead, reached for his jacket.

'Are we leaving?'

'Yeah. Let's get some proper coffee. Come on.'

Chapter 58

IT WAS LATE. HE WAS LATE. The candles had liquefied in their glass jars, and the food was ruined. She'd called and texted him numerous times, but had received only one terse response:

Will get back 2u asap

No kiss. No sorry. It was an instruction to wait, a request not to take action, a plea for patience.

She decided to bake, because she felt unable to concentrate on anything else. She'd left the heart-shaped biscuit cutter in its box, opting for a more neutral round. Shortbread was the only thing she could manage without resorting to a recipe; she had learned it in school and could now do it without weighing or measuring.

She took the biscuits out of the oven. She turned the ringer and alert sounds up to maximum on her phone, and tried to settle down on the sofa to some film or other.

As the shortbread cooled, she unlocked the studio and looked at the portrait. She could see now that she'd probably added an inch or so to his height, and almost certainly more definition in his arms and abs.

There was only one thing worse than everything falling apart, and that was being in the hell of suspecting that everything was about to fall apart.

A text pinged in.

Will txt tmrw. Sorryx

There was a kiss, which was promising, but he wasn't coming this evening and intended only to text her tomorrow, so probably not then either. Her heart started to pound. Her thumb hovered over the contact icon. She pressed it. The call went straight to voicemail. She hung up, and texted him.

What exactly is happening?

No response.

Call me

No response.

I need to speak to you NOW

Her phone rang.

An urgent whisper: 'I can't speak for long. I'm in the bathroom.'

'What's happening?'

'I can't come over. Mia's fractious.'

'I'm fucking *fractious*!'

'Yes, I know, Ruby! We all are. But my daughter,' — he placed such weight on the word — 'who is still jaundiced, scarcely sleeping, and hardly feeding, needs me here.'

Boom.

•••

She ate all of the shortbread, glad, at least, that they were not heart-shaped. She popped the final couple into her mouth as she lay on the sofa. Crumbs fell onto her clothes, into her hair, but it didn't matter. She just carried on looking straight up at the ceiling, making shapes and stories from the damp stains, and studying the overpainted egg and dart architrave, as people in the upstairs flat danced, getting ready for a Saturday night in the city.

chapter 59

IT'S NOT VERY SISTERLY. That was the verdict, verbatim, of yet another one of Ruby's friends who had hiked up to the moral high ground, joining the majority. Her lack of sisterliness bothered her – of course it did – although the word seemed of another time. The most irksome aspect of these conversations was that people — friends — assumed she was unaware of the potential impact of her actions. They hadn't taken into account, or had long forgotten, how easy it is to be blind and deaf to the truth when the alternative is so much more attractive.

You're leaving a baby fatherless, said a new mum, now former friend who'd been cradling her baby at the time, supporting its too-heavy head. You can't argue with that.

She saw Mark fleetingly now. He looked dog-tired every time.

'I hardly see you any more.'

They were sitting on the catholic cathedral steps, sipping hot chocolates. He had two huge John Lewis carrier bags at his feet, filled with baby paraphernalia.

'I can't just go out. It was easier when I was at work.'

'Say you're going for a walk or something.'

'Mia's quite demanding. It takes two of us to…'

Two. Two of us.

'When do you think you'll be able to talk to her?'

'I need to get the christening out of the way. Then there's gonna be this big family gathering at New Year — relatives from all over the bloody world are flying in for it.'

'That's three months away! You're gonna still be there in three months?'

No response.

'I thought you were going to talk to her, like, soon!'

He ran his fingers through his hair. It looked like it hadn't been washed for days.

'Can I wash your hair?'

'What?'

'Ten minutes' walk to my flat. Half an hour, max, to wash and dry your hair. Cab home.'

●●●

Just before Mark put his key in the door, he took a deep

breath. He'd tried all the way home to shake himself out of Ruby mode. When it had come time to leave her flat, she'd broken her usual pattern of withdrawing and had promised to tell him a funny story when she next saw him, involving someone he knew slightly. Instead of taking the opportunity to bolt out, he'd stayed longer, listened to the story. Also, for the first time, she'd closed the door before he was out of sight.

He put the key in the lock and messed up his hair before shuffling in. The rain had disguised the fact it had been lovingly washed just an hour earlier.

He dropped the carrier bags in the hall and walked through to the kitchen where Sadie bobbed Mia rhythmically around in laps.

'Oh, hello!' he cooed, stretching out his arms to take Mia from Sadie. She didn't hand her over.

'Where've you been?'

Mia burped loudly.

'Oh, burpy-burpy! Has my girl got a bit of wind?' He laughed and Mia smiled, causing him to feel strangely relieved.

Sadie was staring at him.

'You know where I've been. Getting everything on the list. Then I went for a quick drink. All right?'

'Someone just rang the landline but hung up when I answered. I thought it might be you. I was feeding Mia. I had to stop feeding her to get it.'

Mark swallowed. 'Probably someone trying to sell us something. A new kitchen or something.'

'There's nothing wrong with the one we've got.'

He held his arms out for his daughter again.

'Wait till you've dried off. I don't want her getting wet.'

He shrugged off his coat, threw it across a chair. 'Shall I start cooking?'

'No.'

'Shall I get Mia ready for bed?'

'No.'

'Is everything all right?'

'Yes. Why?'

'You just seem a bit...'

She looked exhausted. Her hair was pulled back into a scruffy bun, she had no make-up on and a couple of tiny scratches on her cheek, courtesy of Mia. Her clothes were loose and creased, and a greying bra strap was visibly digging slightly into her shoulder. Nothing about her had been done for his benefit. She was refreshingly, honestly guileless; transparent. She wouldn't embellish any stories for his amusement tonight, but she'd let him gallop through a few of his own far-fetched tales with dodgy punchlines without so much as a raised eyebrow. He knew that if he opened the fridge, it would be stocked with nutritious ingredients and healthy snacks — organic carrot batons, washed celery, smoothies. She kept him on the rails, and she would keep Mia on the same track. Beneath the ubiquitous smell of sick, he knew that if he got close enough to her later her skin would smell earthy, woody.

'I'm going to get her ready for bed,' said Sadie.

'OK.'

Mark kissed his daughter goodnight. He gave a cute wave and pulled a funny face, even though his guts were churning. He walked backwards towards a kitchen chair, felt for its edges and dropped into it. He stared into mid-air.

Fifteen minutes passed. Fifteen minutes of sitting and staring and not cooking. The landline rang.

'Hello?'

Nobody at the other end.

'Hello?'

'Hello. Mark?'

'Yes.'

'Hiya. Is Sadie there?'

'What?' The room started to spin.

'Is Sadie there? Her phone's switched off. It's Nancy.'

Nancy! 'Hi. Yes. No. She's just–'

'Is it a bad time?'

Sadie appeared from nowhere and took the phone from him. 'Hi, Nance.' She sat down as Nancy spoke. 'Uh-huh. Uh-huh. Right. OK.'

Mark took the stairs two at a time, shed his clothes, jumped in the shower, tried to keep his breathing steady, his heart-rate down. He picked up a shower gel with the word RELAX on the front, but it slipped out of his hands and clattered into the shower tray. Gloopy, purple liquid oozed out, and the smell of synthetic lavender made him feel nauseated. He bent down to pick up the bottle and, as he clicked the lid back on, he slipped, fell flat on his arse, banged his head against the shower door, and scraped his elbow on the plughole. That's how Sadie found him, in an ungainly tangle. For a brief moment, she looked scared but, once she realised what had happened, she laughed. She laughed till she clutched her sides. He would gladly do it again, night after night, to hear that laugh.

●●●

It was just after four. From her bed, Ruby could make out tiny dawn streaks of pale turquoise illuminating the horizon and the quarter moon, pale and fading. The heat of the previous day's sun and the scent of Mark lurked deep in her pillows and bedding. She kicked the duvet off.

There were final touches to be done to the painting. She'd noticed more grey in his hair today, and a faint line had formed a tiny diagonal crease in his left earlobe. She placed a short diamond-blade knife on her table, and stroked a fine sable brush gently against the canvas.

Chapter 60

It was Tony's best yield yet. His ultimate aim was to provide enough fruit, vegetables and herbs so that none of the family had to buy any. He made up two large bags each weekend: one for Sadie and Mark, the other for Nick and Lenny. The rest were eaten or blanched and frozen, and put in the specially bought chest freezer in the garage.

He was brushing soil off a crop of new potatoes.

'It's like the seventies!' said Violet. 'I'm amazed you can even buy chest freezers these days.' She was scrambling eggs to go with the bacon that was sizzling under the grill.

'You'll thank me when half of these things are out of season,' he said.

'Nothing's ever out of season now, Tony. You can get

anything all year round.'

'Aye, nothing that tastes like this stuff.'

They both knew that the weekend bags, stuffed with goodness, were added incentives to bring the family together at least once a week.

'I think Ava's still seeing Michael,' said Tony. He banged the brush on the worktop.

Violet remained silent. She divided the eggs between two plates.

'You know?' he said.

'It wasn't his fault.'

'What if he persuades Ava to pose for...'

'He didn't persuade Bryony. And it turns out she'd been sending photos like that to a lot of boys. And men.'

'Christ. What kind of girl..?'

'A lost one, Tony. That's all. She's lost, and sad, and angry.'

Ava walked in as Violet set the plates on the table.

'Anything for me?' she asked.

'Of course,' said Violet. She kissed the top of her daughter's head, took the plates back to the worktop, put on two more slices of toast and redistributed the eggs over three plates, taking care not to give Ava any egg that had touched the bacon.

'Have you seen my walking boots, Mum?'

'Under the stairs,' said Tony. 'Are you going walking?'

'I'm going on a march,' said Ava, jutting her chin out defiantly.

'What kind of march?' said Tony.

'Anti-austerity,' she said.

'Oh, yeah, put us all down for that,' he said.

'You should come, then, Dad. You, too, Mum.'

'Will Michael be there?' asked Tony.

'Yep.'

'Bring him round for tea afterwards, then.'

Ava laughed.

'I'm serious,' he said. 'Bring him round. If I like him, I'll give him some new potatoes to take home.'

A couple of hours later, Ava and Michael squelched in, bringing a gust of wind and torrential rain into the hallway.

Tony grinned at the sight of them.

'Dad, this is Michael.'

Michael smiled as he dripped.

'I've probably got some trackie bottoms and a jumper you can borrow. OK?'

'Thanks.'

A few minutes later, Ava and Michael sat at the table, drinking hot chocolate and eating buttered crumpets, courtesy of Tony.

'So the march still went ahead?'

'Yes,' said Ava. 'Although not everyone who signed up was there.'

'How many of you were there?' asked Tony.

Michael and Ava looked at each other.

'Six,' said Ava.

'Six people?'

'Seven, if you include the organiser.'

'Yeah, seven,' said Ava. 'We're doing a food bank collection next weekend. Have we got any spare food?'

'What do you need?'

'Tinned stuff and dried stuff,' said Michael.

'Yeah, we'll do you a box of stuff. What about my veg? I've got a glut of spuds.'

'No fresh food,' said Ava.

'Do you want to take some home with you, Michael?'

'Er, OK. Thanks.'

Tony went off in search of a sturdy bag.

'I know him,' said Michael, pointing at one of the photos on the wall. 'He comes into the café sometimes.'

'Mark?'

'Yeah.'

'He's Sadie's husband,' said Ava.

'He tips really well. He once gave me a fiver.'

'Who?' said Tony, walking back in with a large carrier bag.

'Mark,' said Ava.

Michael peered closer at the photo. 'Who's that with him?'

'Sadie, Ava's sister,' said Tony. 'Now, if I fill this with spuds and other veg, and give you a lift home, how does that sound?'

'Yeah, great, thanks,' said Michael, before looking again at the photo of Mark and the woman who'd never been into his café.

chapter 61

SADIE'S HIGH BLOOD PRESSURE; Mia being sick; Sadie's raging hormones; Christmas; Hogmanay. Mark tipped the last of a bag of Twirl bites into his mouth, glad of a couple of hours of alone time.

A French flag appeared on his phone. Ruby had said something or other a few days ago about applying for a job in Marseille.

•••

'They're doing the interviews on Zoom.'

'Right.' He licked his finger and dabbed a few chocolate shards off his trousers.

A pause.

'If that's what you want.'

'I can't have what I want. Because I think after Hogmanay, it'll be something else. I think things'll keep stopping you from leaving. Mia's birthday, Nick and Lenny's wedding, Mia's first day at school, Ava playing Wimbledon or saving the world — I think they'll all roll by, and you'll feel you can't leave until each one has passed. And I'll wake up one morning and realise I'm staring down the barrel of fifty, and seeing less and less of a married man with three kids.'

Chapter 62

THIS IS EXACTLY HOW SADIE had imagined it. The baby, the pram, all of it. Bright sunshine, windless, although the chill of autumn was already nipping at the heels of summer.

All the headstands, the unbearable hormonal swings, the crazy food restrictions, the endless IVF bills — they were distant memories now, and she held no truck with dwelling on the past. They were back on track. She kept an eye out for better-paying and higher-status jobs for Mark; it would be a mistake for him to get stuck at Re:Klein. Every week, emails from job sites would drop into her inbox and she'd forward them to him. He needed to move onwards, upwards. She'd managed to delegate her own workload to a brilliant freelance stitcher, to give herself a decent maternity leave, and had plans to expand the business once she returned. In the meantime, she'd hired a PR and social media consultant on a small retainer, just to keep things ticking over.

She edged the perimeter of the Botanics, invisibly doing pelvic floor exercises and holding her core tight as she pushed the pram along and through to Stockbridge, stopping off for fresh bread and cheese, returning the smiles of shop staff. It occurred to her that having a baby was similar to having a very cute dog, in that most people smiled at it, and then at its owner. She'd never experienced anything like it; almost everyone seemed pleased to see her. She particularly loved it when people asked the baby's name — it was impossible to say 'Mia' without smiling. Somehow the clichéd comments seemed fresh and original: Yes, she was a beautiful baby; yes, she had her mother's smile; yes, what a head of hair for such a tiny one.

Sadie was deeply in love with this tiny human being who was smooth as a nectarine and smelled of milk and lavender and shit. Although Mark still baulked at the full nappies, she was adept at them now, and had the whole process down to a swift couple of minutes. Things had turned out just as she'd always imagined. And, once Mia was in full health, they could start talking about a brother or sister for her.

chapter 63

'*Merci, je serai ravie de vous rejoindre en novembre.*'

Ruby gazed at the phone long after the gallery owner had hung up. Eventually she called Mark.

'Can you speak?'

'Hi, yeah, Sadie's just gone shopping with her mum.'

The cry of a baby in the background.

'She's left the baby with you?'

'I'm her dad.'

Silence.

'I got the job.'

She heard the baby's breath near the phone. Mark had obviously picked her up to stop her crying.

'Will I see you before I go?' she asked.

'Of course you'll...'

'Tonight?'

'No.'

'The weekend?'

'I might be able to get out on Monday.'

'Right.'

There were muffled sounds at Mark's end, followed by a groan. 'Oh, sorry, gonna have to call you back. Mia's been sick.'

He didn't. He sent some sorry-arsed text an hour later, accompanied by a photo of baby-sick on his shirt, which she supposed was meant to be funny, or proof that it had really happened, or just something to say that wasn't as awkward as what needed saying.

•••

Monday.

'I've made the cauliflower couscous thing you like.'

There was no cauliflower couscous thing he liked, and he spotted spinach that he'd also have to negotiate.

'Oh, wait! Cherry tomatoes! I forgot to buy them!'

'It'll be OK without,' he said.

'I want it to be right. Let's run to the corner shop.'

Mark shivered as the chilly air hit them.

'It's twenty two degrees in Marseille.'

'I'll miss you.'

They stopped walking. Kissed.

•••

It was the final of the inter-schools tennis tournament. At the end of the day, either Ava or Orla Densmore would fall asleep, after a marathon selfie session, with their arms around the trophy. Ava sat next to Emma on the school bus.

'How are you feeling?'

'OK,' said Ava.

She hated it when Emma got jittery. She was a great coach — she had all the tips for play and technique — but she had a real issue with anxiety. Ava could always tell when it started to kick in because Emma would start to chew the skin on the side of her thumbs. It was disgusting to watch.

'Why are you rubbing your ankle?'

'I tripped earlier. It was nothing. Just a stumble.'

'What!?'

The driver turned around briefly.

'I'm OK. Really. It just feels a bit sore. It'll be fine.'

Emma put her thumb to her mouth. Ava now wished she hadn't said anything.

'Do you wanna just…?' Emma stood up in the aisle of the coach and signalled for Ava to put her foot on her knee.

'Really?'

'Slip your shoe off. Let me see it.'

Ava obliged, rolling her eyes.

'What happened?'

'I told you. I tripped.' Explaining that she'd been pushed by Bryony wouldn't help right now.

'How exactly?'

'I don't know. I just kind of…'

'Was there a bend at the ankle? Did you fall inwards or outwards on it?'

'Inwards, I think.'

Emma took hold of Ava's ankles. 'Point your toes for me. Then flex. Then point.'

Ava did as she was told.

'Any pain?'

'It's fine.'

'Do you want to talk strategy?'

'Actually, I just need a bit of silence, if that's OK.'

'Sure. You get yourself into the zone,' said Emma.

Ava smiled.

'Do you want an apple?' Emma pulled out a plastic bag of apples. 'They're washed.'

'I really just want to sit here, quietly.'

Emma gave her the thumbs up, then took an apple from the bag, bit into it and crunched loudly. She hummed as she checked her phone. It seemed that Emma had selected all the various noises it was possible to enable on her phone: keystrokes, message arrivals, sent messages, tweets.

Ava tuned out, and focused instead on watching people going about their business: a man pushing a three-wheeled buggy, a couple kissing, two toddlers on leads. She craned to check that they were actually on leads, like dogs. Cute. The couple had stopped kissing now. The woman leaned her head against the man's shoulder. Against Mark's shoulder.

She leapt up and pushed past Emma. She ran down to the back window, and jumped knees first onto the seat, between two boys. Her head bobbed around as she peered out.

Emma appeared at her side. 'Ava, what's happening? Are you OK?'

Ava pulled her phone out of her pocket and started to text.

'Is everything OK?' said Emma.

Ava ignored the question.

Just seen Mark KISSING a woman.

As soon as Violet read the text, she knew straight away that it was true.

Where? Has he seen you?

Leith Walk. On way to match.

●●●

Violet called Tony. 'Listen, don't explode, but Ava's seen someone who looks very like Mark on Leith Walk with a woman.'

'A woman?'

'Kissing her.'

'He's what?'

She could imagine Tony pulling on his jacket, halfway out of the door.

'Tony, listen: we need to get our facts straight before we go barging in. It's possible it wasn't even Mark. We need to talk to Ava when she gets in. I'll be home early.'

As soon as they heard Ava's key turn the lock, Violet and Tony rushed into the hallway. She was carrying a trophy.

'Oh, you won!'

'Is Mark having an affair?' Ava seemed shaken. Violet took the trophy from her, slid her kit bag from her shoulder, and put her arm around her.

'If he is, you can guarantee that...'

Violet made a face for Tony to shut up.

'Come and sit down, and tell me what you saw,' she led her to the sofa.

'OK. So, where were you?'

'On the school bus going to the match.'

'And what exactly..?'

'He was kissing this random woman. It was so weird, Mum. Just, like, kissing! Proper kissing! In the street!'

'And it was definitely Mark? You're sure it was him?'

Ava nodded.

'And he didn't see you?'

'No.'

'And you're sure?' said Violet.

'Yes. The bus moved so I ran down to the back to see them, to make sure, but they'd gone.'

'So you're *not* sure?' said Tony.

'Yes, I'm sure.'

'You said you ran down the bus to make sure.'

'I did.'

'But they'd gone. You said they'd gone. So you couldn't make sure.'

'It was definitely him.'

'And this other woman was definitely not Sadie?' said Tony.

'Definitely not.'

'OK.' Violet leaned back, sighed and rubbed her face with both hands.

'Are you going to ring Sadie?'

Violet gazed out of the window.

'Mum?'

'No,' said Violet.

'You don't believe me?' Ava jumped up.

'Ava, sit down. Of course I believe you!'

'It's not that we don't believe you,' said Tony.

Ava perched on the arm of the sofa. 'What, so you're just going to deceive her?'

'No, of course not,' said Violet. 'We're going to take some time to think about it. We can't just muscle in. It's complicated. We need to get our facts straight before we jump to conclusions. She could have been a colleague. Colleagues often kiss each other.'

'With tongues?'

Tony had spent most of the evening deliberating on the many ways in which Mark had betrayed his daughter and their family, and was now riffing on suitable forms of punishment for the little bastard. He and Violet were on their third medicinal scotches.

'You do realise you're talking about seriously harming the father of our grandchild, Tony? And, to be honest, I'm not sure some of those things are physically possible.'

'You forget that I know people, Vi. People who can

do things.'

She cast him a sideways glance. 'All right, Al Pacino, calm down.' She downed the last of her whisky and rolled the empty glass around between her palms. 'Ava won't keep it to herself, so Sadie's going to find out either from her or from us.'

'I could speak to him.'

'And say what?'

Tony shrugged.

'Brilliant.'

'Well, I don't know… I could go over there tonight, get Sadie out of the way, and have a word with him. Find out if this woman…find out if it's serious, or if it's all just a…'

'It's half-past nine – you can't just turn up at half-past nine! They'll wonder what the hell's going on.'

The doorbell rang, and they both looked at each other, blankly, before Tony jumped up to answer it.

It was Nick and Lenny.

'Sorry, Mum, I know it's late.'

'It's half-past nine,' said Violet.

'I know, I know, but—' Nick shrugged, palms up.

Ava ran downstairs.

'What did you see?' said Nick.

'Mark kissing a woman.'

'You're sure it was him?' asked Lenny.

She nodded.

'I think the only thing we can do is give him the opportunity to explain, before we go off at the deep end,' said Violet. 'We believe you, Ava, but there could be a…reasonable explanation.'

•••

Mark didn't respond to the text Violet sent him, asking him to ring her. Neither did he respond to the one from Nick, asking him the same thing, only less politely. So, following a very brisk twenty-minute walk, Tony knocked softly at Sadie and Mark's door, holding — at half-past ten at night — a bag of raspberries from his garden and three cut hydrangeas.

'Evening,' said Tony, pushing past Mark. 'I didn't think the raspberries would keep till tomorrow, and Violet doesn't want these on the coffee table,' he said, holding up the hydrangeas. 'She says they get in the way of the telly. Is Sadie in?'

'She's in bed,' said Mark.

'Thought she might be,' said Tony, 'because it's you I want a word with.' He plonked the fruit and the flowers on the table. 'Sit down.'

Mark sat.

'You were seen kissing someone this afternoon. Not Sadie.' Tony's voice was two notches above a whisper.

Mark stood up.

'Sit down,' said Tony, through gritted teeth.

He sat.

'Who is she?'

Mark stared at Tony. He shook his head. 'I don't know.'

'Are you in the habit of kissing women you don't know?'

More staring.

The baby monitor gurgled, but Sadie's breathing was steady. Tony walked up to it, looked back at Mark and whispered, 'This thing two-way?'

Mark looked puzzled.

'Can they see or hear us?'

Mark shook his head.

Tony looked at the monitor before turning back to his son-in-law.

'Not enough for you, those two? Needed a bit on the side, did you?'

Mark had not known Tony when he was in his heyday, although he suspected he'd been utterly terrifying.

Tony leaned over him. 'Here's what's gonna happen. You ring her and you tell her, right now, that it's over.'

Mark opened his mouth to protest.

Tony dropped to his haunches: 'This is not a request. Not a discussion. Got it?'

Mark nodded.

'Do it. Now,' said Tony, standing up.

'What, now?'

'I want to hear you say the words.'

Mark looked around the room.

'Or I can ring her,' said Tony.

Mark rang her.

'And keep it down,' said Tony, glancing upstairs.

'Ruby, listen, I need to talk to you. I have Sadie's dad here…'

Tony snatched the phone from him, and spoke slowly and quietly.

'Ruby. This is Tony. I believe you've been shagging my son-in-law. Now, there's no accounting for taste, but you need to know that it all stops now.'

There was a pause.

'*I'm* telling you it's over. And I'm also warning you — don't even think about doing anything stupid that will upset my daughter. Got it?'

He hung up, pushed the phone into Mark's chest, and walked quickly to the window, where he stood with his back to Mark, his head in his hands. After a few moments, he took a deep breath, expanded his chest, pulled back his shoulders and turned to face Mark. As he spoke, tears rolled down his cheeks.

'If I find that you have been back in contact with this woman, I will end you. Do you understand me? I will end you.'

•••

Mark called her back as soon as he could be sure Tony was away. She sounded more bemused than scared.

'Shit. I'm glad I took the job.'

'I don't know what to do. He threatened all sorts. He knows people.'

'What people?'

'Villains.'

'How did he find out?'

'No idea.'

•••

'It's sorted,' said Tony, as he walked back into the house.

A chorus of *How? What's going on? What did he say?* erupted.

Tony looked around at them all. 'It's sorted, and that's the end of it. And you,' he looked directly at Ava, 'Schtum, now. OK? The fire's out. Nothing to see.'

Later, in bed, Tony assured Violet that Sadie could sleep soundly at night. There was no way Mark was going to risk anything stupid now.

Chapter 64

YOUR HUSBAND IS having an affair.

They sent it from Michael's phone, then blocked Sadie's number so she couldn't ring or text them back.
Michael deleted the message and made a cringe face.
'She deserves to know,' said Ava.

Sadie dropped her phone. It bounced onto the sofa, where it stayed face up, the text still readable. It briefly occurred to her to flush it, or bin it, or stamp on it, as though the phone itself had caused her the deep, sharp pain. She rushed to the landline and tried to remember her parents' phone number. Her breathing was laboured and she was covered in a cool layer of sweat.

'Mum.'

'Sadie. Are you OK?'

'Can you come over?'

'What's happened? Are you OK? Is it Mia?'

'It's Mark.'

'Mark?'

'He's been having an... I just got a text.'

'Have you spoken to him?'

'He's at footy.'

'I'm on my way.'

Violet sped through the streets, zooming past the 20mph signs, clunking the clutch at every gear change, cursing every light that wasn't green.

'Let me see the text.'

Sadie was in shock. She hadn't cried or spoken to anyone else. Mia was asleep, so she'd been able to sit quite still until now. She pointed to the sofa. Violet picked up the phone.

'Do you recognise the number?'

Sadie shook her head.

'Have you tried ringing it?'

Sadie stared into the middle distance.

'Sadie!'

She shook her head.

Violet rang the number from her own phone. Michael picked up.

•••

'So, Ava saw this man who looked like Mark, but it

was from a moving bus, and it just seemed so unlikely, and you were dealing with so much that we thought it best to just ignore it.' Violet tried to convince Sadie that they'd withheld the information because they hadn't believed it was true.

'So why would she text me if she wasn't sure?' asked Sadie.

'You know Ava. Black, white, no middle ground.'

Sadie started to cry.

'You want my advice? It's a little flag. A reminder that you're married to a fallible human being.'

Sadie looked at her mum, waiting for her to tell her about her own flags.

'Remember that superintendent? Your dad started to slip her name into conversation just a little too frequently, and I knew, I just knew. Red flag.'

'Did he..?'

'Not as far as I know. Two of the switchboards girls were in the choir, and they kept an eye out. Apparently, she had most of the lads like rabbits in headlights. Very striking, very clever.'

'I don't want to go through marriage looking for red flags.'

Violet put her arm around her daughter.

'You don't need to. You'll just know. And you might create some little red flags of your own. We're human. Our heads can be turned. Mark's. Yours.'

'I don't think so. I would never —'

'Believe me. This is nothing. Best thing you can do now is get some rest. Have an early night. Get yourself off to sleep before he comes home.'

Sadie rested her head on her mother's shoulder.

'I'll stay here for a bit,' said Violet. 'It's been ages since I did any batch cooking. I used to love it, but your dad does all that now. I'll make you some stuff for the freezer. What time's he due home?'

'Half-nine.'

Violet kissed Sadie goodnight, and started a long shift of cooking, ironing and seething. She left at nine.

Chapter 65

ONCE SHE'D DROPPED OFF several bin bags at the charity shop, Ruby's possessions fitted neatly into two pieces of mismatched luggage: one hold, one carry-on.

She printed the lengthy note she'd drafted over several days, instructing her tenants on how the boiler worked, how the shower wouldn't flow if the dishwasher was on, and vice versa, where the stopcock was, and several emergency numbers, including her new work number in Marseille.

Mark should have arrived an hour ago, *definitely, absolutely,* to say a proper goodbye. She'd bought Au Gourmand croissants. She'd made, poured away, and made another cafetière of coffee. She checked her phone again. Nothing.

She consulted her checklist of everything she needed to keep in her hand luggage, made sure her suitcase was securely fastened, then checked her phone again. She rang him. Voicemail. She unplugged the television, the radio, the kettle. She poured the last of a carton of milk down the sink. She texted Maurice and asked him if he could give her a lift to the airport. Of course he could. She gave him instructions for where and when to pick her up.

She pulled the painting from behind the large wardrobe and wrested it into the hallway. She wrapped it in a sheet, securing it at the back with several large knots and strategically placed safety pins. It wasn't heavy but it was awkward, so she was going to have to carry it by the chunkiest knot, bending her arm so her hand was at ear-level, to take the weight and keep it stable.

She needed to move fast. No taxi could take the size of the painting, so she had to walk. It wasn't far but it was tough, and she stopped every now and then, to adjust the sheet and to get a better grip. Occasionally, the frame would scrape against the pavement and she would resign herself to a little more damage before hoisting it up again. As she reached the corner of Mark's street, she paused. She rested the painting against a wall and examined her hand; it was deep red and sore with white indented lines where the folds of sheeting had dug into her palm. Adrenaline and imaginary dialogue had carried her this far, but the sight of their car, their house, their front door, their garden, their curtains – the sight of it all had brought everything to a silent standstill. A gust of wind rustled the trees, stippling her exposed neck and wrists with goosebumps.

Maurice's car pulled around the corner. She gestured for him to wait there. *One minute.*

As Mark opened the door, the top corner of the painting, no longer wrapped in a sheet, fell into the hallway causing the door to bang loudly against the wall.

'What's going on? You'll wake Mia!' said Sadie from the living room.

He let out a gasp as he realised what this was: a life-size, fully naked portrait. He could feel his heart starting to pound in his throat. He pushed the canvas outside, flipped it face down and tried frantically to slide it under the car, scrabbling around on his hands and knees. It wouldn't fit, but it could stay there for now. He stood up and craned around for any sign of Ruby.

'What's that?' Sadie appeared in the doorway.

'It's nothing.' He brushed tiny sharp stones from his palms.

'So what's it doing under our car?'

'It's just… Go inside, Sadie. It's nothing.'

She stepped outside and peered at it. 'Well, either you can pull it out or I will.'

Mark stood on the driveway, his arms folded across his chest. He was trembling now, and waves of nausea churned around his body. Sadie walked over to the car.

'Leave it, Sade. Just leave it where it is.'

She crouched down and hooked her fingers around the frame. She slid it towards her. Once it was almost out from under the car she looked up at Mark.

'What am I going to see?'

'Don't turn it over.'

'What am I going to see?'

'Please. Don't turn it over. Let's go inside.'

She lifted a corner of the frame, and angled her head to get a better view, a split-second of curiosity and artistic appreciation.

'I don't know anything about it,' said Mark. He took a couple of steps backwards and stumbled.

Sadie dropped it to the ground. 'Bring it inside,' she said, and walked back indoors.

He brought his hand up to cover his mouth, and noticed he was bleeding. He pulled out a sliver of glass from his palm, feeling nothing.

Eventually, he dragged the painting indoors. Sadie was waiting in the kitchen, leaning against a cupboard. The colour had drained from her face and she was trembling.

'The truth,' said Sadie.

'It's a painting of me.'

'I can see that. Who did it?' She whispered the question, as though she'd run out of sound.

He didn't answer.

'Who has seen you naked?'

'Lots of people.'

'Narrow it down.'

She was glaring at him, visibly shaking now.

He started to breathe heavily.

'I made a mistake.'

Her fierce expression was fixed; he attempted to start again.

'I made a massive error, and...'

'"Error"? You made an "error"?'

'A mistake! I made a mistake. I don't know what else to call it.'

'An affair? You had an affair?'

'No! I bumped into her...'

'And all your clothes fell off, did they?' she said, looking over at the painting.

He didn't answer. Part of his brain was working out how this had happened, when Ruby had painted it, why she'd painted it. He knew why she'd delivered it, of course.

Sadie moved towards him and whispered loudly: 'You fucked another woman?'

'It wasn't like that.'

'Did you or didn't you?'

Silence.

She picked up the nearest thing to hand — a sourdough baguette — and hit him around the head with it. He protected his head, then grabbed the bread from her and threw it across the room. She lobbed a pack of flour at his head. It exploded on impact, enveloping him in a cloud of white dust. She started to sob, she doubled over. Putting one hand on the floor, she slumped down into a crumpled heap, defeated, broken. He made his way towards her, rubbing his eyes clear of flour, spitting out lumps of the stuff.

'Get up off the floor, please, Sade, come on.' He bent

over to help her up.

She swiped him away. He caught sight of a varicose vein on her leg; it had appeared just a few weeks ago, along with the scarlet and silver stretch marks that now ribboned her belly. She looked up at him. A white, Halloween spectre, both hands cupped around his nose and bleeding mouth.

'I know I've let you down,' he said. 'I know I've broken our marriage vows.'

'Is that what you think you've done, Mark? Broken vows?'

'I... Yes.'

'You — YOU have broken everything! Everything!'

'I know, I know.'

'Our family. You've broken up our family, Mark.'

He stepped back. 'No, it doesn't have to be like that.'

'Oh, what, you want to stay? You want to be forgiven? Perhaps you'd like us to hang that fucking thing over the mantelpiece while we're at it!'

A few moments of silence, as the baby monitor gurgled and snuffled. Eventually, there was a little snort, then regular breathing.

Sadie started to sob again, hard. She pulled at the tablecloth and retched into it, wiping the tears and snot from her face. As she pulled it again, crockery started to fall off the table. She paid no attention to any of it as she wrapped the tablecloth around her. Mark jumped as the fruit bowl inevitably crashed to the floor, sending glass, apples, pears and bananas everywhere.

Sadie rocked, gently, insistently.

'When I first met you, you were lower than a fucking

snake.' Her voice was lower now, in volume and tone.

'I know.'

'Drugs, drink, the lot. You were a fucking mess.' She drew it out, slowly, deliberately.

He nodded.

'I made you what you are today.'

'If it weren't for you, I'd have been dead by now.' The phrase came out of him as though it had been learned by rote.

'Does she know? This painter woman? Does she know about me and the baby?'

The unmistakable silence of no right answer; she had him in a corner.

'Yes.' The wrong answer.

'How DARE you discuss our child with some fucking tart!' She grabbed at the leg of a chair and slid it across the floor; it toppled over and skittered toward him but didn't quite reach. He walked past it and put out his hands for her to take them and stand up. She refused; she stayed on the floor with the upturned chair, undone, sprawled, flattened.

Eventually, she went upstairs to check on Mia, to cry, to think.

When she came back down, there was hissing from her, quiet pleading from him. There were hardboiled threats through gritted teeth, harrowed tears and streaming snot. It all went on until Sadie put the baby and the pram in the car and set off. Five minutes later, she pulled in to a garage forecourt, took off her hoodie and cried and retched into it. And, although she knew where she was going, she took the long way round because she thought, if she just allowed a bit more time, she might arrive at her parents' house looking anything near normal, even though three weeks of driving wouldn't achieve that. And, thankfully, Mia slept because the universe does have a beating heart after all; there's only so much it can throw at someone in any given day. She arrived with her eyelids like marshmallows, her hair matted with snot. The texts clearly hadn't prepared Violet or Tony. They became more ashen-faced as they lay Mia on the sofa, swaddled, as they brewed tea, made toast, held their broken daughter's hand, stroked her poor aching head. Eventually, as it grew light, Sadie crashed into a deep, dead sleep. They took the pram upstairs and kept the baby with them.

'Why are you here?'

Sadie turned to see Ava standing over her. She sat up and looked around for Mia.

'What's happened?' said Ava.

'You know what's happened,' said Sadie, her hands covering her entire face.

'Have you split up?'

'Can you get me a glass of water and some paracetamol?'

Later, once Mia had been fed and bathed, once the breakfast dishes had been cleared away, and conversations heavy with dead-end sentences had been had, Sadie and Violet headed out for a walk along the sea front.

'Your dad can go over there later, pick up some clothes and bits for you and Mia.'

Sadie didn't respond.

'Best to do it when Mark's at work. You don't want your father coming face to face with him.'

The wind stung Sadie's cheeks, raw with all the crying and rubbing. Her hair started to stick to her face and she realised that tears were leaking out of her now, that she was crying without even knowing it.

'Not that your dad would do any damage to him — not really — but...'

Sadie wiped her sleeve across her face.

'We'll get the spare room properly set up for you this afternoon. I've been meaning to clear a lot of that stuff out of there, anyway. Old files and goodness knows what.'

They walked in synchronicity, their footsteps slow and heavy.

'He's known her since school.'

Violet stopped filling in the silence.

'She was there when he killed Fergus, and he decided she could—' she laughed, 'that she could — I don't know — absolve him of the guilt, or some such shit.' She paused briefly as they passed a happy-looking family. When she started speaking again, she was louder, angrier. 'It's not like I've not said, a million times, that it wasn't his fault. Nobody blames him. I've said that.' She turned to Violet, who was quick to rush to her defence.

'Of course you have. Of *course* you have.'

'I've said it over and over. What else could I have done? What else?'

'Nothing.'

Later, Sadie and Mia returned home. She took a pair of scissors to Mark's clothes because she needed to do something with her anger and she didn't have the energy for any original thought.

Chapter 66

IT ALWAYS STRUCK MARK that a rocking chair was a deeply unsuitable seating choice for a therapy room. He didn't want to lie back on a Freudian couch, but he did feel as though something static would at least help clients feel more dignified. For starters, the first time he had sunk into it, years ago, he'd grabbed at its bentwood arms as it rocked back alarmingly, causing him to bite his tongue. He had bled before he had spoken.

'Good to see you again, Mark.'

His feet twisted as they remembered how to stabilise the chair. 'Yes, sorry it's been a while. I...' He trailed off. Examined his shoes.

'How have things been?' Anders poured two glasses of water from a cheap Ikea carafe.

'Mixed.'

An encouraging nod.

'I got caught up in something.' He locked eyes with Anders. 'I had an affair.'

Anders gently pushed one of the glasses towards him and made a short closed-mouth sound.

'She — Ruby — was there when I...when Fergus died.' He leaned forward. 'She was at the game. She saw everything.'

Anders nodded.

'I know we kind of established in here that it was never my fault, what happened, but, to be honest, Anders, you weren't there. Outside this room, it still felt like it was all my fault. I was just able to put it on pause in here.'

'Right.'

'I feel bad saying that.'

'You have to be honest. We agreed that, remember?'

'Yeah.'

Anders smiled benignly and turned his palms upwards, signalling that Mark should talk.

'I bumped into her. We had lunch. I started seeing her more regularly. I didn't tell Sadie. And...'

He looked at Anders for a long moment, in need of a question, a prompt.

'OK. How do things stand now? What's brought you here today?'

'Well, when you last saw me, I was a mess. Now I'm a bastard. Turns out that's just as hard to live with.'

'Sadie knows?'

Mark nodded. 'I didn't mean — I know everyone

says it — but, genuinely, I look back and I just don't know what happened. It's like a whirlwind picked me up and…'

A meaningful silence. Mark knew this meant he was supposed to do a bit of digging around on his own.

'She made me feel…'

Anders took a sip of his water. Mark looked out of the window at a recycling bin so full that the lid didn't close properly. The wedge of Amazon packaging and plastic milk cartons obscured his view of the park across the road.

'I have no excuse, really, do I? I've been a twat, yeah?'

'I'm not here to judge you.' A pause. 'Do you remember we used to talk about appropriate levels of responsibility? How sometimes you took responsibility for things that weren't your fault and, at other times, you went the other way? You did a lot of work on that.'

Mark nodded, and Anders responded with an expectant look.

'So when I said I didn't mean to have an affair, that's me not accepting an appropriate level of responsibility, isn't it?'

'It sounds as though Ruby fulfilled something that was missing for you. That you made a choice to get closer to her, maybe because you felt it would reduce the pain you still felt over the accident?'

'Yes, but that's passing the buck, too, isn't it?'

'Accepting that you weren't passive, that you made a choice, and understanding why you made that choice — that's not passing the buck.'

'The whirlwind thing — it wasn't like that exactly —

it was more that she had this big warm cloak or blanket or something, and she opened it to let me in, and I just wanted to feel that warmth. Whenever I was with her, I swear I was measurably degrees warmer. My whole body felt so relaxed around her. She didn't care if I had marbles rolling around my head. She didn't want anything from me. She was always happy to see me.'

'That sounds pretty compelling.'

'Can you understand why...'

Anders smiled. 'Can you take me back to that moment when you bumped into her?'

Yes. Yes, he could. He wanted to talk about that moment to someone who wouldn't judge him. And all the other bits he couldn't face admitting to anyone. He wanted to say out loud things he had barely admitted to himself. He could do that here.

chapter 67

'SHE'S JUST LIKE HER MOTHER.'

Some seemed to say it for want of something, anything, to say, whereas others — mainly Sadie's family — seemed to chant it as an optimistic prayer. Although nobody actually said they hoped Mia would be nothing like her father, the implication hung around like the smell of a full nappy.

The visits from family and friends were much less frequent than they had been at the start, but Sadie hadn't felt ready to take Mia out much in the cold weather, so still they trickled in at weekends, often on their way to something or other. Mark wasn't sure who knew about the affair and who didn't, so he thought it best to be acquiescent around everyone. It didn't always pay off. His keenness to take people's jackets as they arrived wasn't matched by his ability to then place them somewhere suitable. Olive oil, crumbs and spilt milk ended up on several cuffs and collars, which made returning them somewhat awkward. He burnt the biscuits he'd attempted to bake, and tried to compensate by sprinkling granulated sugar and edible glitter on them. He made tea and coffee for everyone, but invariably managed to mix up the orders.

When Sadie's family visited, he noticed that Violet made no eye contact with him whatsoever, and certainly didn't hug him hello, congratulations or goodbye. Tony took the opposite tack; whenever Mark glanced over, his father-in-law was looking intently at him as though the only thing stopping him from tearing Mark limb from limb was the thin veneer of civility. Nick and Lenny pretended not to know about the affair, and acted accordingly. Ava's response was characteristically blunt. She followed Mark into the kitchen on one of his tea-making excursions, and quizzed him.

'How long were you having this affair?'

He hummed and hawed.

'Did you not love Sadie any more?'

Of course he did.

'Why did you like Ruby more than Sadie?'

Things weren't that simple.

'Was all the sneaking around exciting?'

No, it was exhausting.

'Did you plan it?'

Of course not.

'Would you do it again?'

No.

'How do you know you wouldn't do it again if you didn't plan it the first time?'

Sigh.

Everything seemed to come naturally to Sadie. She knew how to work all the various bits of baby kit they'd amassed, but he couldn't get the hang of it, no matter how hard he tried. She would ask him to pass her a wipe and he'd hand over a muslin square, at which point she'd roll her eyes and grab a chunky pack of wet wipes. He'd tried to put a nappy on Mia at the start but, once he finally got it on the right way, she did a determined shit in it before he'd managed to get it fastened. In a flash, Sadie scooped up the baby with one arm, and changed the nappy one-handed.

Mia would be the reason he'd never stop trying to make everything right again. It would never have been easy to walk away from Sadie, but it was now impossible. This kicking, crying, shitting bundle made his stomach ache with love.

His morning erection was less insistent now, and he ignored it. Also, he stopped flirting, and felt bad that he'd ever done it, particularly with bar staff who were paid to tolerate such crap. He didn't dare touch Sadie. He guessed that she would be sore and sad and feeling a whole load of other stuff he couldn't name. He suspected she hated him, which was fair enough. She was civil, but she only cracked a smile at Mia and visitors. And she hugged her parents extra hard as he stood holding out coats and umbrellas, like some scruffy butler. There was a terrible weightiness to everything now, as though they were wading about on the sea bed. He had laughed out loud a day or so ago at a story Nick was telling, about Ava's boyfriend going to Mars, and everyone had turned to look at him, so he decided to stick to silently nodding and making tea.

He'd ditched the Ruby phone. As Sadie was sleeping one night, he dismantled it as best he could, immersed the component parts in water and bleach, because he couldn't think of what else to use, then wrapped it in newspaper and shoved it to the bottom of the outside bin. As he closed the lid, a bat flew past his head at speed, causing him to duck and cry out. He put his hands on the ground, slid his legs out, sat on the grass and wept.

Chapter 68

HE HAD AN ALBUM OF baby photos on his phone, ready to pass around on his first day back from paternity leave. He bounced back into the office, ready to turn over a new leaf.

Nisha was waiting in reception for him.

'I wanted to catch you before you came in,' she said, manoeuvring him into a corner.

Mark's smile slipped. He couldn't face a job in sales. 'Don's dead.'

His mouth dropped open, but no sound came.

'Died at the weekend,' said Nisha, loving the drama. 'Shit.'

'Yeah.'

'What was it? The bleeding?'

Her excitement was palpable. 'Heart attack. He was

driving.'
   'Driving? Was anyone else...?'
   Nisha nodded. 'No. He hit a tree.'
   They both struggled not to laugh.
   'God.'
   'I know. It had a preservation order on it.'

A fortnight later, all staff were offered a half day's paid leave to attend the funeral. Some went. A handful sneaked off to the pub. Most, Mark included, stayed behind to catch up on their workload; a new soft-furnishing collection was due for arrival any day.

Chapter 69

The Health Visitor, Janice, was golden.

'It can be hard work, can't it?'

Sadie nodded, realising that even strangers could see the damage inside her.

'Harder than you expected?'

'Mark had an affair.' She blurted it out, as though the words had been waiting for her mouth to simply open.

Janice screwed the lid onto the jar of Sudocrem, and put it into the changing bag.

'I'll make some tea. You see if you can settle Mia.'

Mia quietened in her crib, and amused herself with something bright and soft. Janice returned from the kitchen with tea and biscuits.

'Would it be useful to know it's not uncommon?'

'When your wife's pregnant?'

'Happens more often than you might think.'

'But we'd gone through all the IVF, and…' she curled up, hugging herself as she started to sob. Janice stroked her back, her head; she would be forty minutes behind schedule for the rest of the day.

'Are you talking to anyone?'

'My mum.'

'Good. And friends?'

'Not much. Too embarrassed.'

'Have you thought of counselling?'

Sadie scraped her hair back, twisted it into a tight knot.

'I don't know how we got here. I had it all planned to the nth detail − I mean, it took me three weeks to decide on the nursery wallpaper. We used to joke about that. We can't joke about anything now.'

'Not yet.'

'It'll never be the same.'

'No. No, it won't. But you'll be able to laugh again. It takes time, and work. I'm going to give you some numbers, website addresses, and my direct line. I drive past here most days. It's easy for me to nip in.'

Sadie didn't believe they'd ever laugh again. Right now, she hated him for daring to smile, even at his own daughter.

Janice stood up to leave, but Sadie hadn't finished.

'It had been going on for months.'

Janice nodded. 'And it's all over now?'

'I think so.'

'Good.'

'What shall I do about the cradle cap?'

'Well, you've tried all the usual things. One of my mums said she'd used something from Atkinson's, the herbalist on Bristo Place. It cleared her baby's up straight away. I'll find out what it was.'

Sadie smiled a thank you.

Janice opened the door, then closed it over again, keeping hold of the handle.

'Have you had any sexual contact since the birth?'

Sadie shook her head.

'None at all?'

'Can't face it.'

'Physically or psychologically?'

'Aren't they connected?'

'Yup. We'll talk some more about that next time.'

Janice dropped off a sample of the cradle cap cream a few days later. She checked if Sadie had contacted any of the services she'd recommended. She had. And she gave her a leaflet about a new parents' pilates class that was opening up in a local studio.

'I've signed up for that,' said Sadie. 'And I've hired the pilates teacher's partner, Greg. He's a cleaner. Very thorough, apparently.'

Janice smiled.

'My mum and dad have paid for us to go on a weekend couples retreat I was thinking about. Counselling, zip-wiring, all that kind of malarkey. They're going to have Mia; they're actually looking forward to it.'

'Sounds brilliant.'

'I'm not sure these things work, but I could do with

a weekend away.'

'You deserve it.'

'Do you think they'll have a magic wand there?'

Janice smiled.

'Or a time machine, so I can go back to the day before he started the affair.'

'What would you do?'

Sadie fell silent.

'It wasn't your fault. A time machine couldn't stop it.'

She looked intently at Janice.

'No use looking back. Get the counselling, throw yourselves into it, be honest, go on the zip wire retreats, have date nights, talk, give him the opportunity to make amends, give yourself time to heal, don't expect too much too fast. Baby steps. If you fall on your bum, have a wee cry then get back up.'

Chapter 70

HERE'S THE THING ABOUT couples who go on relationship retreats: everyday reality is off the menu. It's replaced by a belief this could be the answer to everything, that candlelight and teambuilding exercises could relight the fire, erase the affair, reanimate tired bodies, that this could be a springboard to future happiness.

The journey was awkward. In the past, in advance of long car journeys, Sadie would have programmed the route the night before, while Mark downloaded a playlist. Prior to setting off, final adjustments of seats and mirrors would take place, so everything was just right. The petrol tank would be at least three-quarters full, the tyres, oil and screenwash checked. There would have been healthy snacks and bottled water in a padded cool bag. Today, they filled the tank at the local garage, where they fumbled for their Nectar card, and picked up machine-dispensed coffee and a pack of tissues. The engine noise drowned out the radio, so all they heard clearly were beeps on the hour. There were attempts at conversation, but they were stilted, as though Ruby was in the back seat, naked and grinning. Now and then, they would spot something, a murmuration of starlings or a workman's bumcrack, and they would connect over the beauty or otherwise of the sight, occasionally laughing, but without much heart.

'Welcome to Mason House.' The receptionist's blinding teeth gleamed in the landscape of his bewildering facial topiary, although his eyes remained fixed on the screen in front of him. 'We hope you enjoy your stay with us, Mr and Mrs Darling.' He looked up. 'We scan your car registration as you come in. I have all your details in front of me,' he said, with a threatening smile. Clearly, there would be no stealing of towels from here.

'Now, we recommend you download our app to book into workshops, activities and events. All free. There are also iPads in the bar and other relaxation areas that you can use. Or you can use our booking screen over there.' He pointed to a poster-sized screen. 'It's very user-friendly.'

'What kind of events?' said Mark.

'All kinds. Kayaking, zip-wiring, climbing — all done at your own risk — Latin dance with Rino and Adrianna, who've done all the cruises. And there's drama, tango, archery — although you need to sign a waiver for that.'

Sadie looked at Mark for a long moment. Her fingers secretly made a bow-holding shape.

'But we don't recommend you overbook yourselves. It's important to leave some space for quality time together,' said the receptionist, and he winked.

A porter carried their cases to their room. They dropped behind and started to whisper.

'Did you see that guy *wink*?' said Mark. 'A full-on-Sid-James-Carry-On-Up-The-Khyber-wink!'

They both did a mock-appalled face.

'Do you think they have cameras in the rooms?' said Mark. 'Checking we're having the requisite *quality time* together?'

'I wouldn't be surprised if they hold up scorecards as we check out,' said Sadie.

'You leave the world behind when you come here,' said the porter, as he held the door open, waving them through ahead of him.

Sadie and Mark nodded as though they had received an instruction.

Inside their room, the colour of most things could be described as taupe or neutral, apart from a large glass vase of red roses, some still tightly budded, and a vast abstract painting. A black-framed foxed mirror was fixed to the wall instead of a headboard. The duvet cover seemed to be stuffed with at least two king-sized duvets, and there were countless pillows in various shapes and sizes, artfully arranged over the top half of the bed. The entire suite was an ode to Kelly Hoppen. A bottle of unremarkable champagne sweated in an ice bucket branded with the name of a better champagne. The fruit bowl contained kiwis, paw paw, guava, rambutans, black figs and kumquat.

'The bathroom is through here,' said the porter. There was no door to it. It was simply an area behind a frosted-glass-brick curved wall. A giant circular bathtub was surrounded by bottles of oils and lotions, rolled-up towels and flickering storm lanterns.

'And this...' he said, indicating for them to peek behind another, smaller, screen. He didn't finish the sentence, and they duly smiled at finding the fairly unremarkable toilet.

'I hope you enjoy your stay. If there's anything else...' the porter smiled, expectantly, prompting Mark to fish a note out of his pocket and thrust the crumpled thing into the man's hand.

Once the door had closed behind him, Mark did an approximate impression of the porter's bashful reveal of the toilet, as Sadie sniffed at the contents of the various bath oils. They moved onto the fruit bowl, turning the various pieces over in their palms, inhaling their unfamiliar scents.

Sadie opened the balcony doors, and stepped out into the cool air. Below, there were couples cycling, couples running, couples walking hand-in-hand, couples as far as the eye could see.

'It's punctured, Nigel! Face it!' The strained voice of a long-suffering woman floated up and through the foliage.

'Yes, and I'm telling you I can fix it, Bridget!' was the hissed response.

Sadie stepped back inside, leaving the doors open.

Mark faffed around inexpertly with the champagne bottle and sent the cork flying across the room.

Sadie rushed to position a glass underneath the frothing bottle, and necked the contents in three large gulps. 'No breastfeeding for a whole weekend.' She took a deep breath, and allowed herself to melt a little.

They finished the bottle and, almost as soon as they sipped the last drop, they crawled under the toasty duvet and promptly fell asleep.

'Mark?' Sadie had woken up with a stiff breeze in her face, whooshing in from the balcony. Her voice was hoarse, her eyes barely open. She propped herself up on one elbow.

Mark grunted.

'I think we've wasted our first day. We fell asleep.'

He rolled over and put his arm around her waist. 'How's that wasting the day?'

'We should be kayaking or doing something with ropes.'

Mark sat up slowly and squinted at the fruit bowl. 'Is there anything edible in there, do you think?'

'Depends how hungry you are,' said Sadie.

'I'm hungry enough for room service. You?'

Sadie winced. 'We should really try and at least leave the room. We could do this at home.'

An hour later, they were in a dining room filled with couples, almost all of whom were chatting animatedly. Some had bonded with other couples over risky outdoor pursuits, and had requested for their tables to be joined so they could talk to their new friends over dinner. Sadie and Mark surveyed the room.

'Are they all on something?' said Mark.

'Must be the fresh air,' said Sadie.

Just then, a waiter placed an espresso cup of broth in front of each of them.

'Compliments of the chef,' he said. 'An amuse-bouche.'

They eyed the cups warily.

'Broth,' he said, before smiling indulgently, turning on his heel and gliding off.

Mark sniffed at it. 'I reckon this might be the stuff that's got them all perky.'

Sadie tested the temperature with her lips before drinking it in one go.

'Any good?'

She nodded.

'Feeling perky?'

'Perkier than of late,' she said. 'Sleep. Champagne. Broth.'

'All set for the zip-wiring and…'

'Archery,' she said.

'Yeah. I'll stand still, so you can get a good shot at me.' He smiled ruefully before returning to his broth.

An awkward silence.

'I fancy the Latin dancing,' said Sadie.

'Rino and Adrianna?'

'They *have* done *all* the cruises,' said Sadie, mocking the receptionist.

'You're right. It'd be rude not to.'

The turndown service included the lighting of a five-wicked scented candle in a container the size of a bucket, a faux-fur throw artfully placed on the sofa, and a smores set-up. Outside, on the balcony, a couple of hundred tiny fairy lights twinkled in the otherwise absolute darkness.

'Do you think they'll make us stay until we actually have sex?' said Mark, picking up a handful of marshmallows.

Sadie lay on the bed, hands on her stomach. 'I've eaten too much.'

'Space for a marshmallow?' said Mark.

She shook her head.

'Isn't there a test? An experiment they did with kids where the scientists left the room and made them wait with a marshmallow in front of them?' he said.

'Immediate or delayed gratification.'

'That's it. And the kids who ate the marshmallow right away…' he said, with two in his mouth, 'were less successful in life because…'

'They couldn't resist temptation.' She sat up, swung her legs off the bed, put her head between her knees, and released a low groan.

'You OK?' He kneeled, pulled aside the curtain of hair hiding her face, and peered at her.

'Sade?' She was pale, and pinpricks of sweat had

formed on her forehead. Suddenly, her shoulders lifted towards her ears, and her face lengthened as her chin dropped. Mark dashed for the first vessel he could find, put it at her chest level, and with the other hand swept back her hair, just in time, as Sadie extinguished the Diptyque flame in one momentous heave.

The balcony chairs had quilted wraps draped over them. Mark cocooned Sadie in one, and brought two glasses of water from inside before settling on the other chair. They sat in silence for a while, their outbreaths making clouds in the cold night air.

'I'm the marshmallow kid. That's what you were thinking, wasn't it?' he said, eventually.

Sadie took a sip of her water.

'Thing is —'

Sadie raised a hand to stop him talking.

'Can you get me a damp facecloth, please?' she said.

He quickly made his way to the bathroom, ran two facecloths under the twin handbasins, and returned to her.

'One hot, one cold,' he said, handing them to her.

She ran the hot one all over her face, then the cold one, moaning gently.

'Better?'

'Better.'

'Why don't I tidy the place up, put the tray outside the door, and do something with the candle, and you get yourself settled down for a good night's sleep?' he said.

She gave a weak smile and stood up. As she turned

to go inside, something under her foot cracked. She'd half-stepped on a snail.

'Shit! No!' She put her hands over her face.

Mark crouched down. 'It's still moving. It's OK.'

'I've not killed it?'

He stroked his finger across its cracked shell.

'No.'

He stood up, and led her by the elbow to bed.

'You look like a movie star,' he said, as she slipped a sleep mask on, and sank herself into the mound of pillows. Seconds later, she was asleep.

The next day, Sadie woke up to a note:

Thought you'd like a lie-in. Gone for a bike ride. Back at 10ish.

She stepped out onto the balcony. The sun was trying its hardest but there was a definite chill in the air, and Sadie wrapped her robe more tightly around her as she sat down. The breeze carried the distant shouts and screams of today's zip-wiring couples.

A few centimetres away from her chair, watery sunlight glinted off…what? She peered at it, trying to make out exactly what it was. Four tentacles wormed around mid-air. The snail. Foil from the top of a champagne bottle had been carefully applied, kintsugi-style, to its shell.

Chapter 71

MARK DIDN'T CARE TO calculate the number of weeks since they'd had sex. It pained him to think that the last time *he'd* had sex was with Ruby. The weekend away worked, in as much as it had served to remind them who they had been as a couple, before Mia, before Ruby. Subsequent counselling had been hit and miss. Often he would leave sessions feeling emotionally battered. His late-night conversations with Dean offered some insight, although his friend was heavily distracted by his own life, particularly his impending wedding, and offered little by way of comfort. 'Your own fault.' 'Suck it up.' 'And how do you think Sadie must feel?' were phrases that would ring in Mark's ears for days afterwards.

'She's doing well.'

Mia wrapped her tiny fingers around the paediatrician's forefingers.

'How's she feeding?'

'Great,' said Sadie.

'And sleeping?'

Sadie turned to Mark.

'Her sleep's improving. We take it in turns to do the night feed, and she's getting better at settling after that. We bought a low-light lamp — that's helped.'

'Good idea,' said the doctor.

An unmistakable smell suddenly rose from Mia, and the doctor laughed. She picked her up, and passed her to Mark.

'I think Daddy can deal with this,' she said. 'The changing facilities are next door. There are plenty of nappies; everything you need's in there.'

Once Mark and Mia had left, the doctor quickly typed something into her computer before turning to Sadie.

'And how's Mum?'

'Better.'

'Good. You might want to keep on top of her nails,' she said, pointing at the tiny scratches on Sadie's face. 'Cut them after she's been in the bath, and gently file them so you don't leave any sharp bits that can catch you.'

Sadie put her hand up to her cheek and nodded.

'Just battle scars,' said the doctor.

Chapter 72

THE CHRISTMAS DAY DINNER was a family tradition that could be broken only by death. If you were an earth-dwelling, living, breathing member of Sadie's clan, or attached to one, you would be seated in your place in the family home, in the leafy heart of Trinity, on Christmas Day, surrounded by people who would always love you. Or tolerate you, in Mark's case.

They were getting ready to go. Mia was napping. Her wee rubbery arms were outstretched, her eyelashes flickered like moth wings, and a gentle snore gurgled in her throat. Nearby, Sadie struggled to wrap festive tissue and red ribbon around a floppy toy hare; she always gave the best and most beautifully wrapped gifts.

Mark walked past her, naked, and dropped a bundle of clothes into the laundry basket. 'I'm going to jump in the shower,' he said. 'What time are they expecting us?'

'Noon,' said Sadie. 'Plenty of time.'

She looked him up and down as he left the room. He'd lost weight over the past few weeks, his bottom had lost its pertness, and his skin had loosened. She was inexplicably overwhelmed by a raw and urgent desire for him.

His eyes were closed, his hair and face covered in lather. He wasn't singing — he hadn't done that for a while. He bent over to spread lather down the length of his legs, and was startled when the shower door opened.

She stepped in.

•••

The elements of Christmas Day dinner never changed: the oversized turkey, the dented tree baubles, the thirty-year-old homemade paper-chain decoration pinned millimetres away from previous years' pierce-points. Sprouts were boiled to the point of collapse, the sole vegetarian catered for, but not expertly so.

Nick and Lenny were the golden boys this year, taking responsibility for topping up glasses, tidying away discarded wrapping paper and being generally amusing. Nothing funny was expected from Mark today. He'd been asked by Nick to put together the playlist. Traditionally, everyone was asked to pick two or three songs and, as each tune started, the chooser explained why they'd selected it. Rather liking the tune counted as a perfectly good reason; heavy elucidations were discouraged. It made for an eclectic soundtrack and interesting chat.

'This is a song by Lizzo,' said Ava. 'It's called Tempo.' As the ribcage of her tiny frame began to expand and contract more quickly, her bony fingers curled under the edge of her seat. The option to abort her mission, to skip to the next track was still open to her; the first few bars had given nothing away yet. She chewed at the inside of her cheek. A few seconds in, the first instance of *bitch* was virtually inaudible to most around the table, but the *fucks* soon came thick and fast.

In her attempt to reach the OFF button as quickly as possible, Violet elbowed her daughter in the head. An accident, of course, but one of those secretly satisfying parental moments.

'Mark, did you not check this playlist? Nick, can you skip to the next song, please? And can you delete Ava's stuff?' said Violet, urgently.

'You don't even know what my other song is!' said Ava.

'I don't want to know. You've forfeited your right to another song.'

'My "right"? What are you on about, Mum?'

Violet glared at her.

'Why can't I have the music I've chosen? Everyone else does! I have to listen to all your shit!' She stomped out to the back garden. The air crackled in her wake.

Sadie gave Mark a look which he mistook for the 'Let's go home' signal. He half-stood to say thanks for the meal he had not yet eaten, only to be pulled back to his seat by a gentle tug.

Tony eyed Mark. 'Did you not check the playlist?'

'Check it?'

Nick chipped in. 'Sorry, I should've said. You're supposed to *check* the songs, then put them in order — Mum's first, then Dad's — then…'

'Check them for what?' he asked.

'For things like this,' said Tony.

'To be fair, Dad—'

Tony closed Sadie down with a wave of his arm, and sauntered off to the kitchen, shaking his head.

Lenny refilled the glasses, as Nick aligned cutlery in the manner of a royal butler, having stopped just short of donning white gloves.

Eventually, Violet and Ava returned from the garden, and Tony shepherded everyone to the table, before picking up the carving knife.

Sadie nudged Mark, and he cleared his throat.

'I…erm…I want to make a toast.'

He half-stood, and looked nervously at Tony, who had a firm grip on the knife.

'I want to make a toast to this family…'

Sadie stood up beside him, Mia on her hip, and took over.

'We need to put the old year behind us,' she said. She looked around, raised her glass tentatively. 'So. To the future.'

The response was strained. Tony took an extra-long slug of his wine, the others nodded and murmured variations on 'cheers', and Ava smirked.

'Mark, why don't you carve?' said Sadie.

It took all Tony had to pass the knife handle-first to him.

•••

Hours later, after the crackers and the hats and the Queen's Speech, as ice sparkled on the pavements, Mark secured the baby seat into the car, while Mia wriggled and squealed in Sadie's arms. Eventually she was strapped in, and hugs were exchanged to varying levels of enthusiasm at the garden gate. Mark checked the rear-view mirror before driving off. He could see his in-laws waving, receding into the distance. Mia's piercing cry dwindled to a disgruntled grizzle.

'She'll be asleep in no time, once we get on a clear stretch,' said Sadie.

He turned onto Ferry Road and put the car into fourth gear before resting his hand on the gearstick. He took a deep breath. Sadie reached out and stroked his fingers.

•••

Later, once Mia was in bed and asleep, they would sit side by side on the sofa. She would have a large gin and tonic, and he would drink two or three measures of whisky barely diluted with water from a small white jug. They would half-watch *Love Actually* again, and talk about the day, the presents, the tree, and how cold it had turned, how slippery the path was. After a while, she would tip her head towards his chest, and he would stroke her hair with taut fingers. They wouldn't be aware that their ligaments and muscles had adjusted to an infinitesimally tighter set point, or that they would never again sprawl quite as carefree, loose-limbed and intertwined as they once had. It would hardly matter now; they were back in the hullabaloo.

Acknowledgements

The tricky second novel. It took me seven years and a deep dive into academia to lose and re-find my writing voice. Thank you to those who helped.

My heartfelt gratitude goes to Scott Pack. Every writer should have access to someone so wise, kind and real. One hot summer afternoon, when no part of me could see the sunshine, he picked me up, dusted me down, and has stood by me ever since. He also makes excellent cake.

Thank you to everyone at Lightning Books. It is a truly wonderful thing to be part of this warm, talented and welcoming family.

Scottish Book Trust saw something in the early drafts of this novel, and awarded me the services of editing guru, Sophy Dale. Thank you to all at the Book

Trust, who do amazing work, and to Sophy for being rigorous and honest and steadfast. Golden.

Five days fangirling with the wonderful Melissa Bank gave me the confidence to start my next book. Finally, momentum. More on that soon. But not here.

It's easy to disappear down a research rabbit hole, but visits, phone calls and emails to some key people have saved me hours of trawling the internet. Greyfriars Art Shop in Edinburgh allowed me to handle and gad about with various-sized canvases, to test their weight and manoeuvrability. Thank you to spellcheck for helping me spell manoeuvrability. Thank you to Rob Harris from Harris Moore Canvases who provided excellent advice on Ruby's choice of paint colours, and had endless patience with someone who has only ever painted using a three-inch brush and five-litre cans of emulsion.

Thanks to Emma from The Lawn Tennis Association, who enlightened me as to how a child might progress to become a Wimbledon champion, and explained the various options open to those who don't make Centre Court.

Mia from Marks & Spencer in Manchester's Trafford Centre tracked down the pyjamas I wore a lot as I wrote this book. Never underestimate the power of comfortable workwear. Or Mia.

Ian Webster, Isabel MacNeil, Euan Tait and Marie Moser have been the most enthusiastic book-selling, book-reading, book-loving champions. Huge thanks. Huge thanks to all booksellers everywhere. You rock.

Thanks also to Hannah Hargrave and to Emma

Welton, for everything they have done to help push this book out into the world.

Lovely friends and beta readers — there are too many to name, but you know who you are. I know who you are. And thank you to Sarah Cairncross who read and enthused over the final, final, absolute final draft.

Thank you to Charlotte Halliday for offering bird advice. Despite her expertise, I still have a rogue nightjar swooping over Salisbury Crags. Poetic licence. Speaking of which, eagle-eyed jazz fans will know that Bill Kyle could not have been on drums in The Jazz Bar when Mark and Ruby were there, but his inclusion is a tribute to the stardust that he was and is. RIP, lovely man. I miss you and everything you made happen in that amazing space.

My love, always, to David, who nodded, smiled and laughed out loud (in all the right places) as he read sections of this book over and over, in all their incarnations, and to Tom for his unwavering honesty, unrivalled research skills and fast typing of the beats.

And, finally, to Luke de Castro, whose sensitivity and understanding of human nature was second to none, and whose writing will always blow my mind. I am forever grateful for his support and kindness during an utterly bleak academic year. He had a rare talent, and was lost just as he was about to take the literary world by storm. He lives on in many hearts, in his words and, thankfully, on YouTube.

If you have enjoyed *The Darlings*, do please help us spread the word – by posting a review on Amazon (you don't need to have bought the book there) or Goodreads; by posting something on social media; or in the old-fashioned way by simply telling your friends or family about it.

Book publishing is a very competitive business these days, in a saturated market, and small independent publishers such as ourselves are often crowded out by the big houses. Support from readers like you can make all the difference to a book's success.

Many thanks.

Dan Hiscocks
Publisher
Lightning Books